OWEN (SPECIAL FORCES: OPERATION ALPHA)

BLUE TEAM BOOK 1

RILEY EDWARDS

This book is a work of fiction. Names, characters, places, and incidents are products of the author's imagination or used fictitiously. Any resemblance to actual events or locales or persons living or dead is entirely coincidental.

Dear Readers,

Welcome to the Special Forces: Operation Alpha Fan-Fiction world!

If you are new to this amazing world, in a nutshell the author wrote a story using one or more of my characters in it. Sometimes that character has a major role in the story, and other times they are only mentioned briefly. This is perfectly legal and allowable because they are going through Aces Press to publish the story.

This book is entirely the work of the author who wrote it. While I might have assisted with brainstorming and other ideas about which of my characters to use, I didn't have any part in the process or writing or editing the story.

I'm proud and excited that so many authors loved my characters enough that they wanted to write them into their own story. Thank you for supporting them, and me!

READ ON!
  Xoxo
  Susan Stoker

For Susan

PROLOGUE

Life is about choices.

I'd read that somewhere.

Every choice you make, makes you.

I'd read that, too.

It was bullshit.

Obviously, the Maxwell guy who wrote that in one of his books about growth and leadership didn't take into account there were some people who didn't have choices.

I was one of those people.

I didn't have *choices*.

Not if I wanted to stay alive.

My whole life, I was a woman whose decisions had been made for me. I had no choice but to follow the rules. This wasn't a cop-out, it wasn't a way to dodge responsibility, and it wasn't because I was weak or stupid. In the world I grew up in the only *choice* you had was to learn and do it fast. Learn to keep your head down, keep your mouth shut, and do as you're told. If you didn't, you'd find yourself swimming with the fishes with a pair of lead boots on your feet.

I wasn't sure if my father, the crime boss, or my uncle, the new boss when my father bit the bullet—not literally but close enough—actually said stuff like 'swim with the fishes.' But in my head, it sounded better than what it really meant—murdered. Which was how people in my world ended up when they didn't follow orders. When they thought for themselves, when they had morals, when they tried to escape, when they talked.

My father had tolerated me. This was because I was smart and kept my mouth shut. I did as I was told, didn't question anything, and mostly stayed out of sight.

My uncle despised me for a variety of reasons. His biggest issue with me was that I was breathing and not just currently—that started when I drew my first breath. No, that wasn't right. My uncle's hatred started when I was a bundle of cells. He had a wife, though she wasn't my aunt—she was the woman of the house. And like all the ones before her she was disposable. Some of them had more freedom than others. After my uncle divorced them, some were set up in brownstones close to where he lived, some disappeared and were just gone. I assumed they were swimming with the fishes, though I never asked.

I did know the ones who were left breathing all lived on the same block. It was like my uncle was taking over a section of Chicago and making it his personal community of available pussy. That was what he called women—available pussy.

Unfortunately when my father died—meaning murdered by his brother—I was given to my uncle. Yes, the man who had killed my father.

Takeover.

It was the way of the world. When you're the king, or The Boss as my father liked to be called, there is always someone plotting and planning to take you out. My father was a lot of things, all of them despicable, but I never thought of him as stupid. However, in the end, he proved to be a total idiot and never saw the knife his younger brother—The Advisor, his second in command—used to stab him in the heart. So, really it wasn't a takeover as much as it was a hostile-takeover-slash-murder..

No choice.

No life.

My uncle took possession of me and made it known he wasn't happy. I'd been twenty-five. I figured he would've married me off as soon as he could to get rid of me. But he had bigger plans. And when I no longer fit into those plans, or more aptly when I saw something I shouldn't have, he sold me.

No choice.

Then I was saved from a life of being some sick, deranged man's real-life sex doll. And now I lived in a new kind of prison. One that was far, far worse than my uncle's. I was not being held captive by sex traffickers or vile men. Yet, I was still a prisoner. Sure, the locks on the doors were meant to keep people out and not me in. Sure, I knew the code to the alarm which was set to keep me safe. I had access to the phone, the outside world, anything and everything I could want, but I couldn't leave.

Not if I wanted to stay alive.

I suppose that was a choice. If one could call choosing between life and death a choice. Not that my life was worth much. I went from my father's chilly disposition to my uncle's cruelty, to the possibility of being a sex slave, and I now lived with a man who had risked his life to save mine. He'd cared for me, nursed me back to health, had tended to my injuries with a gentleness I'd never known, and if all of that wasn't enough, on the nights I woke up screaming, terrorized by nightmares he held me.

Owen Cullen.

The man of my dreams. The only man who'd ever touched me with kindness in the thirty-two years I'd been alive. I was far from naïve; I knew there was no such thing as happy endings. People in my world tended to have a low life expectancy so it was doubtful I'd reach my fortieth birthday. But Owen made me want to believe I had a future that didn't include a pair of cement boots and a swim in Lake Michigan. Though knowing my uncle he'd play it safe and dump me somewhere in Indiana—probably Cedar Lake—and some fisherman would be traumatized when they found my stiff, bloated body on the shore.

So, I was in a new prison with a man who was kind and gentle. In other words, Owen was the most dangerous man I'd ever known. He and his team of brothers.

Men who fought evil.

Good men.

Clean men.

A man who would be horrified if he knew I was in love with him.

I was Sarah Pollaski. Daughter of a crime boss. Niece of Wilco Pollaski the reigning king of Chicago's underworld. I came from filth. My family's crude, profane, vulgar deeds had leached into my skin, coating me in the most putrid stench that would never wash clean.

Owen would set me out of his house if he knew. So I did what I'd been trained to do my whole life—I stayed quiet. I didn't touch things that didn't belong to me—which meant I touched nothing because I had nothing. I didn't look around his house. I didn't make myself comfortable even though he'd told me to.

I certainly didn't tell him I was terrified every waking moment of every single day.

I didn't tell Owen that my nightmares weren't nocturnal figments of my imagination but very real things I'd seen.

I didn't tell him he was the first man who was not related to me by blood who hadn't looked at me like I was what my uncle called me, available pussy.

I didn't tell him my tale of woe to protect myself; I stayed silent to protect *him*.

Even though I wanted to believe, I was constantly reminded I had no choice.

My life had been predetermined.

I was owned. My life was not mine and it never would be.

Those were my thoughts as I sat on the floor in the corner of Owen's bedroom staring at an envelope with my uncle's address embossed on the left corner, my name neatly printed a little off-center mid-height, and a postage stamp on the right.

He'd found me.

My hands shook as I held the envelope, trembled so badly it took me two tries to engage the cell phone Owen had given me, and even longer before I was able to tap on his name.

It rang once before his deep voice came over the line.

"Hey."

"He found me," I told him.

"Who found you?" Owen asked.

Gone was the smooth baritone that never failed to soothe me and in its place was a rumble of concern.

"My uncle," I whispered as if saying his name would magically make him appear. The man was like the Boogeyman, Bloody Mary, and Freddy Krueger all wrapped up into one demonic nightmare. Only I lived my nightmare.

Wilco Pollaski was a living, breathing, walking demon.

"Is he there?"

Through the phone I heard something scrape, then footsteps.

He was coming. Owen would come.

"No. I checked the mail. There was an envelope with my name on it. Posted from Chicago."

I was so stupid. Owen normally checked the mail; it was his house after all. But Eva told me she ordered me a bottle of nail polish and it was being shipped to the house. Months ago, Eva Brown sort of saved my life—actually there was no 'sort of' about it. Eva was a pilot who'd been kidnapped by a man who wanted to use her skills to run drugs into Canada. I was supposed to be on the flight, too. But Eva was strong and brave and fought. I had not. I begged her to let me die. It was my last chance—death was my *only* chance to be free. That was the first time Owen had shown up to save me. He and his team swooped in to rescue Eva.

My rescue had been accidental. Then he didn't know what to do with me. I refused to tell him my name or where I'd come from. So Owen brought me home—to his home and promised me a safe place to heal.

Anyway, back to the mailbox. I'd checked the mail instead of waiting for Owen for a stupid bottle of nail polish. Something so trivial but I that wanted desperately. That was what my life had come to, a bottle of polish so I could have something pretty.

"The house locked up? Alarm on?" His words came out in fast pants.

He was running. I closed my eyes and answered, "Yeah."

"Where are you?"

The only place in the world that makes me feel safe when you're not home.

I didn't tell him that. Instead, I said, "In your room."

"Stay there. I'll be home in ten minutes."

I screwed my eyelids tighter in an effort not to cry. I hardly ever cried, and only twice over something I loved. The first time, I was maybe eight or nine when my cat died. I'd been devastated; Peaches was the only thing I loved, the only thing that kept me company. I cried and cried until my father backhanded me and told me Pollaskis didn't show weakness and they never cried. I'd never wanted to be a Pollaski but right then, holding my dead cat with my father's mark on my face, I'd wished I was never born.

I didn't want to think about the second time I'd cried. It was worse, and not that long ago.

"Thank you, Owen."

"Ten minutes, honey. Sit tight."

Then the line went dead.

I sat tight. I didn't move a muscle.

Owen wasn't home in ten.

He was there in five.

Which made the only decision I'd ever made for myself harder than I ever thought.

CHAPTER 1

He found me.

Christ, I couldn't get the sound of Natasha's terrified voice out of my head.

I checked my rearview mirror. My team leader Myles was in his beat-up Bronco and behind him my teammate Gabe was in his flashy, yellow Lexus with Kevin in the passenger seat. That was all the reminder I needed I wasn't alone.

My team had my back. They always did. Not that there was much they could do. Nat wasn't talking. Hadn't talked since I'd found her in Alaska, and after the last attempt on her life she'd shut down. Not that I blamed her. There weren't a lot of people who could say they survived being sold into the sex trade, and were rescued from that living nightmare only to be kidnapped by someone who they thought was a childhood friend, beaten to shit, almost shot, and witnessed their so-called friend killed in front of them.

But even with all of that, Nat hadn't broken—she'd just clammed up. She'd cried when she saw Ashaki die in front of her, but not a single goddamn tear shed after that. The woman was stone cold.

I pulled into my driveway, heard the screeching of tires as both Myles and Gabe slammed on their brakes at the curb.

The drive from Z Corps' headquarters to my house had been ten miles of pure hell. I was no less calm now that I was unlocking my front door than I was when I got Nat's call. No less scared at what I would find. I was halfway through the living room when one of the guys unarmed the alarm and the beeping stopped. I was in front of my bedroom door when I heard the front door close. I paused just long enough to regain a minute bit of control so I didn't scare the shit out of an already terrified woman.

I slowly opened the door and found her immediately. Ass on the carpet, knees bent, arms wrapped around her legs, her chin resting on her knees, and her eyes on the door. She didn't move, not a muscle, not even to blink. Stone cold dead eyes stared at me.

And that was when I vowed to kill Wilco Pollaski.

She wasn't faking her fear. There was no faking that kind of fear, it rolled off her and filled the room.

"Nat?"

"Sarah," she corrected.

It had been months since I'd learned her real name was Sarah. For months before that, I knew her as Natasha. The name she'd given me when I found her in Alaska. I'd never stopped calling her Natasha and she'd never before corrected me.

"He's given me twenty-four hours to come home."

I didn't bother asking her who because I knew.

"You *are* home," I told her.

"No, Owen," she whispered. Her big green eyes finally lifted and our gazes locked. "This isn't my home."

My mind seized on a memory; one that all these months later still plagued my thoughts and made my heart clench. The first time I'd looked into those soulful eyes. She'd been scared stiff as I cleaned the gash on her forehead. At the time,

I'd been running on adrenaline and relief after the team and I had successfully rescued Max Brown's woman Eva. Natasha was an unknown, she wasn't even supposed to be there. I didn't know *why* she was there. But the fear couldn't be missed. It shone in her eyes. It was in the rigid set of her shoulders. But if I tried real hard—and I did, frequently—I could still hear her soft voice telling me she had no home. And the deadened tone when she'd told me she was from nowhere.

I'd done everything I could think to do to give her a home. Gabe, Kevin, and Myles had followed my lead along with Eva, Max, Tatiana, Brooks, Emmy, Thad, Anaya, and Kyle, all doing their part to make her feel safe. Give her something to hold onto—friendship, trust, compassion. Each and every one of them had reached out to her.

I don't have a home.

That was what she'd said.

"Nat, this is your home. You're not going back to your uncle."

"Sarah," she angrily corrected and tagged an envelope from beside her foot before she unfolded and surged to her feet. "My name's Sarah. There's no point in pretending anymore."

"What are we pretending exactly?"

"That I'm not a Pollaski."

I felt something unpleasant start to coil in my chest.

"What's that mean?"

"You know what it means," she spat.

"No, babe, I don't."

"I'm filth."

Like a dart, her words pierced my heart, making that unpleasantness turn nasty. She believed that, believed she was filth, believed she'd been pretending to be someone else when she wasn't. But she was dead wrong. She couldn't hide the goodness inside her, even in the beginning when she'd refused to talk about herself, what had happened to her, and how she'd ended up on a tarmac in Alaska awaiting transport to Canada where she'd be delivered to a man who'd bought her. She couldn't hide her kindness.

Nat hadn't been concerned about her situation. All her anxiety had been for Eva and her sons Eli and Liam. Natasha asked about them every day—how the boys were doing after their mother had been kidnapped, how Eva was coping. She'd even asked about Max.

Sarah Pollaski—or Natasha No-Last-Name-Given—cared, and she couldn't hide it.

It spilled out of her.

"Babe, you're not."

Nat winced and I was reminded there were times it hurt to look at her because another thing she couldn't hide was her pain. There were times when she smiled and it looked almost genuine but it wasn't. All she'd done was momentarily staunch the flow of anguish. And like any wound that was left untreated, the gash would continue to bleed.

"It doesn't matter. I have to go back."

"You don't and you're not."

With narrowed eyes, she took a wooden step toward me, and the ever-present ache to pull her close started to uncurl until my fingertips tingled with it.

This was my plight.

Need and sensibility.

The longer I was around her the harder it was to remember. The harder it was to hold on to my restraint. My need now outweighed my sensibility, turning my dilemma into a battle of self-control.

"You don't get it," she huffed and ran her fingers through her long sandy-blonde hair. Her movements were jerky and agitated. "I lied."

"Lied?"

"To Amie. I knew. I knew everything. I knew what my

dad was doing. I knew Amie's parents worked for my dad. I knew what they did for him. She was right. I lived in that house and I saw it all. I lied and said I didn't know, but I knew. I just kept my mouth shut because I'm filth like the rest of them."

I didn't want to think about the day the rogue CIA agent bypassed my security, broke into my home, and took Natasha. By the time we'd found her, Amie, better known as Ashaki Maloof, had beaten the absolute fuck out of Nat and was readying to kill her. That day still played out in my nightmares. I hadn't forgotten a single second of it, and the vivid way I remembered told me I would until the day I died.

"That bitch—"

"Was right about everything," she cut me off. "You don't know."

"Five months ago—hell, two months ago—I would've agreed with you. I didn't know jackshit. But now, I do know. I know about your dad. I know about your uncle. I know your dad and uncle started their racket when they were in their teens and built from there. Small-time burglary to start, worked their way up to bigger jobs. Shit was different in the seventies when they started. Easier to fence what they stole. Stay under the radar, especially in Chicago. The murder rate had hit an all-time high, and Barny and Wilco used that to their advantage. Once they had the funds, they started in the business of high-risk loans. In other words, high-interest returns. That venture earned them the money they needed to buy muscle and get into the drug trade. They played it smart, stayed on the fringe, and didn't make their play for territory until they'd built an army. Once they had the men, the guns, and the cops in their pocket they went for it and won a few blocks. It took them years but they gained more and more ground doing that bloody and ruthless. In the nineties, they added a stable of women and raked it in. Drugs. Women. Gambling. Loans. That's how the

Pollaskis made their money. How your uncle still makes his money."

"How do you know all of that?" she asked, her face pale.

"What do you think I've been doing?"

"You shouldn't know that," Nat whispered and dropped her gaze. "You *can't* know that."

"Why's that?"

"Because…because…he's dangerous."

"Yeah, babe. I know he is. So what I don't get is why the hell you'd think I'd let you go back to him."

"*Let* me?" Color rushed to her cheeks and fire sparked in her eyes—a flicker of anger I'd never seen come from her. Something that pleased me a great deal. "I didn't know I was being held captive," she finished.

"That's how you're gonna play this?" I shot back. "Months, Nat, you've been here and when have I ever treated you like you were my captive? Or better yet, when have I treated you less than someone I cared about? I've done the best I could keeping you safe even though I was in the dark and had no clue what I was protecting you from. We all have."

"You can't protect me from him."

"Wanna bet?"

"No. Me winning that bet means someone's dead."

She was perfectly serious.

Something else she believed, something I needed to correct.

"Wilco isn't some supervillain, Nat. He cannot hurt you. Now that we know who we're up against, we can make you safe. Trust us to do that," I pleaded.

The pink in her cheeks slowly receded and her teeth sank into her bottom lip. And not for the first time I wished I could pull her into my arms and comfort her, lick the sting away, kiss her abused lips, take her worry, and make her forget. Even if it was for a couple of hours. If there was ever a woman who needed to get out of her head it was Natasha. And I knew the perfect way to make that happen. Neither of us would be thinking about anything other than the pleasure I could deliver.

But that wasn't going to happen for a variety of reasons. The biggest was when all of this was over and she was free and clear of the Pollaski crime family, she deserved a happily ever after. Something I knew better than to believe in. I'd blown my chance and had no interest in finding a future ex-wife. Sure, in the beginning, it would be good, it always was, then the veil would lift and all of the politeness would slide away and it would go to shit, ending in ex-wife number two.

Been there, done that, got royally fucked, and would never do it again.

"I can't." Nat's quiet words pulled me from my thoughts about her pretty mouth.

"Why not?" I gently asked, doing my best to hold on to my irritation.

I'd given her no reason *not* to trust me. My team had worked their asses off to help her. My boss Zane Lewis had sunk money and resources into helping her. Everyone had been patient when she wouldn't tell us who she was or where she came from. All we'd known was she was a victim; she'd been bought and sold and was getting ready to be sold a second time.

All of that, unacceptable. All of it despicable.

"If it were me—my life—I'd trust you. I'd stay. I'm not worth much anyway so it wouldn't matter."

Nat paused and was going to say more but I couldn't let the jab at herself stand.

"Honest to God, Nat. Stop saying shit like that."

"No, Owen, it's true. You're the one who needs to stop living in this fantasy world where you call me Natasha and think you're some dark knight riding in to save the day. I. Am. Not. Worth. It. You have to believe that I'm telling you

15

the truth. I'm dirty. I come from filth and the Pollaski stench will never wash clean. It will never go away because I'm one of them. It's in my blood. It's who I am."

Christ. Without her knowing she was doing it, she sank her blade in deep. *Dark knight*. I'd heard that before, only my ex-wife had called it a savior complex and she'd accused me of riding a white steed. Of course, I was young then, I hadn't been jagged by war. I hadn't earned the darkness that now lurked in me.

"But this isn't about me," she continued. "My uncle's not coming for me, he's coming for you, and Eva, and Emerson, and Ivy, and Violet, and whoever else stands in his way."

I didn't have to look behind me to know my team had been giving me the appearance of privacy while still listening. Hearing Nat—no, Sarah…she was right. I needed to pull my head out of my ass and start paying attention—hearing Sarah say our teammates' women were in danger, they'd filed in behind me.

"Why would you say that?" Myles asked the question I couldn't.

"Because that's what he told me."

Sarah lifted her hand and offered me the envelope, but it was Myles who stepped forward and took it.

"He'll send a plane," she carried on. "If I can get to an airport in Easton, he'll have his pilot pick me up. Then you'll all be safe."

Pinpricks of unwanted awareness tingled over my scalp and I shook my head.

"Let me get this straight. Your plan is to go back to the man who you know is dangerous. A man who either gave you to Ashaki Maloof or sold you to her, putting yourself in grave danger so Eva, Ivy, and Emerson will be safe. Do I have that right?"

"And you. I want you, and Gabe, and Myles, and Kevin… I

want all of you to be safe. Everyone, Zane, and the rest, too. If I go back then my uncle will leave you alone."

"And that right there proves you are wrong. You are not one of them. You're not Pollaski filth. You'd give yourself up to protect people you barely know."

"I know you," she murmured and my spine shot straight. "And I know you don't deserve whatever he has planned. I know Eva has two little boys. I know Emerson is pregnant and so is Anaya. I know that there are kids around, good men, good women, and none of them deserve to be in harm's way. My uncle is a lunatic; he won't care who he hurts to get his way."

"Keep talking, babe, because the more you say the deeper that hole gets. You are not like them. You are nothing like your uncle, who is indeed a lunatic and doesn't care who he hurts. But you? You care and you can't deny it. If you didn't, you would've kept that letter a secret, stayed holed up in my house, and not given us the information we need to keep the others safe while doing the same for you."

Sarah's lips pinched together and her gaze slid to the floor.

Yeah, that was what I thought.

She cared.

"I need to call Zane," Myles announced.

"How about we all go into the living room?" Gabe suggested.

The men filed out of my room leaving me alone with Sarah.

"Trust me, Sarah. Trust *us*."

She slowly lifted her head and dull, dead eyes met my gaze.

Christ, what had she been through?

Which one of the assholes in her life had taken the light and snuffed it out so completely?

CHAPTER 2

Trust?

I couldn't begin to understand the concept. But I couldn't deny I desperately wanted Owen to teach me. So it was seriously unfortunate I didn't have the courage to tell him that.

"Sarah?" he prompted and my belly clenched hearing him call me by my real name.

I hated that name.

A long, long time ago I had loved it. Sarah was my mother's name and my grandmother's name. Though I'd never met my grandmother, when I was little—very little—my mom used to tell me stories about how beautiful my grandmother was. How kind and smart and how she'd wished I could've met her. That was before life had beaten my mom down. No, before my father had crushed my mom's spirit. Then he ended her life altogether.

Now I hated the name, hated the reminder.

"Okay, now you're worrying me," Owen went on. "Need you to say something."

"I don't know how," I blurted.

"Don't know how to do what?"

"Trust." Then since I was being honest I decided to keep

blurting stuff out. "I don't know how to do any of this. As far back as I can remember every decision was made for me. I was told what to do and how to do it. I wasn't allowed out of the house without a bodyguard. Not for my protection but as a babysitter. Someone to watch me and make sure I stayed in line. Until you brought me here, I'd never been left alone *in* the house before. I'm thirty-two, Owen. Thirty-two years old and my whole life I've been treated like a child. I can't trust you because I never learned how to do that. I can't stay here and trust you to keep everyone safe. I can't continue to lie to you. It's not right. None of this is right. You have to let me go back to Chicago."

"Then let me teach you."

God, why was he making this so difficult? He should've been happy my uncle had found me. Now he could get rid of me. He could have his house back, his freedom, his…heat hit my cheeks and I quickly glanced away.

"Sarah?"

"Huh?"

"Babe, look at me."

"Owen—"

"Nuh-uh, look at me."

Shit. I didn't want to look at him now that I was thinking about it. One of the many things I'd shoved aside, placed in the Do Not column of my mental spreadsheet, which was next to the To-Do column, and two over from the Maybe column. That was how I'd lived my life, rows and columns. Do-nots and to-dos. Thinking about Owen and his sex life was a Do Not. I should never, ever think about it but there had been many days when I held my breath and wondered if that day would be the day he called to tell me he had a date, or maybe that would be the day he came home from work, checked on me, then headed out to meet a woman. But days had slipped into weeks, then weeks into months and he never called to tell me he had a date, he never came home then left. He'd spent every night with me.

Well, not *with me*, with me, but he was home every night. We ate dinner together, we watched movies together, we watched bad reality TV together, and on more than one occasion I'd accidentally woken him up with one of my nightmares. Those nights he crawled into bed with me and held me. What we didn't do was talk—not about anything important. I didn't know Owen and Owen didn't know me.

So thinking on it now, me leaving meant Owen could get back to his life in all ways. He was gorgeous with a capital G and two lines underlining the word and an exclamation mark to drive the point home. And that being, Owen could get any woman he wanted. Yet he was stuck home with me. That wasn't right. He should be out doing what hot men do and not sitting on his couch with a basket case who was marked for an early death.

"I think we should go out into the living room," I told him, still looking at the carpet.

"Not until you tell me what you're thinking about."

That was never going to happen.

"I was planning my escape and wondering if I could outrun you," I lied.

"And that turned your cheeks pink?"

Dammit.

I couldn't think of another lie, mainly because I sucked at it, but also because Owen was close. So close I could smell his soap. *Pine Tar*. God, I was going to miss that outdoorsy, fresh scent. I was going to miss Owen coming home from work telling me about his day. I was going to miss the normalcy. And I was seriously going to miss him coming home to me, laughing his ass off, handing me a bar of soap then including me in his team's inside joke by showing me a Dr. Squash commercial.

Something ordinary, Owen made extraordinary. He

21

would never know I'd never been included in anything. He'd never know how special that made me feel. He'd never know that laughing with him watching a soap commercial was one of the best nights of my life.

I was totally pathetic.

It was time for me to stop being selfish and let him go so he could get on with his life.

"And just so we're clear, you can't outrun me. You can try, but I'll always find you."

He had to stop; I could feel my heart cracking. Tiny fractures that would allow the unthinkable to happen. Fissures that would leave me vulnerable to the hope that wanted to grow.

"Owen," Myles called from the other room. "Z wants to talk to you and Sarah."

My eyes drifted closed when I heard my name. I really wished I hadn't reminded them I was pretending to be Natasha.

"Come on."

Without waiting, Owen grabbed my hand and led me out the door, down the hall, and into his living room. At some point, I'd opened my eyes but I refused to take in the room. I didn't want to look at his comfy couch, or the recliner that sat off to the side, or the big coffee table. I had it memorized, every inch of his house. The first place I'd ever lived that felt like a home and not a penitentiary. I would miss all of this, too. There wasn't a single space in my uncle's brownstone that felt homey. It was cold and stark. A grand display of wealth and power. Same as my father's house when he was alive.

"I'm thinking west."

Hearing Zane Lewis's angry voice fill the room, my eyes went to Myles who was holding his cell phone out in front of him.

"That's what I was thinking," Myles said. "Abe's got that cabin—"

"Hell no!" Zane boomed. "Last time we used Abe's cabin as a safe house it cost me a goddamn fortune to rebuild the thing. Those southern California contractors bend you over and do not provide Anal-Ese, they just slam it home and wait for the tears to start. And for the record, I'm not sure how honest Abe is. You shoulda seen the contents list he provided. No way. I'm not building him another cabin. You're taking her to Idaho."

Her? Was Zane talking about me?

"Idaho?" I croaked. "I can't go to Idaho. I have to go to Chicago."

"Christ, here we go," Zane mumbled. "You're not going to Chicago."

"Why not?"

"And so it begins…again." I didn't understand Zane's sarcastic remark and he didn't give me time before he launched in. "Here's how this goes. You and Owen dance around each other, for how long is anyone's guess that part of this game varies. What doesn't is there's gonna be a whole lot of bitching and moaning. Lots of moaning actually— Kevin, Myles, and Gabe, I highly recommend Bose noise-canceling headphones, it will be the best three hundred bucks you've ever spent. Especially when it comes to the bitching you'll have to endure that'll likely take place over breakfast after the sex has worn off and Sarah starts in about how she should turn herself over to save everyone."

Throughout Zane's speech, I found myself getting annoyed. The mention of sex embarrassed me, but thankfully he finished with the topic at hand, giving me the perfect opportunity to voice my objections.

"This isn't a game, Mr. Lewis. My uncle has requested me to come home, if I don't he'll carry out his threats. That's not me bitching, that's me being honest. He'll do every last thing in that letter."

"I see we haven't gotten to the sex part."

Zane's nonchalance made me snap. Years of bottled-up fear rushed to the surface and exploded out of me in a rush.

"This isn't fucking funny. My uncle is the devil. He has no morals or compassion. He will not blink at hurting Ivy. My guess is that's where he'll start. His philosophy has always been to start at the top. Cut off the head of the snake and the rest will fall. He doesn't believe in showing his enemy mercy, he will take everything. Dismantle your business, ruin you professionally, but his kill shot will be your family. He'll leave you breathing so he can watch you crumble to your knees after he's taken your wife and kids. That's what he does. He likes knowing he has the power to bring down powerful men. All of this will end as soon as I'm on the plane. Everyone can get back to their lives and forget I existed."

The room was silent, but that didn't mean I couldn't feel the pissed-off vibes rolling off Owen. I hated he was mad at me but this was for the best. Everyone needed to be free of me.

"If that's the case, then why have you been camped out on Owen's couch?" Zane inquired, his voice deceptively even.

I'd only been around the big man a handful of times—he was gruff, mildly obnoxious, completely sarcastic to the point one would have to ask if he knew how to have a normal conversation—but there was no missing the fact he loved his wife. As in, *loved* her. Fight and die kind of adoration. Me mentioning my uncle's perverse inclination of killing women as a way to control men should've sent Zane Lewis through the roof.

What I wasn't going to do was tell him the truth about why I'd stayed. Even though that might have made him instruct his men to put me out on my ass and let me hitchhike to the airport. It would've been safer for all involved, but

I could barely admit my reasons to myself. Saying them out loud for Owen to hear would never happen.

"Because I thought my uncle was done with me," I lied, knowing Wilco Pollaski was never done with his toys—even after he broke them he still liked keeping them around. "He wanted me out of his house and he finally found a way to do that. Lucky for him Amie was willing to pay. Apparently, he's changed his mind."

"Why'd he want you out?" Gabe asked and my gaze skidded to him.

Damn, out of all of Owen's friends Gabe worried me the most. He was the quietest which meant he listened more than he spoke. It seemed he paid attention to everything, he caught even the smallest nuances.

"What?"

Gabe merely shook his head, catching on to my stall. I needed to get better at this lying stuff.

"You're a bad liar and you know it."

Boy, did I know it. But I was still delaying so I lied some more. "I don't know what you're talking about."

Gabe gave me a small, disappointed smile.

"You're such a bad liar you can't even successfully lie about lying. Just to move things along, I'll tell you how I know. When you're getting ready to lie you pause and think about your lie instead of it rolling off your tongue. You also pinch your thumb and forefinger together." I immediately ceased pressing my fingers together and he continued. "I don't know how you survived in that den of vipers not knowing how to lie—all I know is you're shit at it. My guess is, just like you've done with us in an effort not to get caught in a lie, you stayed silent. So, I'll ask again, why'd he want you out?"

This time my silence wasn't because I was thinking of a lie; it was because I didn't want to tell the truth.

"Sarah?" Owen rumbled and I lost it again.

"Stop calling me that," I snapped, and Owen's hand convulsed around mine. Then I straightened my shoulders and decided the truth was my best play. I needed them to let me go. "My uncle hates me. I'm the reminder that he lost the woman he loved to his brother."

"The old love triangle," Zane rejoined.

God, did he ever take anything seriously?

"So, your uncle Wilco was involved with your mother?" Kevin inquired.

"Yes. They were together until my father, being the eldest, declared she was to be his. My uncle begrudgingly stepped aside."

"If that's the case why would Wilco want you back?"

My gaze went to Myles and I shrugged. "I don't know why he does anything he does."

Only, I had my suspicions and I was keeping them to myself. Voicing them would put everyone around me in further danger.

"She knows," Zane contradicted. "I'll call Rhode and make the arrangements. You're going to Sandpoint. I suggest you pack your cold-weather gear."

"I can't—"

"Listen up, Sarah," Zane cut me off. "This is my one and only bit of advice—okay, that's not true, I'll likely have to give you more, but this is the one time I'm gonna give it to you gentle. Pull your head out of your ass before you martyr yourself and end up dead. Wilco Pollaski is on borrowed time."

That was gentle?

Zane paused and when he spoke again his tone was dark and ominous. "No one threatens my wife. No man threatens to take out my men and their families without retribution. I give less than two fucks about my business or my reputation. Wilco Pollaski isn't the first to try to bring Z Corps down and he won't be the last. But what he will be is dead—he bought that sentence the moment my wife's name crossed his mind. I'm not one of his dirty politicians he keeps in his back pocket. I'm not a cop on the take. I don't fuck the pussy he rents. He doesn't have a damn thing on me because I'd never leave my family vulnerable. He's a man who is currently breathing his last breaths on this earth, and while he's doing that, you're going with Owen and the team to Sandpoint, Idaho. While you're there, if you feel like helping us out and wanna fill in the blanks I'd be obliged. You wanna sit back while I engage my men and remain silent, that's on you. Bitch, moan, complain, I don't give a shit. Thankfully I won't have to hear it because your ass will be in Idaho and I'll be here saving your ass from a lifetime of misery."

"Why?" The stupid question was out of my mouth before I could think better of it.

No one except for Owen had ever tried to save me from anything. Well, maybe that wasn't completely true; Owen's team had helped him, and I suppose Zane being Owen's boss had as well. But I didn't understand.

"I guess with you growing up with Barny and Wilco you can't begin to fathom there are decent people who don't sit idle when innocent lives are being destroyed. The men standing there with you are four of them."

"And you," I murmured.

"There's not a damn thing decent about me," Zane returned. "Pack. I'll call you back in twenty with instructions."

Myles pocketed his phone and speared me with a cold stare.

"Why'd he want you out?"

"He didn't. He wanted me dead. Amie gave him a better option so he took it," I admitted.

"So you knew all along Amie was behind everything?" Myles pressed.

I tried to fend off the memories of that day, but like

27

always they came crashing in. Owen had unknowingly held me through nightmares that were not figments of my imagination but of a day that I couldn't stop living.

The day I realized I didn't have a single friend in the world and the girl who I'd thought was the only bright spot in my childhood was not real and true. Instead, she'd be my final downfall.

"I didn't see her, but after a minute of Amie talking to my uncle I recognized her voice. I was so stunned she was there in his house I was oblivious they were talking about me. And when I figured it out, it was too late. The deal had been struck. An hour later I was in a van, then I was put on a plane. Then you found me in Alaska."

That was the CliffsNotes version. The facts. I left out the emotional devastation I'd felt that day learning that my childhood playmate hated me with such a passion she'd offered my uncle a deal he couldn't refuse. It wasn't surprising Wilco would sell me. Horrifying, yes—that was my life—but not surprising. I found it unbelievably disturbing that there was actually such a thing as human trafficking, but I didn't find it shocking that the suckage that was my life, the filth I'd been born into, would end with me being bought and sold like the commodity I'd always been.

My only worth was as a bargaining chip to make my mother behave and that only worked so far. She dished out her own brand of hate. Once she was gone, I was useless.

Utterly.

Until I was old enough to perform.

"That day Maloof had you, you said her parents worked for your dad. We didn't find record of that," Kevin informed me.

His tone sounded accusatory and I didn't blame him. But the day Amie 'had me'—which was Kevin's nice way of saying had me tied to a chair while she beat the hell out of me—I should've stayed quiet and let Amie believe what she needed to believe about her parents. Who was I to shatter the illusion of their innocence?

"I don't know what to say about that. They laundered money for my dad. And Amie's dad sold my father's drugs. She wanted to believe her parents were innocent because she loved them. She needed to believe what happened to her mother was solely my father's fault, and it was, but it was *her* father who put her mother in harm's way. It was Amie's dad that skimmed money. It was Amie's dad that started using drugs. Then it was her mother that paid the price. Then her dad and brother went down, too."

"That sounds like you're making excuses for a man who *sold* a woman," Gabe sneered.

"Excuses for my father?" God, *as if*. The thought made me want to puke. "No. I hope he's rotting in hell. Excuses for Amie, yes. I understood her pain. She needed to hold on to her memories even if they were false because she had nothing else. I shouldn't have told her I knew her parents worked for my dad. That was a shitty thing to do."

"A shitty thing to do?" Owen exploded. "She *sold* you. Do you not understand what that means? Jesus fuck, woman. The life she wanted for you was worse than death."

"She wanted me to live her mother's life, Owen. She wanted me to pay for what my father did to her family. And I can't blame her for that."

"You can't? I sure as fuck can and I do."

"I lived in that house and I knew what was happening but I was too much of a coward to stop it."

And that was the God's honest truth. I was a coward. I convinced myself I didn't have choices when I did. I simply chose wrong.

"You were a teenager. How did you think you were going to stop it?"

"I could've gone to the police."

"And you would've been dead. Your dad and uncle owned the local cops."

"Dead's better than—"

"Don't fucking finish that," Owen snarled then looked at Myles. "We'll meet you at the office in twenty."

Wordlessly, Kevin, Myles, and Gabe shuffled out of Owen's house, and for the first time since I'd met him, I was scared to be alone with him.

I wasn't afraid he'd physically harm me.

But emotionally, he could cut me to shreds.

CHAPTER 3

The front door closed behind Gabe and I waited.

I heard car doors slamming, and I waited longer.

Finally, I heard engines roar to life and that was when I turned to face Sarah.

Fear.

That was what I saw—*all* I saw. And it pissed me right the fuck off. I'd worked hard over the months to ease the look of dread. I'd given her nothing but easy, not wanting to push her. Sensing she needed peace after what she'd been through. Maybe that was a mistake. I should've pushed her for answers. I should've made her face her past, then worked to smooth the trauma.

But I hadn't.

I screwed up, and now I was going to rectify that error knowing full well she'd withdraw and be angry, likely scared, and not giving a single care about either.

It was time.

"Wake up."

"Huh?" Sarah returned, and her brows pinched.

"It's time you woke the hell up and started paying attention."

Her torso jerked and a deep frown marred her pretty face.

"What?"

I took a good long look at the woman who had shared my home but nothing else, and the familiar feeling of inadequacy washed over me. I'd shared a home with Naomi. I'd shared my life, my money, my hopes, and she'd shit all over it. And here I was again, sharing—not to the same extent but in some ways more—and once again the woman before me took, but never gave a goddamn thing back in return.

Not her trust, not her history, nothing.

So what if Natasha stirred long-ago forgotten desire? The spell Nat wove was a different craving. I was forty, not twenty. The thrill of meaningless sex had diminished and the three years I'd spent with my ex-wife dulled the fascination of having a family. Nowadays it took a lot more than tits, ass, and legs to catch my attention. I'd had plenty of relationships since Naomi, none of them deep and abiding, none of them started with the intent they'd last. A step above meaningless. That was all I had to offer. Friendship, respect, and sex.

But Nat, she was different. She gave me nothing, wanted nothing, yet *I* wanted it all.

Her lack of trust and my stupidity pissed me right the fuck off.

"Pay attention! There are a lot of people who are putting their ass on the line for you."

"I know that."

"Then start participating in your life."

"I don't understand what that means, Owen. I tried and got railroaded into going to Idaho. I wanted to go back to Chicago."

Christ, the woman had no sense.

"You wanna die? Is that it? You have a death wish?"

"What? No."

"Then shut up about going to Chicago."

Natasha's shoulders bunched and her arms folded across her waist and the woman shrank back.

Fuck.

"Damn, Nat. I shouldn't have told you to shut up. I'm sorry."

"No. You're right. I need to stop talking. It doesn't matter what I have to say."

"Don't do that. You're not a teenager, don't sulk like one."

"I'm not sulking. I'm admitting you're right. I should stop talking."

"Is this what they taught you?" I asked, even though I didn't need her verbal confirmation. The answer was in the way she held herself.

"I know better than to talk too much."

It was beginning to dawn on me that not only did I not know Nat at all, I didn't have the first clue what her father and uncle had done to her. One would think that would quell my temper, unfortunately, it had the opposite effect.

"No, Nat, you don't talk enough. Christ, woman, open your mouth and stand up for yourself. Speak. Yell. I don't give a shit, just say something." I took a step closer and her flinch set my body on fire. "Do you think I'd hit you?"

"No."

"*Fuck* no. That's the right answer. Fuck no, would I ever put my hands on you in anger."

"Okay."

Her whispered agreement felt like a slap in the face.

"Jesus." My hands went to my hips, and contrary to what I told her I wanted to shake her alive. Shake her until she woke up. Rattle that brain of hers until she lost control.

"What do you want me to say?" she shouted.

Finally.

"Anything. Christ, Nat. Just say *something*."

"I can't."

And just like that, she gave up.

Fucking hell.

"Whatever. Then stay quiet. Let your life roll by. Let me and the team make you safe, then…I don't know, continue to move through the rest of your time walking around with your head down. I wouldn't call that living, but hey, at least you'll be breathing. I won't have to live *my* life with your death on my conscience."

"That's not fair."

"Check it, Nat, life's not fair. There are no guarantees. No promises. Nothing is owed to you. You want something, fight for it. You want better, fight for it. But fuck, woman, you have to fight."

"I don't know how to do that."

"Bullshit, you don't."

"I don't," she repeated.

"Right. See, I don't believe you." I ticked off on my fingers one by one. "Somehow, you lived through your father's abuse, your mother's neglect, your uncle's madness, being sold, a kidnapping, and a beating. And you did that by *fighting*. The war might've taken place in your mind, but you fought it. *And* you won. But standing here with me, a man you know will never hurt you, you lock yourself away and give up."

"You think I won?"

"Hell yeah, I do."

A somber look passed over her pale face and sadness crept into her eyes and I wished I could've rewound the last ten minutes and never opened my mouth.

"Then you're blind, Owen. I didn't win anything. I didn't fight a great war in my mind. I did the only thing I knew how to do, and that was push it away so I wouldn't have to feel. I learned to go numb. That's not winning, that's surviving. And just so you know, I don't have a death wish. I don't want to live with *your* death on *my* conscience. I don't want my uncle wreaking havoc on good people. He's a maniac. He won't care. I'm not worth this."

I was done.

So done.

Over the top, deep in my gut, fucking *done*.

"Pack up, we're leaving in ten."

I turned and made it to the mouth of the hall when Natasha's words stopped me.

"That's it?"

I craned my neck and looked over my shoulder.

"Yeah, Nat. That's it. There's nothing I can say that will make you pull your head out of your ass. And if I have to listen to you tell me you're not worth it one more time, I'm gonna lose my motherfucking mind."

"But—"

"No buts. No more bullshit. If you were my woman, I'd show you a hundred different ways all the reasons why you're wrong. I wouldn't tell you with words, I'd *show* you and I'd do it in a way so you'd never fucking forget how precious your life is. You'd know your worth and you'd damn well know what you meant to me. So do me a favor, yeah? The next time you wanna put yourself down, don't."

I made it to my room, rooted through my closet, found a backpack, and tossed clothes in. Less than ten minutes later, I was back in the living room waiting for Natasha. I couldn't remember a damn thing I'd packed. It was only minutes before and I couldn't recall if I'd grabbed my toothbrush.

My good sense had fled, and at some point, *Sarah* had once again become Natasha.

A smart man would escort her to the office, tell Zane he had to back away from the case, and let Myles take responsibility for her. Myles wouldn't forget she was Sarah. He wouldn't have dreams about her under him. He wouldn't itch to pull her close and taste her mouth. He would be perfectly professional.

Natasha came into the living room with a pack over her shoulder, her movements slow, her eyes deadened, and her presence cold.

I hated everything about the way she looked.

It would seem I was stupid. I wasn't going to drop her off and let my team leader take over. I wasn't going to back off. Not until the woman grew a backbone and told me to fuck off.

Yeah, that was what I was going to do. I was going to push her to the extreme, force her to acknowledge her anger, and keep pushing until she unleashed unholy hell. Then I'd walk away. Then I'd know she was ready to stand up for herself.

"Ready?" I asked.

"Um, yeah. I didn't know if I was coming back here."

I waited for her to say more but she didn't, so I prompted, "And?"

"And, so, I didn't know what to do. I only brought what fit in this." She lifted the strap of the pack. "I left the rest."

I was being a dick, which served no purpose except to be an asshole because my feelings were hurt.

"You're coming back here," I assured her. "And we're going to Idaho, not a deserted island. If we need something we'll go to the store and get it."

"I thought we were hiding."

"Okay, I'll amend. You won't go but someone will. We got everything covered."

"I know."

"Do you?"

Natasha jerked her chin up in defiance. "You asked me to trust you. So I've decided to try to do that."

"Just like that?" I didn't bother to hide the skepticism.

"No, not *just* like that. I know you won't believe me but I don't want to die. But more, I don't want anyone to get hurt either. I've warned you about my uncle. He's crazy, Owen, really and truly crazy. Please believe me."

Oh, I believed her.

"I've done my research on Wilco. I'm fully briefed on his level of depravity. We all are."

Nat was quiet for a beat before her solemn gaze met mine.

"Promise me one thing." It was a demand, not a question, so I remained silent and waited. "Don't get dead."

"None of us are going to die."

"Promise me, Owen."

"I promise."

Relief washed over her features and her shoulders sagged. "I'm ready."

I looked Natasha over one more time and found it doubtful that was the truth. The only thing she looked ready for was more pain, more disappointment, more misery.

She didn't realize it yet, but those days were over for her.

CHAPTER 4

Eight hours later, we were in Idaho. It felt like the hours had passed in the blink of an eye. Yet, somehow I felt like I'd been awake for a week.

Owen had driven us to Z Corps' headquarters, the ride mostly silent. When we got there, Owen, Kevin, Gabe, and Myles met us in the parking garage and flanked me as we made our way through the various security checkpoints. It was not the first time I'd been to Owen's work. However, the first time I'd been so overwhelmed with relief after Owen and the guys had saved me from boarding a plane in Alaska to Canada where I would've been lost forever, I had not paid attention to my surroundings.

And when I'd met Zane Lewis I hadn't spoken a word. Owen and Eva had done all the talking. I hadn't protested when Owen announced he was taking me back to his place. My plan had been to slip out that very first night after he'd gone to bed. But Owen being Owen, he probably sensed my plot and had not gone to sleep. Each time I'd walked out of the guest bedroom under the pretense of getting a drink he was awake on the couch. The next few days were a blur.

Owen hadn't pushed me to talk. He didn't ask me uncomfortable questions. He just let me be. Then days turned into months and he remained the same—gentle, kind, steady.

That was, until he had to rescue me once again. Then he started asking questions, lots of them. But that day, Amie had given him everything he needed to know—my real name. Apparently, he didn't need me to answer the questions he'd bombarded me with. Owen had investigated my family and knew too much.

Now he was fresh out of patience. Not that I blamed him.

The guys had a brief discussion with Zane, and even though the conversation took place in front of me, I was not part of it. No one had asked me a single question and I hadn't offered my opinion. Then we were on a helicopter, and again I remained silent. After that, we were on a private jet to Idaho, and as soon as I could, I feigned sleep. We landed at a small airport south of the place called Sandpoint. During the hour-long drive, I stared out the window. Yes, in silence.

Now we were driving up a mountain road and I had my eyes closed tight.

Owen leaned closer and murmured, "Babe, it's not that bad."

"Um-hum."

He tried again. "Myles is a good driver."

"There's snow on the ground," I lamely retorted. "And we're on a cliff."

"I wouldn't call it a cliff."

"Then what would you call a dirt road with a sheer drop-off?"

It was pitch-black out, so dark that when we'd started up the road I couldn't see anything. Then we hit a switchback and the headlights had illuminated the mountainside and fear struck hard and fast.

"I grew up in Colorado," Myles said. "Wouldn't call this a mountain as much as a hill."

I hummed my disagreement and kept my eyes closed. If we were going to slide off the side to our deaths I didn't want to see it coming. I wanted to be blissfully unaware. And wasn't that just like me?

Eyes closed, ignorant, and mute.

I was doing exactly what Owen had accused me of doing —letting my life roll by me. I was breathing but not living. I was a bystander in my own life, and the hell of it was I was too afraid to fight to be an active participant. I knew the pain it would cause if I spoke up. I knew what the blows would feel like if I tried to escape my circumstances.

The SUV slowed, then finally came to a stop.

"We're here. You can open your eyes," Owen whispered.

While I appreciated his attempt at discretion it wasn't necessary. I had no pride left, not that I really had any, to begin with. These men had seen me at my worst—twice. And it was a toss-up which event was worse. The time they rescued me from a sex trafficker, or the time Owen carried me out of a small bungalow, bloody and broken.

God, I was pathetic.

Yet, not strong enough to change.

I wasn't sure what I'd expected but a beautiful log cabin wasn't it. I could barely make out the A-frame structure, but from what I could see it was huge. Owen opened the door and a rush of frigid air washed over my face, the chill almost enough to make me feel alive, but not enough to make me brave. Just enough to let me know I was no longer in Maryland—a reminder I was on the run from my uncle.

"Thanks," I mumbled as Owen helped me out.

Owen held on to my arm until I was steady on the icy ground. But when he let go, he remained by my side.

"Myles and Kevin went to get the generator started. No sense in us moving through the dark."

What he meant was, there was no sense in *me* trying to

walk through the dark where I would likely slip and fall and break a leg. Owen could make it, no problem.

"Thanks."

A few minutes later, the house lit up and sheer beauty took my frosty breath.

"Come on, I can hear your teeth chattering. Let's get you inside."

"Wait." Owen looked over at me, his brows pinched, and I explained. "It's so beautiful I wanna look at it a minute. I've never seen pine trees so tall before. And the cabin is…magnificent."

"Wait until you see the inside," Owen returned.

"You've been here?"

"A few years back the team and I were stateside and we came out here. Met up with Rhode and stayed a week."

There was something in Owen's tone that gave me pause.

"What happened?"

Owen turned, giving me his full attention. There wasn't enough light, but if there was, I would've been able to see puffs of his breath. But right then, standing in the cold with my fingers going numb, something inside of me warmed. I wouldn't say it was my libido, that had come on station from the first moment I'd been able to have a cognitive thought after he rescued me. From there the lust had grown. Owen was a good-looking man so I wasn't surprised for the first time in my life I'd felt desire. This was something altogether different—it was bigger, it burned.

"What happened?" he parroted.

"Yeah, why'd you and the guys come out here for a week?"

"Why would you ask that?" he asked and narrowed his eyes.

"Sorry. I shouldn't—"

"Don't do that," he rumbled. "Don't apologize, don't stop asking questions, don't stop talking. I was just wondering why'd you ask why we came out?"

I sucked in a lungful of fresh air and gathered all my courage.

"The way you said it…I mean, there was almost sadness in your voice when you said you and the team came out here. Which made me wonder if something had happened. You know, something bad, and that's why you were here."

In the dim moonlight, Owen's eyes bore into mine and I had the strangest urge to roll up on my tippy-toes and kiss him. Well, the thought wasn't strange—I'd been daydreaming about that for months—but the need I felt was like if I didn't give in to the impulse I would explode.

"Yeah, something bad happened," he said, cutting off my inappropriate musing.

"I'm sorry."

Strong fingers threaded with mine and my world started spinning.

And for a moment, standing in the freezing cold with snow under my feet and a sliver of moon overhead, I pretended.

It was dangerous but I did it anyway. I was lost in a dream of make-believe.

A place where I was free. Where I was just me. Where I could love and be loved. Where I was whole and my soul was pure. Where I could have something clean and precious and mine. Where I could touch and kiss and speak. A dream-world where there was no pain and regret.

"Let's get you inside and warm."

I closed my eyes and let my fantasy world drift away. The last vestiges left when Owen tugged my hand and guided me to the porch. I wanted to take a minute, to look around, but Owen was of a different mind. A moment later I was ushered into the cabin.

The big, beautiful, log cabin.

Myles was in a squat in front of the fireplace arranging wood in the firebox. My gaze went to the side door as Gabe walked in with an armful of logs, and without stomping the snow off his boots, he made his way to Myles.

As usual, I remained mute, even if I wanted to scowl at him for tracking snow in.

"It's colder than a witch's tit out there," Gabe mumbled.

"No warmer in here," Myles grumbled the truth.

The only difference being inside where there was no wind, but it was just as cold.

"Kevin turned on the furnace," Myles continued. "He's doing a walkthrough to make sure the vents are open in the bedrooms."

Owen squeezed my hand and my gaze lifted to his. "Why don't you sit down? I'm gonna run out and get the bags."

"I wanna help."

Owen's eyes widened then narrowed. "Ground's covered in snow—"

"Then I can find something to help with in here," I argued.

"Sarah," Owen started and I flinched. I really, really wished I hadn't told him to call me that stupid name. "Babe, it's been a long day. Why don't you sit and relax? I'll grab the bags and when Gabe's done bringing in firewood, maybe he'll take pity on us and cook some dinner."

I was unclear why my feelings were so hurt. Owen was treating me exactly as I'd trained him to do—like I was a helpless, spoiled twit who couldn't do anything but sit on a couch and watch the people around me work.

"I can help."

And without waiting for his rebuttal I toed off my sneakers and marched my unhappy ass to the kitchen. I was admiring the granite countertops when I heard the door open and close. It was then I let out the breath I'd been holding and bowed my head.

What if I tried?

What would it hurt to be Natasha for a little while longer?

What if I could pretend I was a normal person, on a normal vacation in a beautiful log cabin on top of a mountain in Idaho?

Why couldn't I?

CHAPTER 5

The frigid air did nothing to cool my temper.

And the fact I didn't understand why I was pissed only pissed me off more. I knew I was seriously over Natasha's hot and cold personality changes. Her reminding me she wasn't Natasha only to flinch when I called her Sarah. We both knew there was something brewing under the surface—an attraction that I'd thought we'd mutually—albeit silently—agreed we wouldn't act on.

But goddamn if the woman hadn't looked at me like she was waiting for me to kiss her. In the moonlight no less, like a fucking romance movie. More like a horror thriller where the hero bites the dust after the female lead dies doing something incredibly stupid like running back to the crime boss uncle.

Months. I lived with her for months. And in that time, she'd changed a lot. It wasn't lost on me she came from money. In the beginning, it was small insignificant things like her perfectly manicured fingernails and expensive haircut and highlights. Being as I'd been married to a bitch who visited the salon once a week to get her nails done, and once a month for a root-touchup—God forbid a millimeter of brown show—I knew an expensive cut when I saw one. But it was also the things Nat didn't know how to do, little things like how to clean a house. Not that I'd asked her to clean, but when she'd set out on her own to conquer the bathroom she used, I'd caught her reading the back of a Soft Scrub bottle. Yet she knew the perfect wine pairing for scallops. Watching her vacuum was akin to watching a toddler push around a walker—she had no idea what she was doing, yet she delicately held a Walmart wine glass like it was fine crystal.

However, now she was comfortable cooking and cleaning —small changes in her that were actually big changes. We'd never spoken about them, but I knew by the way she smiled when she took cookies from the oven she was proud of herself. She'd taken to watching cooking shows and had even started giving me detailed grocery lists so she could try new recipes. Being as I wasn't fond of cooking and before she'd taken on the role as head chef our meals had been mostly takeout, I didn't complain when a meal was burnt—and in the beginning, there were a lot of burnt meals. I'd simply expressed my gratitude and encouragement.

As much as things had changed, much remained the same. Always closed off and distant, unless she had a nightmare. Then she sought comfort. It was in those moments she let her guard down—not verbally, but emotionally. She'd allow me to hold her while she shook in fear. She'd bury her face in my chest and let me rub her back. But the next morning she'd be locked up tight and the cycle would begin again.

Round and round we went.

Dancing around attraction and what was right.

So her gazing up at me like she wanted me to break the *silent* rule didn't piss me off, it infuriated me.

With more force than was necessary, I opened the back hatch of the Suburban and yanked out the bags.

I could do this.

Now that Pollaski had made his play, it wouldn't be very much longer.

We'd been in a holding pattern waiting to see what Pollaski was going to do. There was no need to stir up a hornets' nest if the man was going to leave Natasha be. That had not been the case; Wilco Pollaski had declared war. It was a fatal error on his part. Zane Lewis was not a man you threatened. But more, he was not a man who took threats against his family kindly. Anyone who was anyone knew who Zane Lewis was, therefore, Pollaski knew and he still threatened Zane's wife Ivy. If that wasn't bad enough he'd threatened Max Brown's wife Eva and their kids. It was debatable which of those two men would come undone first. What wasn't in question was Zane had already put together a team and was making plans.

Pollaski's days were now numbered.

It wouldn't be long before Natasha would be free of her uncle. Yet I didn't know, because she never fucking spoke where she'd go after everything was said and done. Eva and the other women had taken a liking to her, so I'd bet they'd try to talk her into staying in Maryland, though I didn't know what she'd do for work. I'd investigated her, she didn't have a college degree but I also knew that didn't mean shit, she could still find work if she wanted. Thinking on it, the Pollaskis were filthy rich with an emphasis on filthy—dirty money made from prostitution, drugs, and blackmail. But I reckoned some of it would go to Natasha once her uncle was dead.

Why did that piss me the fuck off?

Once again my dilemma slapped me in my face. Natasha *wasn't* Natasha, she was Sarah Pollaski. Heiress to the Pollaski money. The crime family princess, with her crown of thorns.

I did not want that shit in my life.

There it was—the reminder I needed to ignore my attraction.

* * *

I TOOK MY TIME TAKING OUR BAGS UP TO THE MASTER bedroom. I took more time unwrapping the sheets from the plastic that had been left on the foot of the bed by whatever service Rhode used to look after his house while he was away. I'd taken time, a lot of it to tamp down my irritation but it wasn't enough. It flared back to life when I walked into the house and found her in the kitchen. She was speaking softly to Kevin, after months of her not talking to anyone on my team, saving all of her limited words for me I didn't like hearing it. Even if all she was doing was explaining she was heating up soup because there was nothing else in the house to make.

So, yeah, I was taking my sweet-ass time.

I was also trying to build back the wall I needed to keep between us. How I was going to do that while sharing a bed with Nat I didn't know. But there was no way in hell one of the other guys was going to sleep next to her. And none of us was going to share a queen-sized bed in order to give Nat her own room. Which meant for the foreseeable future we wouldn't only be sharing a house but a bed, too.

I made the bed, doing it methodically with military precision, crisp corners like a DI would be inspecting it and I didn't want to get smoked, so the bed was perfect. All of that took a long time, but not long enough. I had to get my shit together for Nat so I could do my job, and when it was done she could move on and live her life.

Without me.

I'd need nor want that hassle. Once was enough. I'd tried, I'd failed, I'd learned. Actually, I'd failed in spectacular fashion. My ex had made known far and wide what a shit husband I'd been. She'd been relentless in this endeavor, so convincing she had me believing it. And I knew the end of our shitty marriage wasn't because I'd done her wrong. But through the divorce I learned—no, I *vowed*—never to do it again. There would be no future second ex-wife for me, no woman who could control my happiness, and no more drama. Not even a hint of it, and Nat had 'drama' tattooed on her forehead.

I made my way downstairs, noting that Myles had a fire going so the temperature in the house was nearly warm enough to take your coat off and not freeze but not quite there yet. There was no TV in the great room, but someone had found a stereo, and rock music piped through the cabin at a low volume. Gabe was stretched out on the tiny loveseat that would comfortably fit two small people, but Gabe's large frame took up the majority of the space. Two other empty recliners sat on either side of the loveseat, facing the fire. They were empty because Myles and Kevin were sitting at the kitchen table with Nat, bowls placed in front of them. Not a single person lifted their gaze as I walked into the kitchen.

That irritated me, too.

And the sudden urge to shake Nat awake washed over me in an unwelcome wave. What the hell did I care if she didn't acknowledge my presence? I meant nothing to her. I was her unpaid bodyguard. Nothing more.

The pan she'd used to cook was washed and set on the strainer next to a cleaned bowl—obviously, Gabe had eaten, as well. The counters were tidied. A towel hung over the handle of the stove the same way Nat did at my house and for some ungodly reason that irked me, too.

"Your bowl's in the microwave." Nat's voice drifted from across the room. "I didn't know how long you'd be."

"Thanks," I returned, and went to the microwave.

"I can make more if that's not enough."

Christ, that pissed me off.

"This is fine," I lied.

After rushing around all day, only snacking on a few protein bars, I was hungry but I didn't want Nat to feed me. As a matter of fact, I didn't want Nat to make dinner or lunch or breakfast for any of us like this was some sort of domestic situation.

"Owen?" Her voice was closer now.

I craned my neck and looked over my shoulder to find her right next to me.

Unfortunately, I was distracted by her nearness, so goddamned distracted by the void of nothingness behind her eyes when she looked at me, I missed her raising her hand. Further, I missed it moving toward me, then lowering and landing on my forearm.

This was not going to work. I should've told Zane to send one of the other guys in my place. I should've stayed back in Maryland and done the jobs I was good at—hunting and extinguishing threats. I was not cut out for close cover. There were other ways I could keep Nat safe and do it keeping me *safe*.

"Yeah?" I forced out.

"There's not much in the house…to eat I mean. But I saw a can of ravioli. I know it's your favorite so I pushed it behind the clam chowder."

I fought against my body going stiff. I failed in this attempt, and Nat felt it. Her left eye twitched, something I'd learned over the months was her tell. A small tic that told me she was uneasy. This was normally the juncture where I'd try to smooth that discomfort, but right then with her touching me, telling me she'd done something thoughtful, even if it was small coming from her, it was huge. All of it. Her taking the chance to lean close, speak softly, reach out on her own to hold on to my arm, something she had never done.

No, I didn't have it in me. Not when there was a riot of thoughts running through my head.

"I know you have to be hungry, and not that I want the others to go without, I just thought..." Nat trailed off, leaving me hanging.

I didn't know what she thought.

I had no fucking clue what was going on in her head.

And I wasn't sure I wanted to know.

Especially when my gut was clenching.

How the hell did she remember something so stupid like I only like canned ravioli? I barely remembered telling her about the guys making fun of me because I refused to eat MREs. If we were only in the field a few days I always packed ravioli and I'd eat them breakfast, lunch, and dinner. I'd take the hit of a few extra pounds in my pack if it meant my stomach wasn't cramping with shit Meals Ready to Eat that should've been call Gut Busters in a Bag.

"Thanks." I barely got the grunted word past my lips when she removed her hand.

And you guessed it, that pissed me way the fuck off.

I didn't want her touching me, but I did. More than anything I wanted her hands and mouth on me. I wanted to live in a perfect universe where I'd never met my ex-wife and Nat was not the daughter of a slain gangster, niece of the current king of the Chicago crime world. Just for a few hours, I wanted to live in a fantasy.

Dangerous thoughts for a man like me.

I had to be ready. I had to be steady. I had to have my shit wired tight.

I ruthlessly shoved those thoughts aside and grabbed the bowl of soup.

I didn't bother taking it to the table like civility called for. I stood at the sink, lifted the bowl to my mouth, and swallowed the lukewarm broth in a few gulps. I ignored Nat and the rest of the guys as I searched for the can of ravioli she'd hidden.

I needed time to myself, something I wouldn't get. Not with Nat sleeping next to me. I dumped the contents of the can into my dirty soup bowl. Alarm bells rang and a feeling I knew well stole over me—bad shit was coming my way.

I could feel it deep in my bones.

CHAPTER 6

Hell had frozen over. I was thinking that was literal, considering I was currently living in the second circle, and each day I figured I continued down this hellish path—final destination the ninth and final circle of hell. I hoped it was blazing hot down there, because up here I was living in a frozen hell. It was only my second day and I was over it.

My nerves were shot, my emotions wrecked, and I wanted nothing more than to run away.

Two nights I had slept next to Owen. That wasn't hell; that was unparalleled torture. Last night when I offered to sleep on the tiny loveseat in the living room Owen had grunted something I couldn't understand then disappeared into the bathroom. Ten minutes later he'd come out hair wet, chest bare, with a pair of sweatpants on. He'd muttered his apology for forgetting to grab a shirt. After that, I slipped into the bathroom, did my business, and by the time I was done, he was in bed, his back to me. Unfortunately, he'd found a shirt. I stood silently in the dimly lit room and wondered how'd he feel if I took all of his shirts downstairs and tossed them in the fireplace. As quickly as I had that thought it fled, that would only further *my* torture.

Just like yesterday morning, I'd slipped out of bed before Owen could awaken and made my way downstairs to start coffee. Only this morning, Gabe had beaten me to it.

His brown eyes lifted from his cup and his gaze raked over me from top to bottom. He didn't bother hiding his scrutiny or his suspicion. I didn't know the man all that well but I knew he didn't trust me. *Smart.*

"Morning," I mumbled. Gabe's chin lifted and I took that as his returned greeting so I continued. "Do you mind if I have some?"

"Help yourself."

He stepped out of the way but not out of the small kitchen which meant I felt his eyes on me while I opened the cupboard and grabbed a mug. Then I felt those eyes boring into the back of my head while I poured my coffee.

At this point, a normal person would ask what the problem was. A normal person might even reprimand him for staring. It was rude. It was also disconcerting. Yet, I said nothing because I knew better than to speak my mind, even about being examined like I was a piece of garbage. Which in a way I was, so it was good I remained silent. I didn't need the reminder. I knew who I was.

"Kevin and I are going down the mountain. Anything you need from the store?"

Gabe's innocuous question took me by surprise and my gaze shot to his.

Big mistake.

He had big brown eyes, and from the way he was looking at me, they were far too knowing. I wasn't sure what exactly he knew but whatever it was, I was sure I didn't want him to know.

"Groceries?" I asked.

"Yeah, and we'll hit a store if you need clothes."

I needed clothes desperately. I was freezing. Luckily, Rhode had some gloves and beanies stashed in the closet. But my thin coat did nothing to fend off the cold which meant I could only go outside for short periods before I got so cold I had to come back inside. The truth was, I could layer on every piece of clothing I had with me and I would still be too cold to explore around the house. And being stuck inside close to Owen was wearing on me. That meant I spent a lot of time alone in the bedroom staring at the ceiling because there weren't any TVs in the cabin.

"Thanks for the offer but I'm fine," I lied, not wanting to take any more charity.

"Listen, Sarah—" Gabe abruptly stopped and his all-too-knowing eyes once again took me in. "I heard what you said."

"What?"

"About you pretending to *not* be a Pollaski."

My insides seized and my breathing picked up. Not liking the direction of the conversation but not having any way to stop Gabe, I remained rooted in place. Silent, like always.

"I don't get you," he muttered and I got the sense he was disappointed in me.

Which was absurd.

When the silence stretched way beyond uncomfortable I broke.

"What don't you get?" I whispered.

"Why you're making everything so hard."

"I'm not…" I stopped before I could finish my lie.

I was making everything difficult but I wasn't doing it on purpose. At least I didn't think I was.

"I don't know what to say," I admitted. "I don't understand why any of you would help me. That doesn't mean I'm not grateful, especially to Owen. But I don't get it. I'm trash, and when you all had the chance to get rid of me, you didn't. Why?"

"I think that's the only time since I've met you, you've answered a question honestly."

He probably wasn't wrong but it still hurt to be called a

liar, even in a roundabout, back-handed way. Though I was that, too.

"You don't think you're worthy of kindness?" he asked instead of answering my question.

"No."

"More honesty," he mumbled and I shrugged.

"You do remember my own blood sold me, right? I don't believe anyone does something for nothing. That's not the way the world works. But for the life of me, I can't figure out why Owen would take me in. Why all of you helped him. Why Zane Lewis would pay for all this." I stretched my arms out and motioned to the room. "All he had to do was let me go back and the nightmare would be over."

"And you'd be dead."

Well, there was that. But I wasn't going to confirm or insult Gabe by denying that would happen when we both knew that was a very high possibility.

"My suggestion—stop trying to figure out the why and start paying attention to what's going on around you. The way you grew up is not the way of the world. It was fucked and only got worse for you. I get you don't want to trust what's happening but if you opened your eyes you'd see it. Not a single one of us wants a damn thing from you. Most especially Owen."

Damn, that hurt so bad it sizzled down my spine until I had to slump forward to alleviate some of the pain. It was good Owen didn't want anything from me because I had nothing to give.

"Natasha?" Gabe rumbled and my gaze sliced back to his. "I see you misunderstood what I meant."

"I didn't," I rushed out. "I know he's a good man and I'm sorry if I insinuated something different. As much as I can trust, I trust Owen. I know he'd never want anything in return for being nice to me. I don't have anything to give and he knows that. He took me and gave me a safe place. I appreciate that more than I can say."

"Nat—"

"Have you ever needed help?" I whispered.

"I'm—"

"Like, really needed it? Been forced to accept charity because you had nothing?"

Oh, God, what was I doing?

"Babe—"

"It's hard," I choked out. "It's so hard because I *need* help. I have nothing and I'm so tired. So I took everything Owen was offering. I took the safe place because I've never, not once in my life, laid my head down and known I was safe. I've never woken up without crushing fear about what that day would bring except the mornings I've woken up next to Owen. I don't mean to be difficult. I don't mean to make everyone's life hard but I'm scared straight down to my soul that if I let myself believe when the pain comes back—and it always does—it will be more than I can bear. I need silence, it's the only protection I have. I learned early on I'm to be seen and not heard. I learned to keep my mouth shut no matter what. No. Matter. What."

"Okay, Nat. I'll give you that for now. But just to say, at some point you're gonna have to explain what that means. And not to me, to Owen. I think you know he deserves to hear that from you. But I'll leave you with this—yes, I've needed help. Yes, I know the bitter taste when you're forced to take handouts because you have no other choice. So from where I'm standing, consider my part in keeping you safe payback. Me paying back the kindness strangers showed me when I had nothing, allowing me to have what I have now. That's how the world works, Nat. Give and take. And one day, when you're clear of this you'll find your way to pay back the kindness you received by giving it to someone who needs it."

Before I could come up with something to say Gabe stepped around me and strode through the living room then disappeared. A moment later I heard the front door open and I stood there thinking Gabe had the right idea. I really wished I had a warm coat so I could go for a long walk to clear my head.

That was twice in so many days that two separate people essentially told me the same thing. Okay, there was no *essentially* about it, Owen and Gabe had both told me to start paying attention. The issue was, I *was* paying attention.

I knew my place.

Or did I?

No, of course, I did. I was not to be heard. Little girls who made too much noise got punished. Women who spoke without permission or when not directly spoken to got pain. I knew this. So why did I want to scream at the top of my lungs? Why did I want to rage at the universe for sticking me with people who were filthy, nasty demons? Why did I want to explain everything to Owen so he'd understand I wasn't trying to make his life misery, I was trying to protect him the only way I could? I was keeping him safe by not telling him my secrets.

Lies.

All lies.

I wasn't telling him because if he knew, he'd turn his back on me and I couldn't stand to see him look at me like I was less than the nothing he already thought I was.

I glanced at the smoldering embers in the fireplace and let my imagination run free. What if I was free to be me, the me I wanted to be, not who I was born as? I wouldn't ever have wanted to live in a cold, sterile brownstone. I wouldn't have wanted marble floors, or wainscoting, or crystal chandeliers. I looked around the living room of the cabin and took in the log walls and the wood floors, then up to the planked ceiling. Beautiful to visit but too rustic. Too much brown. Too earthy, even though it was homey. No. If I wasn't born a Pollaski and I was free to be *just* me I would choose Owen's home. Roomy but not too big. Four bedrooms. No formal living room or dining room no one spent any time in. No library, no parlor, no fancy dressing area. Just a pretty home on a nice street. Comfort all around. Safety. Love. Home. That was all I'd ever wanted.

"Babe?" Owen called and I jerked from my silly daydream.

"Hey."

"You okay?"

Concern.

That was all I saw. Gone were yesterday's impatience and the day before that's irritation.

Just concern for *just* me.

"I'd never worn sneakers until you bought me my first pair," I blurted out bizarrely.

"Come again?"

"Well, when I was a little girl I might've, though I doubt it. I was always required to wear a skirt or a dress. Sandals. Ballet flats. Mary Janes. And always heels after I turned eighteen. Even in the winter when there was snow on the ground. Pumps or heeled boots. Never flats and certainly never sneakers. And jeans were only to be paired with a blouse and a blazer and only if staying in and there wouldn't be guests. Skirts and dresses for leaving the house and entertaining. So I owned a few pairs of jeans but I was never allowed to wear them like I do now. And I always had to have my hair and makeup done. A minimum of three pieces of jewelry. Ears, throat, wrist. No exception, staying in or leaving the house. Though if it was formal, it was always diamonds. Ears, throat, and wrist. I could add a strand of something else if it complemented my diamonds but a Pollaski never attended a society function without diamonds. Wealth and manners were always to be on display. Both my father and uncle demanded it. Pussy was to remain silent until spoken to. Pussy was to accept whatever form of appreciation offered, be it a lewd comment, invitation to dinner, or a fuck in the coatroom. Compliance was non-negotiable, but gratuity was expected. Pussy wasn't limited to my father's stable; it included his wife, then his daughter, our household staff, anyone and everyone under the umbrella of Barny Pollaski was available for a price. I had no choices in his house, none in my uncle's. So thank you for buying me my first pair of sneakers. I appreciate them more than I can express."

Owen's green eyes bore into mine. The longer he stared at me without blinking the more turbulent they became. Then without a word he turned on his bare feet and stomped away. I held my breath wondering what I'd said that pissed him off so badly when the bedroom door slammed violently and I exhaled.

"Damn, woman," Gabe grunted from the doorway and I jumped. "I told you to give him something but I didn't think I needed to explain how to deliver that blow."

"Huh?"

"Nat, seriously. The shit you said was fucked-up. No man wants to hear that. But a man who cares about a woman really doesn't want to hear that fucked-up shit happened to *her*. Next time you share, cushion that, at least with a warning so he can prepare."

"Huh?"

"This. Right here. What just happened was what I was talking about when I told you to start paying attention. He cares, and Owen doesn't care about a lot. He trusts us, he trusts Zane, and to a certain extent he trusts the other guys who work at Z Corps. But he does not ever get in deep with a woman. Not since Naomi. The bitch did a number on him. You living with him is not something he'd normally do. The fact that it even happened in the first place shocks me. But more, when Myles offered to have you go live with him, Owen nearly took his head off. Which tells me he cares about you. So next time, Nat, for the love of all things holy, give a guy a break and warn him."

Naomi?

Did a number on him?

Why did I suddenly want to find this woman and knock her around?

"I just wanted to thank him for buying me sneakers. I don't know why I told him the rest. Once I started it just came out." Stupid, stupid me. "I shouldn't have—"

"Oh, no. Don't do that. You should've. And you should tell him more. Just go gentle like. You know, ease into it."

I thought about what Gabe said and it was probably good advice, he seemed like a smart man. But I had no idea what he was talking about.

"I don't know what that means. I know how to be quiet. That's all I know."

Gabe let out a long-suffering sigh and shook his head. "Then forget what I said, and just go with it. Blurt out what you need. But, babe, don't be surprised when he storms off."

I didn't want Owen storming off. I didn't want him mad or upset at me. Worse, I didn't want him to feel sorry, or sorrier for me. No. Quiet was the right way to go. This wasn't my imaginary dream world where I could just be me.

"Nat—"

"I'm fine, Gabe. Thank you for your advice and wisdom. It's appreciated."

"At the risk of sounding like a total asshole, I'm gonna leave you with one more thing."

I held Gabe's eyes thinking I didn't want him to leave me with one more thing. I didn't want more advice. I didn't even want to be in the same room as him. "Grow some balls, woman, and take control."

My eyes narrowed and my shoulders tensed. That wasn't

very nice to say and he certainly didn't know me well enough to say that to me.

"You know?" I snapped. "Something I never understood, why do people say that? Grow some balls? Why would I want to grow two soft, delicate testicles when all it takes is a tiny flick and excruciating pain follows? At least a vagina can take a pounding…"

Gabe's lips twitched before they curved up. His eyebrows hitched up and when I didn't continue he smirked.

"Go on, finish. A vagina can take a pounding…"

"I didn't mean it that way."

"No? Pray tell, Nat, how did you mean it?"

I felt my cheeks heat and my eyes darted around the room in an effort to hide my embarrassment. I didn't want to talk about vaginas with Gabe. I don't even know why I said what I said. And now I had a feeling he was teasing me, but I'd never been teased before so I didn't know how it was done. But Gabe was smiling and his tone was light.

"Are you teasing me?" I asked on a whisper.

"Yeah, babe. I'm teasing you. Though you do have a valid point, vaginas are much tougher. But just so my suggestion's not lost—I was being serious. While we're here…no, scratch that…anytime you're with Owen or the rest of us, you are safe to be you. Whoever you want that to be. You can say what you want, act like you want, dress as you want, and you can trust we'll protect you while you're doing it."

"I'm not—"

"Don't answer, Nat. Just think about it."

I nodded, happy to end the discussion. Gabe turned to leave but before he got too far something hit me.

"Why are you calling me Natasha?"

"Because despite what you said to Owen, you're not Sarah. And my guess would be you never were a Pollaski. Not in any real way. You're you, the name you gave yourself —Natasha."

Gabe left me in the living room and my gaze went back to the dwindling embers in the fireplace.

Maybe I could just be Natasha for a little while longer. Owen liked Natasha. I liked Natasha; she didn't belong to the Pollaskis. The only problem with that was I didn't know who Natasha was, not exactly. I didn't know what *she* liked, what *she* wanted. But if Gabe were to be believed they'd all make it safe for me to find out.

CHAPTER 7

Envy wasn't something I was prone to. But hearing Natasha talking to Gabe made me green with it.

All those words, all at once.

Other than her fucked-up story about sneakers I don't think I'd heard her speak that much all at once. Hell, I don't think she'd spoken that many words all in one day before. Though maybe she had and I was just jealous as fuck that she was talking to Gabe. I was greedy, I wanted all of her words.

My day got worse when Gabe and Kevin left to go down the mountain and Nat went back to silence. She uttered a few words to Myles about his pancakes being in the microwave but said not a word to me. Then after breakfast, she promptly cleaned the kitchen and disappeared upstairs.

It wasn't until hours later when Gabe got back to the cabin, dropped a bag full of clothes on the table, and yelled up the stairs did she come back down. That was the first I'd seen of her in hours. But she certainly scuttled her ass when Gabe bellowed for her. Not that I'd attempted to talk to her but it still pissed me off. Then she'd proceeded to argue with Gabe about the jacket, boots, and fleece-lined Carhartts he'd bought her. That irritation was two-fold. I didn't want Gabe buying her anything. I wanted to be the one to give all the firsts. And I could safely guess she'd never owned a pair of Carhartts before. However, bigger than the new clothes was the fact she was arguing. Hands on her hips, face red, deep frown on her pretty face, she'd said more words. Words that I wanted to belong to me.

In the end, Nat had no choice but to give in when Gabe pulled a knife out of his pocket and cut all the tags off proclaiming they couldn't be taken back. Then he left the room. She gave it a few minutes just standing there in front of a pile of clothes before her gaze went around the room. I waited for her to say something to me but she didn't.

Now I was outside, in the freezing-ass cold splitting wood for no other reason than to blow off some energy. Later I'd go for a run and if that didn't burn out the fire in my stomach I'd do a full workout.

Bottom line was something had to give. I was damn close to my breaking point. Being out of control was not a feeling I was accustomed to and now that I'd felt it in excess I *really* didn't fucking like it.

I heard snow crunching and looked up from the log to find Nat bundled up walking my way. Christ, I was going to kill Gabe. There wasn't a damn thing that should've been sexy about a woman wearing coal-colored canvas work pants and a black puffy North Face down jacket but fuck me running the woman looked like a sexy mannequin for cold-weather gear. Yeah, I was going with that thought because the only other way to describe what I was seeing as she slowly made her way to me was she looked like a woman I wanted to strip down so I could see what she was hiding under all those layers. And those types of thoughts were hazardous.

"Hey," she quietly greeted.

"Everything okay?"

For once Nat's face didn't close down and she didn't

blank her expression. Instead, she stopped in front of me and didn't hide her nervousness. I didn't know if this was because she'd decided to take Gabe's advice, even though I'd told her the same thing but she hadn't listened to me, or if she was so overwhelmed she could no longer push it aside. For my peace of mind, I was hoping it was the latter.

"I...um...may I help?"

"Help?"

"I've never chopped wood before." She tipped her head to the log. "I know I won't be any good at it and I don't want to mess it up, so if you don't want to show me I understand."

"Can't screw up splitting a log, Nat."

She didn't smile, she rarely did, but her lips did twitch and I felt that tiny movement straight in my balls.

Fuck.

I glanced down at her glove-covered hands and pulled off my leather work gloves.

"Can't swing an ax with those on," I told her. "Put mine on."

"Never mind then."

What the hell?

"You gotta problem with wearing a pair of gloves that have been on my hands?"

"What? No. But I don't think mine will fit on those big paws you have and I don't want your hands getting cold."

I wasn't going to go there, where my mind wanted to go, wandering to all the places I'd like to touch with my big paws. So instead I focused on her use of the asinine word.

"Paws?"

"Well, that's what you call abnormally large hands."

There was nothing abnormal about my hands. But I liked that she'd considered them. Liked it in a way that made it hard to ignore how much I wanted her to experience all the ways I could pleasure her with my hands.

"Babe."

"What? They're man's hands. Rough and…well, just rough I guess." Then to my absolute horror, she mistook what I was sure was a stunned expression and started to backpedal. "I don't mean to offend you. I just mean…I don't know what I mean."

"You didn't offend me. I get what you're saying."

"All my life I've been around men, no, not men—males. Who got their nails manicured." Nat shrugged and I begged, albeit in my head, for her to continue.

She didn't.

"Manicured?"

"Yeah. A trim, file, and buff. Part of the manicure is a soak and lotion to keep their hands soft."

"That's jacked."

My off-handed comment made the corner of her mouth tip up and I begged again wanting to see her smile.

She didn't smile but she continued. "Yeah, well, I'd guess soft men like soft hands. Real men have work-roughed hands. Rugged and strong. I'd never felt hands like that until you."

Jesus, she was killing me. I didn't need the reminder she'd already felt my hands. Though the only time I'd touched her was after she'd had a nightmare, and even if it made me a son of a bitch, at those times I was very aware I was stroking her back or holding her hand as she calmed herself down. Mind, body, and soul. Each time I'd held her the awareness was crisp and had me hardening in all the wrong places. Seeing her now, looking like a wet dream, I didn't need the reminder.

"Come here, I'll show you how to split a log."

My change of subject was abrupt and maybe even rude but I doubted Nat would find me sporting a hard-on polite, therefore, the change of topic was very much needed.

"Are you sure I'm not bothering you?"

The fact she asked that made me feel like a dick. We'd

been in Idaho for two days now and I'd avoided her the best I could. This was not done because I was busy, it was done in an effort to fortify my resolve knowing she'd be climbing into the same bed as me. The temptation of her so great I needed hours to talk myself out of rolling her close and pinning her to the bed. And more hours still to remind myself of all the reasons kissing her would be a bad idea. My cock didn't agree with my head. And my heart was warring with my good sense.

How everything had become a tangled mess was beyond me. But for the life of me, I couldn't find a way to untie the tether.

"Come here and put these on." I held up the leather gloves and waited for her to pull her knitted ones off and shove them in her coat pocket. After she'd stowed hers she took mine and shoved her hands in the too-big gloves.

"Um…" She waved her hands and the leather tips flopped. "I think these are too big."

It was then I was reminded of how small *her* hands were. Tiny hands I'd felt hold onto my forearms, felt the softness glide over my skin while I'd held her.

Jesus fuck.

This was a bad idea. All of it. The worst.

Yet I didn't put an end to the madness, instead, I picked up the ax and handed it to her. Then I proceeded to step behind her, wrap my arms around her, and place my hands over hers. Once I had her in the position I wanted her, I lifted the ax over her shoulder and helped her cut through the log.

"Like that," I told her and realized she'd gone stiff in my arms.

I started to slide away but froze when I heard her whimper.

Goddammit.

I was not some adolescent boy who could not control his

body. But with Natasha pressed against me I was finding it hard to will my cock to stay soft. Who the fuck was I kidding? I was half-hard and getting stiffer by the second. I blew out a breath, fighting for control when Nat shivered in my arms. Just that minuscule movement caused her ass to lightly brush against my crotch and I growled my disapproval. The growl was a miscalculation on my part. The moment the sound emitted from my throat everything about Natasha softened.

"Nat," I warned.

"Just this," she whispered and I swear to God her soft plea pierced my hardened heart. But more, those words shot straight to my cock and I lost the battle. There was nothing left to fight—I was hard as a rock and there was no way for me to hide it with her leaning against me.

"*This* isn't smart."

"Then I want to be stupid. Just for a minute. I just want to know what it feels like."

All sorts of dirty thoughts raced through my head, each of them driving the last delicious fantasy to the back, one image after another of Natasha laid out before me, naked, exposed, opened, and waiting for me. Those didn't concern me as much as the visions of me holding her, stroking her silky hair, gently kissing her neck, breathing in her scent.

Fucked.

I was so fucked.

Yet I didn't deny her and move away. I stood still and allowed Natasha to feel whatever it was she wanted to feel. The whole time praying it was the feel of my desire pressed against her ass and not something else. All of it dangerous. But attraction was one thing. Intimacy, now that would be perilous—deadly even. That was something I could never give another woman.

"Thank you," she murmured then asked louder, "May I try again?"

"Yeah." I cleared my throat. "This time by yourself."

I let go of the ax handle and stepped aside.

"It's heavier than I thought."

That's what she said.

Jesus fuck. What was I, thirteen?

"Let the blade do the work," I told her.

She gave a solemn nod, lifted the ax the same way we'd done, and grunted when she brought it down, missing the log altogether.

"Oops."

Shit. She could be cute. Something I absolutely didn't need to know.

I set the piece of wood back up on the chopping block and said, "This time keep your eyes open and focus on where you want the blade to hit."

"Okay."

It took two more tries before she made contact, and when she did I wished she hadn't.

"Did you see that?" Nat beamed. "I did it."

"Yeah, you did."

"One more?"

Hell no.

No more.

I could take no fucking more of her wide smile and shining eyes.

"Sure."

I set up another log and waited. This time she didn't miss.

"Damn, I'm good," she chirped.

Christ. Sweet Jesus. Why was I being punished? What could I have done that was so terrible to earn a bouncing, happy, smiling Natasha?

"You are," I agreed and watched as Nat tipped her head back.

"It's snowing again," she noted.

Thank fuck.

"Come on, Paul Bunyan, let's get you into the house before you start chopping down trees."

Natasha's smile widened and I wanted to punch myself in the face for being a wiseass. One more big, open, easy smile like that and I'd toss her ass in the snow and I wouldn't be responsible for my actions.

"I'm taking these."

Nat bent and picked up the wood she'd split. All six pieces, including the two we'd done together, and started marching toward the cabin.

Thankfully, she was too far away to hear my groan when I caught sight of her ass in those damn Carhartts. What the hell was wrong with me?

She was still stomping the snow off her boots when I made it to the back porch. And I closed my eyes like a child blocking out her ass as it jiggled.

Straight. To. Hell.

That was where I was going. Not the slow ride. I was on the fast train.

"Can you get the door?"

As carefully as I could since she was standing right in front of the damn thing I reached around her and turned the handle and gave it a push.

"Look what I did," Nat announced as we entered the house.

Gabe, Kevin, and Myles all turned in unison.

Gabe smiled, Kevin's brows snapped together, and Myles frowned.

Apparently, Nat didn't notice or was too happy to care about the men's reactions because she continued.

"Owen taught me how to split wood." She gave the pile in her arms a shake. "Tonight we're gonna burn this."

No one spoke and to my shock, Natasha walked to the fireplace, set the wood on top of the small stack that was already there, and continued to ramble.

"Now I can take a turn. Though don't expect much. I miss more than I hit but I can totally bring in at least a few hours' worth of wood. Right, Owen?"

Her question jolted me from my stupor.

"At least," I agreed.

"I'm gonna go warm up, then I'll start dinner."

Jesus Christ, who was this woman?

Nat's smiling face turned my way and I felt that smile stab through me.

"Thanks again for teaching me."

"Anytime."

And with one last beautiful smile, she pranced out of the room and up the stairs.

"Did that just happen?" Kevin broke the silence.

"Yep."

"Jesus. I've never seen her smile," Myles added.

"Nope."

Gabe didn't say a damn thing. He let his smirk do the talking.

Asshole.

"So... you're giving lessons now, lumberjack?" Kevin joked.

"Don't."

"Lighten up, brother. It's nice to see the woman happy. Now if someone could pull the two-by-four out of your anus perhaps we could have an enjoyable stay."

"That sounds like a plan. Then I can shove it up your ass for being annoying," I returned.

"Don't take sloppy seconds, bro, and you should know that. Like my toys firsthand and out of the package."

I wasn't going there and Kevin knew he had me when he busted out laughing.

"No one wants to hear about your ass fetish," Gabe joined. "Not the giving or receiving."

"Not my fault the rest of you don't appreciate—"

"Maybe the rest of us simply like to keep our kinks private," Myles cut Kevin off.

I tuned out the guys' banter. I heard it a million times before. Kevin would call Myles out on his lie because Myles was a gossip and had zero trouble talking about his kinks. Gabe however would be tight-lipped and just laugh while Kev and Myles argued and reminisced.

Wherever Natasha was I hoped she couldn't hear the rude comments. I'd successfully pushed her earlier speech out of my head. But now, I was having trouble stopping her words from invading my mind.

Lewd comments. Appreciation. Quick fuck. Gratuity.

Everything slammed into me at once.

"Quiet," I demanded. "Nat's upstairs and she does not need to hear this shit."

Gabe smiled. Kevin snickered. Myles looked thoughtful.

Whatever.

"Owen—"

"It's under control," I told Myles.

"Brother, I saw," he pushed.

"Saw what?" I asked, hoping he didn't see Nat pressed against me.

"The smile."

Damn. *Shit*. Fuck.

"Not many men could resist a smile like that. Knowing it's rare, knowing he had to earn it, and once he did, fight to keep it. Just saying—"

"It doesn't belong to me and it never will."

It being her smile. And it hurt like a motherfucker to admit that because Myles was absolutely right.

CHAPTER 8

I had no idea what had gotten into me but I knew it felt good.

Damn good.

So good that I was going to continue to live in my make-believe world.

I would use this time to bank as many good memories as I could so when I didn't have Owen anymore I'd still have something.

In real life, I wasn't allowed to keep anything, but not even my uncle could take my memories. So I was going to rack them up and keep them close. I was going to memorize everything I could. I was going to chop wood and wear boots. I was going to cook to my heart's desire. I was going to sweep and clean. And I might even talk more, but I wasn't sure about that yet. That required a lot of courage.

But everything else I was going to do.

I finished with my shower, got dressed, and in the mirror I smiled at my bare face. It had been months since I'd worn a face full of makeup and I liked it. It felt good. I glanced up at my hair and I smiled bigger. Just me. No fancy cut—thank God. No salon-given highlights. Natural hair that was way longer than I normally wore. I liked that, too. I hoped when my uncle got his filthy hands back on me he didn't demand I cut it.

Enough, I chastised.

I was not going to think about Wilco Pollaski.

I was going to live in my dream world for as long as I could.

I was going to be Natasha.

And for once in my miserable life, I felt good.

I didn't miss the flutter in my belly, the sensation wholly new. It was different than the butterflies I got when I was near Owen. I understood what those were—pure unholy need. Straight up desire. Just because I'd never actually felt desire for a man didn't mean I didn't recognize the feeling. This was different, this I couldn't comprehend. This made me feel dizzy with unknown anticipation.

I wanted to twirl around like a child.

A very unwelcomed thought hit me square in the chest. I was a woman. I had been sent to Switzerland for finishing school. I hadn't been allowed to attend college. No, that was a waste of money since I'd never hold a job but I knew useless information such as the difference between a butter knife, salad knife, meat knife, and fish knife. Soup spoon and dessert spoon. I could set a proper table—all twenty-three pieces from a water goblet to a sherry glass. Who needed to know that? Social graces and proper etiquette for every situation. I was refined. I was taught how to walk, sit, stand, and speak. I was no better than a trained dog.

But you know what I *wasn't* taught? How to think for myself. How to be brave. How to live on my own, pay bills, cook, clean. But most of all I had no idea how to be normal.

I was a robot.

The guys probably thought I was silly and immature after my stupidity about the firewood.

Owen probably thought I was an idiot. I mean, who got

excited about splitting wood and owning sneakers. Thank God, I hadn't told him how happy I was to wear a cool-as-hell pair of work pants. And boots. Gabe had bought me a pair of snow boots. I grew up in Chicago, it snowed there—a lot. Yet I'd never worn an honest-to-goodness pair of warm snow boots. I'd never worn leather work gloves. Nor had I ever worn a knitted wool beanie. I had mink hats, cashmere, vintage Burberry. But a regular knit skullcap—no way.

I wanted this life so desperately I could taste it.

I wanted all of it.

And if I was being completely honest, I wanted Owen, too. I wanted to keep him forever but I'd settle for having him only while I lived in my make-believe dreamland.

"Hey."

I jumped away from the mirror and found Kevin standing in the open doorway of the bedroom. "Damn. Sorry. I thought you heard me."

"Lost in thought," I mumbled.

"Must not have been very good thoughts the way you were frowning."

Damn. Now what did I do?

"Um."

"Again, sorry. That was probably rude. I'm not known for my tact. Or maybe my delivery is bad. But I didn't mean to be impolite."

Well, there was some honesty for you.

I didn't know Kevin well. Actually, I didn't know any of the guys well except for Owen and now Gabe. Not that a handful of words made you know someone but Gabe had shown kindness and he'd been sincere and open about something that I'd assume was private. I found it unlikely a man like him would go around telling stories about having to accept food from strangers.

Shit. I hadn't asked him anything about that. I hadn't offered him my condolences. People did that, right? Friends, people who were getting to know each other, they asked questions. God, he must've thought I was an insensitive twit.

"How old are you?"

Where in the world did that come from?

Kevin's lips twitched but he seemed unoffended when he answered, "Forty-five."

"Forty-five?"

My shock must've registered on my face because he smiled huge.

"That surprises you?"

"Well, yeah. You don't look forty-five. I'd guess you were closer to my age."

"I have a lot to say about that, however, none of it Owen would appreciate. So, I'll simply say thank you for the compliment."

What did that mean? Why would Owen care about what Kevin might say?

"You're welcome," I muttered.

"Don't clam up on me now."

"Huh?"

"You get this look, right before you close down. Like you have something to say but lock the words away. Your cheeks tinge pink and it looks painful, babe. As I said, I'm bad with delivery. I'm far too blunt and I know it but I've never understood why people dance around a topic or waste time using five-thousand words when it could've been said in ten. So, I say it straight but for you, I'll try to go easy. You're safe to say whatever you want to say. Act how you want to act. None of us are gonna hurt you. Just don't clam up. Say what's on your mind."

"Everything is on my mind."

"Everything?" he asked with a smile.

"Everything," I confirmed.

"Then you better start talking."

"What if no one likes what I have to say?"

Sweet Mary mother of God. Where did *that* come from?

"You a bitch?"

I felt my body tense and I didn't know how to answer that.

"I don't know."

Kevin busted out laughing. I had the sense he wasn't laughing *at* me but I still got an uneasy feeling.

"You're not a bitch."

"How do you know, when I don't even know? Maybe I am. I've never been allowed to be one. Maybe I'll try being one and I'll like it."

"Right. Go ahead, I'd like to see you try. That'll be fun to watch."

My back snapped straight, I lifted my chin in what I hoped was indignation, and I narrowed my eyes. This had the opposite effect of what I was hoping for. I knew because Kevin started chuckling.

"Yeah, it'll be fun. You should totally try being a bitch for the night."

"Whatever," I huffed. "Was there something you needed?" I asked haughtily.

"Yeah, there was," he told me with his body still shaking with humor.

Damn. I was really bad at this bitch business.

"Well?" I prompted.

"You mentioned dinner. I'm gonna grill steaks. You got everything else."

"Grill steaks in the snow?"

"Rain, sleet, snow doesn't matter. When there are steaks to be grilled you brave the elements."

"Jeez, you must really like meat," I mumbled.

"Again, so much to say. However Owen would kick my ass if I said them."

"Why would you say that?"

"Because I know Owen. He wouldn't appreciate me standing in the doorway of his room making you blush."

"That makes no sense."

"It does to me and does to Owen. But it's cute you have no idea what I'm talking about."

"You're a strange man, Kevin."

"I've been called a lot of things, strange has never been one of them. But we'll go with that. It's safer for me if you tell Owen you think I'm strange rather than you telling him we had a conversation about my meat."

What?

Then a little inkling of what he might be saying tickled the back of my brain.

"Are you trying to make a sex joke?" I asked.

Kevin didn't answer. What he did do was laugh.

"I should be scandalized," I told him and he laughed harder.

"Scandalized," he sputtered.

"And I didn't think men liked their members being referred to as *meat*."

"Members?" he asked through laughter.

"Or junk. Am I wrong? I wouldn't know, but that's what I've read."

"Christ, you're hilarious. You should ask Owen what he prefers his member being called."

Yeah, no.

That was never going to happen.

Kevin pushed away from the doorframe. Still smiling he said, "Meat's going on the grill in ten minutes."

"Steaks," I corrected.

"Right, steaks. Better get your ass downstairs in the kitchen, woman. We're all starved."

"Woman?"

Kevin didn't answer, he walked away laughing.

"I have a name!" I shouted at his back.

"You have multiple names. Pick one and stick to it," he returned without looking back at me and I froze.

I did have multiple names.

One I hated. One I gave myself.

Without thinking I blurted out, "Natasha."

"Good choice."

Good choice.

Choice.

My frozen insides thawed. I made a choice. A good one.

I could do this. I could make choices. I was *going* to make choices. And my first one was going to be… no, my second one was going to be to live in this world. The one that I created in the here and now in a cabin in Idaho with Owen. Yes, that was my choice and I was sticking to it. No changing my mind, no matter what. Even if I got scared I was going to listen to Owen, I was going to stop breathing and start living. Well, I was going to keep breathing as that was a necessity to live, but I was going to live *my* life.

I didn't care I half-skipped down the stairs. I didn't care all eyes—minus Kevin's who was still upstairs—were on me. And when I glanced at the roaring fire I smiled huge. I'd split that wood. Me. With my own two hands. Of course, I wasn't thinking about Owen teaching me how. I wasn't going to think about how good it felt having his big, solid body pressed to my back. I wasn't going to think about how he'd given me a minute to enjoy the feeling that being in his arms created. If I was lucky, he thought I was asking for a moment to feel his hard-on. That was not the first time I'd felt the hard length of him pressed against me. Not even the second time.

"And…she smiles," Gabe noted.

Without looking at him I said, "I cut that wood."

"You did. All six pieces."

That made my gaze slice to his.

"Are you making fun of me?"

"Nope."

"Good. Because Kevin's grilling *meat*. Which means I'm making the sides. And I'd hate for you to have an unfortunate bout of diarrhea."

"Jesus," Owen muttered.

"Oh, now she's got jokes." Gabe laughed.

"*She* has a name. It's Natasha or Nat. And *she's* not joking, *she's* threatening to poison your food. Though I don't think Ex-Lax is high on the Poison Control's list of dangerous substances but I can assure you, your butthole might differ before the night is over."

Utter silence ensued. It was so quiet it was deafening. Only the crackling of the fire could be heard and I was scared shitless—the irony wasn't lost on me—that I'd made a huge mistake.

That was, until the crackling was replaced with raucous, thundering laughter. It filled the room. No, it filled the cabin. And it warmed me straight through.

Straight. Through.

"I've been ordered to the kitchen," I mumbled and scurried away.

Not because hearing their laughter didn't feel good. It did. It was the best feeling in the world. But more than that, it was Owen's smile. The way he was staring at me with approval and pride made me want to flee. I was going to try on this new me. I was going to be brave. But seeing Owen look at me like that made me greedy. It made me want to run across the room, jump in his arms, and beg him to pretend with me. It made me want to invite him into my dreamland where we could live together as a couple. Where he'd pretend to love me and I could tell him the truth about how I felt about him and he'd gladly accept my affection.

But that wasn't going to happen. He'd made it clear where we stood. Friends. Nothing more.

CHAPTER 9

She has a name. It's Natasha or Nat.

I was screwed.

The change in Nat was unmistakable. It was in your face. Punch to the gut. And straight-up beautiful.

So beautiful I knew I was screwed. I was fucked.

Over the months, she'd let some of her light shine through. Tiny pieces that she unintentionally let slip. So I knew she had a sense of humor, but damn, I hadn't known she was funny. And I thought the smile she'd given me earlier was blinding, I was dead wrong.

The woman who had walked into the living room, smiling at the fire, cracking a joke, was beyond dangerous. Beyond blinding. *That* woman, the woman who called herself Natasha, she made you want to fall to your knees.

I could not fall to my knees. I'd never get up. I'd be lost. I'd drown in her. And damn if I didn't want to. Not for a night, but for however long it lasted.

A hand curled around my shoulder and jolted me from my thoughts.

"Brother, your woman poisons my food I'm using your toilet," Gabe said.

My woman?

Nat was not my anything.

I didn't point this out.

"Then I'd go make nice if I were you because you're not using my toilet. As a matter of fact, I'll lock your ass out of the cabin."

"Right," Gabe mumbled and gave me a bone-jarring shake before he let go and walked away.

What he didn't do was comment about me not denying Nat was my woman. Which I should've done. But I was too stunned by her about-face to contemplate why I hadn't.

Kevin came down the stairs, passed me with a lift of his chin and a smile I didn't like. He made his way into the kitchen, and because I didn't like that secret smile of his one fucking bit I followed.

"Need help?" I asked Nat.

She looked up from the asparagus she was rinsing and cut her eyes to Kevin who was unwrapping the steaks.

"I don't. Just going to sauté the asparagus and roast some red potatoes. But Kev might need help with his meat."

Kev?

What the hell?

Kevin snickered and my gaze left Natasha and landed on my friend in time to see him grin.

What in the actual hell?

"What's funny?" I demanded to know.

Surprisingly, it wasn't Kevin who answered since I was looking directly at him. But more shocking because the woman who normally kept quiet did the talking and she did it without pausing to take a breath.

"Your buddy over there has informed me he likes meat. He's like a modern-day Dr. Seuss. He'll grill it in the rain. He'll grill it in sleet. He'll grill it in the snow. I'm sure if I thought about it I could come up with a rhyme about all the places he likes to eat it. Bottom line is I think he *really* likes it. Though I don't think he was talking about steak. I'm new to sexual innuendos, but I'm positive there's a joke in there somewhere and I'm fairly certain it would be offensive. When I think of it, I'll tell you."

Natasha paused, her head tilted to the side and her goddamn cheeks turned pink. I was so mesmerized by how beautiful she was I forgot I was pissed. Then she went on and I remembered. "Come to think of it, maybe you don't want to help him with his meat. I think that's code for his penis."

Did she just say penis?

What the fuck?

"Say again?"

She didn't skip a beat. Not a single pulse when she smiled hugely and said, "Penis?"

Kevin roared with laughter.

I did not.

No, I growled and it sounded furious even to my own ears. But the new Nat, the woman who was standing in the kitchen talking about goddamn meat and penises and sexual innuendoes didn't flinch.

No. Not her. Instead, she swept the smile off her face and glared at me in mock annoyance. I knew she was faking because she was giggling.

Fucking giggling.

The mute woman I'd lived with for months was giggling.

I was beyond screwed. I wanted to scoop her up, take her upstairs, lay her out, and fuck her silly. Fuck her while she smiled. Fuck her while she giggled. Fuck her until she was boneless.

"If you don't like the word penis, you shouldn't have demanded I say it again."

"What the fuck?" I muttered.

"She's not wrong," Kevin put in.

"Do you wanna explain what Nat's talking about?" I asked Kevin.

"Not particularly." He shrugged.

"Someone better explain why the fuck she thinks you like eating meat so much. And, friend, there better be a damn good reason."

"Just to set the record straight," Kevin grunted as he tried to get ahold of his laughter. "I don't eat meat. I eat tacos."

"Are you fucking ten?"

"God, I hope ten year olds aren't talking about eating tacos," he deadpanned.

"Jesus, fuck." I shook my head and looked at the hard-wood floor.

A small hand touched my back and heat seared through me but I didn't move. I stood still waiting for the sensation to pass. It didn't, it kept burning. So damn hot I knew without a doubt she'd branded me. No other woman's touch would do. Never again.

"I don't think he's talking about *taco* tacos," she whispered.

"You don't say?"

Then she giggled again and my night went completely to shit when she rested her breast against my arm as her body shook with laughter.

"Before I don't have any teeth left I'm going outside to grill my—"

"Swear to God, you say meat one more time I'm gonna kill you."

"What's wrong with meat?" Gabe asked as he walked into the kitchen.

No, that was the moment my night went to hell. Complete and utter hell. Natasha dissolved into a fit of giggles. She did this pressed tight, she did it for a long time, and through it all my body was on fire.

I waited until she was done and standing upright before I left the room.

The last thing I heard was Nat's snickered words.

"Owen seems pretty sensitive about meat. Maybe we should turn vegetarian."

Christ.

I couldn't take this new Natasha. I needed her to go back to the soft, quiet woman I met.

The one who absolutely did not talk about meat, tacos, and dicks.

* * *

EACH STEP FELT LIKE I WAS *THAT* MUCH CLOSER TO THE FIERY misery that waited for me behind the closed bedroom door. Dinner had been filled with all sorts of information. Natasha had shockingly answered the guys' questions. None of them had been invasive, mostly they were about the places she'd traveled. No one touched on her family. And by the end of the meal, she'd let her guard down and was talking freely, at least with surface information. Nat had even asked her own questions.

It was unnerving.

But the night took a turn after Gabe and I had cleaned up the kitchen. Kevin had unearthed a deck of cards and poker chips. Natasha's gaze took in the cards like they'd bite her. Then with all of us sitting around the table playing Texas Hold 'em Nat let a little more slip. The first three games she lost, horribly and on purpose. There was no hiding she'd thrown the games. Gabe being Gabe, the shit talker he was, poked fun at her. And if I wasn't actively trying to tamp down all emotion I would've been proud at the way she sat taller, glared, then proceeded to take the next two games like a pro.

Nat knew how to play poker. Not just knew, but fucking

knew how to play. If I didn't know any better, and I was beginning to think I didn't know jackshit, I'd say she was counting cards. What I did know as fact was the woman had an unreadable poker face. Throughout the games, she gave nothing away, not in her body language or expression. It was as if she'd slipped into her comfort zone and three hours later with all the chips piled in front of her she looked crestfallen.

She was not dumb; she knew what she'd let slip. A wealthy woman who lived a sheltered life did not play poker as well as she did. Unless there was a reason. Being as her family were all gangsters involved in selling sex, protection, drugs, and anything else they could, gambling wasn't a stretch. The question was, what was Nat's role? And why hadn't our investigation found the gambling?

Nat's kitchen table winnings equaled nine-thousand-one-hundred fake dollars. Not bad for a few hours' worth of work. At a high roller table, she could make ten times that much. Before she disappeared upstairs she helped clean up, and no one said a word about her skills. Gabe didn't even grumble about losing his ass. It was like the last few hours hadn't happened.

Then she was gone.

Meaningful looks were exchanged between me and the team and I had no doubt Myles would be reporting this new piece of the puzzle to Garrett. He ran all of Z Corps' in-house investigations. If there was something that ran beyond his scope Zane outsourced to a man called Tex. And there was nothing Tex couldn't hack. One of the two men would get us what we needed once they were pointed in the right direction.

In the meantime, while we were waiting for Zane to make his move, I was living a nightmare with a woman I wanted but would never have. And right then I was walking toward the bedroom I shared with her, where she was undoubtedly already in bed. A bed we shared. A bed that I would get into and fight against the pull of her. A bed we'd use to sleep in but a place where I wanted to do other things to her.

Fuck me.

Zane better find his way in and do it quickly.

I was fighting a losing battle and I knew it.

CHAPTER 10

Another day down. Another night lying in bed feigning sleep. Owen was kind enough to let me go upstairs first, get ready, and crawl under the covers before he came up. He also gave it enough time that a normal person who wasn't a ball of stress with everything weighing her down would've already been fast asleep. But, no, not me. I had way too much on my mind. Especially right then.

As soon as the poker chips came out I should've lied and said I had a headache. But I was too caught up living in my dreamland, where I was Natasha, not Sarah Pollaski. I thought I could fool the guys into thinking I didn't know how to play. The first couple of games had been easy to lose, but for some reason when Gabe started making fun of me, I forgot I was supposed to be Nat. Hell, I forgot that I was supposed to be Sarah the cultured woman who…who what? Was innocent? Didn't participate in her family's business? Who wasn't a criminal?

That was a joke. And not the funny kind that made everyone in the room bust a gut and smile. A sad joke that made me want to curl into a ball and cry.

The door creaked open and I held my breath. Owen

walked across the room on near-silent feet and quietly clicked the bathroom door closed behind him.

So began the game.

I willed my body to remain still. Hoped I'd find sleep before he came back out. Prayed he decided to shower, shave, maybe take a long soak in the tub, thus giving me a long time to fall asleep. Minutes later with my hopes dashed and prayers unanswered Owen got into bed.

And like the nights before he was far away from me. I didn't know this for a fact—the room was dark and I would never turn on the light and look—but he was so far away I wondered if half his body was off the bed. Owen was a big guy, it was a queen-sized bed, but it felt like there were yards between us.

I hated it.

Yet it was necessary. Smart even. But that didn't mean I had to like it.

Unlike the two nights before, my body wasn't cooperating, nor was my mind. I was restless, worried, and scared Owen and the guys would figure out who I really was and kick me out. And if I was being a hundred percent truthful, while I shouldn't have ever entertained the thoughts, I was turned on. It had been hours and hours since the wood chopping incident yet I couldn't forget how good it felt to be in Owen's arms.

I needed to forget but I didn't want to. The whole point of living in this new world was to memorize every moment. However, I hadn't taken into consideration that I'd be left aching. And that ache started in my heart but was not limited to the organ. Oh, no, it radiated all over—breasts, core, straight to my legs that wouldn't stop moving. I clenched my thighs and tried to quell the throbbing but it only made it worse.

"Nat," Owen growled, and that sound did unspeakable things to my desire.

"Sorry," I squeaked and rolled to my side. That made my sweatpants push up my legs.

Now I was seriously uncomfortable. I gave it a few moments then used my right foot to catch the hem of the left leg of my pants and tried to smooth it down. This caused the bed to move— no, that caused Owen to move and his movement was what caused the mattress to compress at my back.

"You got restless leg syndrome or something?"

I didn't but that sounded like a wonderful excuse so I went with it.

"Yeah. Sorry. My sweats are bunched."

"Jesus," he muttered but did not move.

I didn't either but I did remind him, "I offered to take the couch."

"You're not sleeping on the damn couch."

"Then don't complain about me moving," I shot back.

"Fix your pants and lie still."

"Sheesh," I mumbled and reached down to do just that. "Someone's got their panties in a bunch."

"Fuck me," he grouched.

Yes, please.

Once I'd rearranged my pants I laid back down expecting him to move back to his side of the bed. He didn't. He stayed crowding me. His proximity ratcheted up the fantasy of him finally doing something more than sleep in this bed. The thought made me rub my legs together.

"Nat," he grunted.

"I'm not doing anything," I rallied.

"You damn well are and you know it."

There was no way he could know what I was thinking.

"I'm not. But if I'm bothering you I'll get up and—"

Then I stopped talking because I was frozen solid. Owen rolled toward me, pushing me mostly to my stomach and pinning me to the bed. One arm over my back, his hand resting by my chest, one thick, muscular leg over mine holding me still.

Welp. That wasn't the fantasy but I couldn't deny it felt good having his heat at my back.

Once I was settled his deep voice rumbled from behind me.

"Babe, stop."

"What?"

"Please, Nat, for your sake and mine stop."

"I don't know what you're talking about."

"You think I don't know what you're thinking, but I do. You think I'm lying less than a foot away and I don't feel you clenching your thighs, but I do. And lastly, you think I don't know why that is, but you're dead fucking wrong. What I'm saying is, I know exactly what we both want but I'm asking you to fucking stop because we are not going there."

Oh, shit. He totally knew.

How in the world did he know?

Because you rubbed up against him like a cat in heat when he was being nice showing you how to use an ax, dumbass. My mind screamed.

Right. Shit. I had done that.

And you were rubbing your legs together to find friction instead of getting up and taking care of your problem alone in the bathroom. My mind reprimanded.

Damn.

Totally busted but I wasn't going to admit to anything.

"I don't know what you're talking about," I lied.

Owen gave me more of his weight, lowered his head so his mouth was right next to my ear.

"Liar." The two syllables blew across my neck and I shivered. "Fuck me."

God, yes! Let's do that.

"Owen," I wheezed. "I really don't—"

"Natasha, you do. You might have a world-class poker

face but you're a shit liar. And I hate to burst your bubble, but your body does not lie."

World-class poker face.

That reminder was all I needed to snap me back to reality.

"I'm not thinking anything."

"Right." He drew out the word sarcastically. "So if I checked you wouldn't be wet."

"Checked?"

"Yeah, baby, checked. You're telling me if I put my hand down your panties I wouldn't find you wet?"

No, he wouldn't. He'd find me *soaking* wet.

That made me shiver again and Owen curse.

"Maybe you should roll away," I told him.

"Maybe I'm gonna stay right here trapping your legs so you stop trying to get yourself off less than a *fucking foot* from where I'm trying to sleep."

Holy Hannah, he *totally* knew.

There was nothing to say, he'd caught me in all my lies, so I stayed quiet.

Silence was my friend. My best option. It always had been and always would be.

After a few minutes, Owen grunted another curse and that was how I fell asleep—Owen half on top of me trapping me between the soft mattress and his hard body. I didn't know how it happened because at the time I never thought I'd find it, but I did and I slept soundly.

Warm and safe.

* * *

Now it was morning and I was alone in bed and the room was bright. Not because there was a light on but the sun was shining in. I didn't need to look at the clock to tell me I'd slept in. I rolled to my back, stretched, and before I could talk myself out of it my hand pushed down the front of my sweatpants. I glanced at the bathroom door—it was shut but there was no light coming from under the door. The bedroom door was also closed and I didn't hear any noise.

The guys were all downstairs being quiet, or some of them had left the house.

Thank God.

I needed five minutes to myself, then I'd get up and start my day. Hopefully in a good mood. One that would allow me to ignore the tension building between me and Owen. He was right, I needed to stop. I had to ignore pent-up emotions.

On that thought I gently teased myself, searching through my memories of Owen, and decided to focus on last night. My finger pushed through my wetness and I barely stifled a moan. I was primed and ready and all it had taken was the thought of Owen's big body over mine. Only in my fantasy, I was on my back and it was his fingers dipping into my pussy and his tongue was swirling my nipple. On that thought, my other hand went into my shirt. I pinched my nipple.

So close but not enough. I closed my eyes and Owen's face filled my mind. His green eyes full of hunger as his fingers plunged in and out. *Holy shit, I was so, so close.* He smiled before he lowered his head and sucked my nipple into his mouth, letting his teeth graze the sensitive bud. *Almost.* Strong, thick fingers continued to thrust, the sound of my moans filled the room. *There. Right there.* My hips bucked and my climax washed over me but Owen didn't stop, his thumb pressed over my clit rubbing hard until one orgasm slid into two.

Then I heard it. Owen's deep growl, and I moaned again wanting to feel the rumble against my over-sensitive clit. I wanted his mouth between my legs. I would beg if I had to, I'd do anything to have his mouth on my…

"What the fuck?"

My eyes snapped open, my hands stilled, and my world shattered.

Oh. My. God.

The haze of my orgasm cleared with lightning speed. The door to the bathroom was open. Owen was next to the bed staring down at me with a frown. No, not a frown, with a *horrified* frown. His eyes were not filled with hunger, they were filled with anger. His chest was bare, his hair was wet, and the lounge pants he wore to bed were on but riding low on his hips. And lastly, he was not wearing anything under those pants because I could see his erection tenting. That should've taken some of the sting out of his expression. Maybe he wasn't horrified, maybe he was just angry I had masturbated in the bed we shared while he was in the bathroom.

I, of course, didn't know he was in there. I most certainly wouldn't have done what I did had I known. But I did do it. Now he was staring at me and one of my hands was between my legs, the other still cupping my breast. And I swear, I didn't want to feel anything other than extreme embarrassment but I felt my pussy clench my fingers and I might've twitched.

"Jesus, fuck, woman."

Okay, there was no might about it, I'd twitched.

It was at that moment I should've moved my hands but I didn't. How did one pull their hand out of their panties with their excitement coating their finger and not make a show of it? I didn't know the answer so I didn't move. I just laid there.

Owen's hand moved and my gaze followed as he grabbed his erection over his pants and squeezed. Good gracious. I wished that was my hand or at least he could've lowered his pants so I could see.

He didn't do either.

But with his hand still on his hard-on, he irately mumbled, "Already took care of this once." Then I watched in rapid fascination as he stroked over those stupid pants. "Come out and find you fucking yourself on the bed, moaning and squirming, now I got a new problem."

I didn't want to know what his new problem was. But I had a feeling he was going to tell me. I had a moment of reprieve, only because Owen was silent as he aggressively, way tighter than I would've ever dared to grip, gave his dick another hard tug.

"Fucking hell, you still got your fingers in your pussy."

I did. But I wasn't going to tell him. Not because silence was my best friend but because I couldn't form words. I was too turned on watching him touch himself. And, I, too, had a new problem. One flick over my clit and I'd come again. That was all it would take. I had his beautiful face, his fantastic chest, his hard dick at eye level, and his rough voice. All of that the perfect recipe for an awesome orgasm.

A whimper slipped past my lips and as a reward he growled.

Good Lord Almighty.

My gaze snapped to his and raw hunger stared back at me.

This lasted a long time. The two of us staring at each other. Both of us challenging the other.

A dare.

A taunt.

Who would do what first?

Then Owen ended the standoff.

"Fuck it."

He yanked the covers off me and I started to disengage my hand but stopped when Owen grunted, "Do not move."

I didn't move. I didn't even breathe when he climbed onto the bed and pulled my sweats down, somehow hooking my panties with them. His head tipped down and his gaze landed between my legs. The hand still covering my sex trembled under Owen's examination. Then he shoved my t-shirt up until the material was bunched under my chin.

"Owen."

His eyes snapped to mine and I forgot what I was going to say. Or perhaps I was going to ask a question. More likely I was going to beg him to do something other than stare but I was lost in his hunger.

"You want this?" he asked.

I nodded my head.

"Nothing changes, Nat."

I nodded because I knew that. Nothing would change. There would be no future. There couldn't be. This would be a fling, maybe even a one and done, but I didn't care. I was used to not getting what I wanted. Long ago I'd accepted I didn't have a future.

"Nothing changes, Owen," I verbally agreed.

"Don't have protection, so this isn't gonna go far."

"I have an IUD. I'm clean. I haven't been with a man in five years," I blurted out.

Then I prayed that in his current state he wouldn't ask me why I'd had a long dry spell.

"It hasn't been five years for me," he returned.

I wanted to know how long it'd been. If he had women since I'd come to live with him. But it was none of my business and frankly, it would hurt so bad knowing he'd been with someone or lots of someones since I'd lived with him I seriously never, *ever* wanted to know.

It seemed our conversation was over and Owen punctuated this by grabbing my wrist and pulling my hand out from between my legs. Then he lifted it and sucked two of my fingers into his mouth.

I was too caught up in the way his tongue felt licking my fingers clean to make a sound. But inside I was shouting for joy.

He pulled my fingers free and asked, "How many times did you make yourself come?"

"Twice."

His eyes darkened and I trembled.

"What were you thinking about?"

"You." My cheeks burned with my admission.

"Don't get shy now, Nat. I walked in and watched you working yourself over. Whatever you were thinking had to be good, you were so lost in it you didn't hear me come in and I was not quiet. So, tell me, what was I doing to you?"

I would think about how rude it was for him to walk in and watch instead of stopping me later.

"The first one you were fingering me."

"That all?" Oh, shit. I didn't think I had it in me to tell him. "You were playing up top, Nat. I watched you pulling your nipple. Were you thinking about my mouth being there?"

"Yes."

"And the second one? What were you thinking about then?"

"I don't think I was thinking about anything as much as I heard you growl because that's what started the second one. Hearing you. Or maybe it was just one long one. But hearing the sound of you is what did it."

"Christ," he bit out. "I want you playing with your tits while I eat you. Both hands, Nat."

Owen let go of my wrist, and before my limp hand could fall like a ton of bricks, I took control of the limb and lowered it to the bed.

"I don't know if I can do that while you're watching."

"You already did," he reminded me.

Conflicting emotions warred in my head. I wanted this. I wanted to be brave enough to do what Owen asked. Hell, I wanted to let go of all my inhibitions and just feel. Let Owen guide me wherever he wanted to take me.

Slowly I dragged my hand over the sheet then picked it up and cupped my other breast.

"Fuck, you're perfect."

And something inside of me settled. That was what I needed.

"Months I've been wondering."

"Wondering what?"

"What you'd taste like, what you'd feel like, what you'd look like. I haven't touched you yet, but all of it's better than I thought."

"Then touch me."

"Not yet. I want to watch you get yourself ready for me first."

I wasn't sure exactly what that meant but I had a fairly good idea, so in an effort not to delay or chicken out because I really wanted to be touched, I slid my thumbs over my nipples. And because I seriously wanted to touch him I engaged my forefinger and rolled my nipples, pinching and even tugging until I was panting again.

"Beautiful," he drawled and his hands finally touched me.

Feather-light against the inside of my legs from my knee up to the top of my thigh.

"More."

"Slow."

I didn't want slow. I wanted more, and to communicate this wish, I bent my knees and planted my feet on the mattress.

Owen dropped his gaze from my breast to between my legs and I waited.

Then I waited some more until he finally lowered himself between my legs.

"Wider."

I let my knees fall open, then slow was a thing of the past. There was no gentle build-up.

Oh, no, Owen ate.

He licked, he sucked, he nibbled. He didn't use his fingers but his tongue to fuck me, and when I came it was swift and my body was wound so tight before it snapped it was a wonder I didn't fly apart.

But there was no time to recover before he was up and his mouth was on mine and he fucked me with his tongue again. It was a kiss but it wasn't. It was almost violent in its intensity. He was in full control—all I had to do was follow. Something else settled inside of me. Owen would absolutely take me where he wanted to go and I was a-okay with that.

He broke the kiss and I licked my lips tasting myself and I loved knowing it was Owen's lips that had transferred the flavor. I freaking loved the reason why his mouth tasted like me. Later I might wonder if that was strange but for now, I was basking in three orgasms. Two I'd given myself, one from Owen.

"Want more, baby. You ready?"

More?

Oh, yeah, I was ready for more.

But I simply replied, "Yeah."

Owen rolled away, tugged his pants down, and I was positive my jaw dropped. I knew for a fact I blinked, then I blinked again just to make sure I was seeing what I thought I was seeing.

"Um…" I muttered and snapped my mouth closed.

Houston, we have a problem.

That wasn't going to fit.

I know, I know, right about now you're wondering if I'm exaggerating. Telling tall tales. Maybe even bullshitting.

But I was not.

Length, above average but not crazy. It was the girth. Owen was thick. Not just above-average—thick as in a porn star would take one look at his dick and quit over safety concerns. There was no way he'd fit in my mouth, not unless I found a way to unhinge my jaw. And since humans were not capable of cranial kinesis this was an impossibility. Yet for some reason I wanted to test my assumption and put my mouth on him.

Way before I was done contemplating his circumference Owen rolled back, guided my hand between his legs, and my fingers wrapped around his dick. He used his hand over mine to stroke.

"I like it hard, baby, hold on tight," he told me and I tightened my grip. "Oh, yeah, just like that." His hand left mine and I continued to jerk my fist up and down. "Hitch your leg up over my hip, but don't lose my cock."

We were on our sides facing each other but my head was a tad bit higher than his. His face was at breast-level and I had to stretch to keep hold of him. But the moment my leg was where he wanted Owen made the uncomfortable position worth it. In a dual assault, his tongue swiped over my nipple and two thick fingers drove into my pussy. After that, he didn't stop. Just like before Owen didn't waste time, he didn't coax, he didn't charm—he took. And the faster his fingers thrust the faster I pumped my hand on his dick.

I was close and getting closer. My hips were moving on their own reaching for the climax that was dancing *just* out of reach. I wanted it. I wanted to come around his fingers like in my fantasy, but more, I wanted him to. I doubled my efforts and added a twist on my downward slides. This earned me a groan so I did it again only harder. Unfortunately, that made him remove his mouth from my nipple and that was a damn shame because his mouth felt good. He knew what he was doing, suck hard but not painful. Giving me the edge of his teeth, scraping but not biting. I wanted his mouth back desperately but I quickly changed my mind when he spoke.

"Jesus fuck," he rumbled. "Better. So much better. Taste better. Feel better. Look better. Kiss better. Had no clue a woman could feel this good."

The compliment albeit crass warmed someplace deep inside of me that had always been cold. A place I knew was there but I'd locked away because if I didn't I'd freeze to death.

Sex was a weapon.

It was a tool.

A means to an end.

But not with Owen.

"You are so goddamn beautiful, Natasha."

His words slammed into me. Heart and soul. Mind and body. My breasts swelled and phantom twinges pulled my nipples. My pussy clenched and convulsed. And I closed my eyes against the onslaught of emotions.

"Wanna see you, Nat."

I shook my head and let the pleasure he was creating sweep me away. Pleasure, not emotion.

Owen's hand stilled, his fingers deep, his palm pressing against my clit, and my eyes opened.

"Don't stop."

"Keep your eyes open."

I nodded and he went back to work. This time he curled his fingers and my body jerked.

"Oh, yeah. There it is, baby, ride my fingers and come for me."

There was no option but to obey. I kept my eyes open and rode his fingers until my climax built and I was ready to explode.

"Harder, Nat. Take me with you."

I did as he asked and moments later Owen's long, rough groan filled my ears right before I felt warm splashes of his orgasm hit my stomach. I only got to enjoy the excitement of my accomplishment for a few seconds before I was floating in a sea of euphoria. Total bliss.

But the best part was not my fourth orgasm of the day, and it wasn't even nine o'clock in the morning. It wasn't that

I'd stroked Owen's heavy cock until he came on my stomach. It wasn't even that I'd lived a dream I never thought I would.

It was the look on Owen's face. Gone was the hunger that had turned into savage aggression. It was his eyes. The way he was looking at me. Tenderness shone so brightly it seared my soul. No one had ever looked at me like that before. Like they gave even the barest hint of care if I lived or died.

Owen would never love me. But he was giving me a gift. He was giving kindness.

And he thought I was *goddamn* beautiful.

I'd take that to my grave. I'd take it and lock it deep, remember it for the rest of my life. I'd cherish it and recall it whenever I needed it.

Then Owen gave me another gift, this one no less beautiful than the way he'd looked at me. His chin dipped and his lips pressed against my forehead before he lowered them and brushed them over mine. Tender. Sweet. Gentle. I'd never had any of those things. No one had ever brushed their lips over mine.

I swallowed the lump in my throat and prayed now was not going to be the time I broke down into tears.

I didn't know what to say so I followed Owen's lead and softly kissed his mouth, his jaw, and brushed my lips over his cheek. When my mouth got close to his ear I whispered something I thought he should know.

"No matter what I will never forget you. Until the day I die I will remember every moment I spent with you. You're the best person I have ever known, Owen."

I ignored the stillness. I pretended he hadn't turned to stone next to me. I refused to allow what that meant to penetrate my brain. I couldn't—or I would break.

CHAPTER 11

A smart man would get out of bed. *No.* A smart man would never have gotten into bed. A smart man would've quietly backed his ass back into the bathroom and given the woman masturbating on the bed privacy.

But, no, not me. I came back into the bedroom after escaping into the bathroom to do the very same thing Nat had done. The only difference was, she hadn't caught me jerking off. I'd been *smart* enough to go into the bathroom and lock the door.

Then why had I been so pissed when I saw her taking care of herself? What the hell did I care if she was goddamn masturbating? It was perfectly normal, healthy even for a woman to... Christ, I had to stop thinking about Nat and what she'd been doing.

The evidence of orgasm number two was still on Nat's belly and my cock was already getting hard. Something that hadn't happened to me in years.

But I had more to worry about than my thickening cock.

Until the day I die I will remember every moment I spent with you.

What the hell did I say to that? I knew what I wanted to

say. I wanted to tell her she wouldn't have to remember a damn thing because she'd be by my side until the day she died. I knew I wanted to possess her beauty. I knew I wanted to watch her come into her own and flourish. I knew I never wanted to wake up and live in a world that Natasha was not a part of. I wanted her in my home and in my life.

But damn if that was not a possibility.

It was too late for me to pretend I didn't care about her. Well beyond me denying if I let myself I could fall in love with her. The point was I cared, too much. I'd already disappointed one wife. And according to Naomi I'd been such a crap husband, hurt her so badly, that her only option was to hurt me ten-fold as payback. I'd lived through that, and after years of reflection, I hadn't been a great partner to Naomi, and part of the reason why was because I'd been young. The other part was because I'd had no business marrying a woman I could live without. I'd loved her, but it was not consuming. I'd cared, but not enough to quit my job. I married Naomi because I thought it was the next logical step. And we both paid. But if I were wrong and I was straight-up just a shit husband because I was a selfish asshole, I'd never put another woman through that. Most especially Natasha. Once she was clear of the bullshit she deserved the best. That was not me.

So I would never allow myself to fall in love with her.

But I did care, so I would show her kindness and respect.

Once I tucked my dick back in my pants, that was.

Actually, I needed to find my pants first.

No, first I needed to clean my come off her belly.

Christ. I was an asshole and I already behaved like one. I decided to stay the course so I lowered my mouth to hers.

This time, I didn't go at her like a starving man.

This time I went gentle. A soft slide of my tongue over Nat's bottom lip. She tilted her head and returned the gesture. Fucking hell, how could a swipe of her tongue feel so good? I continued to tease—light and coaxing—content with just this, a kiss but not really. Licking and nibbling. Until her hand glided up over my shoulder, around the back of my neck, then into my hair. My scalp tingled as she combed her fingers through it. My intention had not been to go another round. I didn't have any condoms and I'd never had sex without them. Not even with my wife. Part of me was thrilled—divine intervention—the reminder I absolutely should not take us further than we'd already gone.

Natasha leaned closer, her t-shirt still bunched under her chin. And I knew I needed to end the kiss when she moaned into my mouth. It was a different moan than she made when she got off. This noise was full of need, it was a plea, and unfortunately, I wasn't going to give her what she wanted.

I broke the kiss and rested my forehead against hers, needing a moment to calm my racing heart.

When was the last time my heart pounded in my chest from a kiss?

Christ. I could love this woman and it wouldn't take me much to get there.

"Shower time," I told her.

When she didn't move I gave her hip a squeeze.

"Nat?"

"Please let me have this," she whispered.

Fucking hell.

She was killing me. Killing. Me.

"Have what, baby?"

"This. What we shared. Please let me have it and keep it. Don't tell me it shouldn't have happened or it was a mistake. And if you regret it please, I'm begging you, don't ever tell me. Just let me keep this."

Yep. She was killing me. Each word she spoke carved away some of the scar tissue around my heart. Adhesions that had served me well, protected me. Blisters that had hardened into calluses; I felt them when I breathed,

111

cautioning me to never let my guard down, to keep women out.

"I don't regret a damn thing," I assured her.

And I didn't. But I shouldn't have taken us where I did. However, I'd keep that to myself.

She nodded and rolled away. I missed her immediately. With savage force, I shoved those thoughts aside and watched her sit up and pull her tee down, then she threw her legs over the side of the bed, and with the hem of her shirt barely covering her ass she walked to the bathroom.

This was precisely the moment I should get up and beat feet. Leave the room, give her privacy, then find something to do for the rest of the day that would keep me from her. We both needed the physical distance to get our heads sorted.

But I knew I wasn't going to do that.

By my estimation, I was the stupidest man on the planet. My guess was confirmed when I got out of bed and followed her into the bathroom. She had not locked the door, if she had, my idiocy would've been over I would've dressed and left her to it. But she hadn't so I took the unintentional invitation and walked in.

Natasha had wasted no time undressing. Not that she had much to take off but the shirt was on the counter and there she stood naked. I didn't know what I expected her to do—kicking me out would've been a good start, but bold as brass she ignored my presence and stepped into the shower. I took that as my second unwitting invitation and helped myself to her shower.

It was a fool thing to do. And over the next few minutes, I learned exactly how dumb I was. She said not a word when I grabbed the soap and washed her. She remained silent when I rinsed away the suds. I didn't think about how good she felt as my hands roamed her body. I ignored the fast beat of her heart. I pushed away all thoughts about how beautiful she was, how I wanted to be the man who had the right to

OWEN (SPECIAL FORCES: OPERATION ALPHA)

shower with her every morning. The honor of being the man who would care for her in all ways. It wasn't until I was done, standing behind her I kissed her shoulder, did she speak.

"Thank you, Owen."

Fuck. Killing. Me.

I kissed her shoulder again and I hoped she caught the meaning. Then I stepped out, dried off, got dressed, and got the fuck out of there.

I hoped like hell she didn't think to change the sheets.

I hoped she was telling the truth and she'd never forget me because I'd never forget a single moment of her being in my life. But more, when this was done, I hoped she didn't hate me.

* * *

I WAS IN THE KITCHEN EATING THE BAGEL I'D TOASTED wondering why Nat hadn't come down yet when Gabe came in with a wide smile that looked an awful lot like a smirk.

"Mornin'." He beamed.

Yes, he fucking beamed.

Damn.

"Whatever you think you know, keep to yourself."

"Hate to break it to you, but the cat is out of the bag," he returned.

My gut tightened and I was no longer hungry.

And for the record, Gabe didn't hate to tell me anything. He looked mighty pleased to be the bearer of bad news.

"Right. Then how about you help me make sure everyone knows not to mention it."

"Think she knows what happened, brother."

"Don't be a dick." The side of Gabe's mouth hitched up but he wisely didn't comment. "I don't want her to be embarrassed."

"Yeah, I get it. I can totally see how bumping uglies with you would be embarrassing."

I didn't correct Gabe, it would only make it worse. If he wanted to assume I'd fucked Nat, I was going to let him.

"Happy for you," he whispered. "Know what that twat did to you. But it was a long time ago. Too long for you to still be licking your wounds. Glad you found something else to lick."

Jesus.

"It's not—"

"If it's not, then you're a dumb fuck and you need to make short work of turning it into that."

"Good morning." Nat's unsure voice cut off my rebuttal.

"Mornin'," Gabe greeted.

"You hungry? I can make eggs."

"Nope. We've all already eaten."

Nat's gaze shot to mine and her eyes widened. Probably in question, maybe in embarrassment, but most likely she knew everyone had heard us.

Damn.

"Okay. Then I'll just…" She trailed off and I wracked my brain with something to say to ease her discomfort.

"After you eat, bundle up and we'll take a walk down to the creek."

Seriously, dummy, that's what you came up with?

"Creek?"

"Back of the property. Rapid Lightning Creek."

"Okay."

Gabe cleared his throat and my attention went back to him. He jerked his head in the direction of the living room.

"I think you're being summoned," Nat said when Gabe walked away.

"Subtlety is not his strong suit."

"So, Kevin has no tact. Gabe isn't subtle. That leaves you and Myles. What aren't you good at?"

I didn't want to think about how Nat knew Kevin was

mostly rude because he had zero filter. Likely it had something to do with their *meat* conversation and I wasn't going to think about that either.

"Myles's only fault is he's a control freak."

"Control freak? Like he's bossy?"

"No. Like when we're out on an op, he controls the mission. Which isn't bad, he's the team leader, but part of that control is putting himself in the line of fire. The way he controls the outcome is by ensuring if someone's taking a bullet it will be him before one of us."

The color bleached from Nat's face and I mentally chastised myself. We'd never talked about what I did for Z Corps —what the team did. She'd assumed we were in the investigation business and I'd let her think that. It wasn't entirely incorrect but neither was it completely correct.

I'd had no intentions of telling her what we really did.

"Missions?"

Fuck me.

I ignored her question and moved on.

"Grab something to eat. I'm gonna see what Gabe needs."

Nat wasn't stupid; she caught on immediately. She also didn't hide her disappointment. Which made me think about the months I'd spent with her. I'd thought she was shit at hiding her emotions—even if she was silent they played on her face, in the tense way she held her body. Or opposite— when she was relaxed she had ways of showing that, too. But now, after last night's poker game I was beginning to wonder if she wasn't playing me.

"Wait," she called and I turned my head to look back at her. "What aren't you good at?"

"Nothing."

She didn't respond, but her lips tipped up and I felt that movement in my dick. It seemed I did have a regret, a big one. I'd tasted her pussy, her tits, her mouth, but she had not tasted me. And watching that sexy-as-all-fuck mouth smile, I wished I'd had the chance to feel those lips wrapped around my cock. But it was too late for that. We had what we had and it was done. So, hell yeah, I had a regret.

In an effort to turn my thoughts from what she'd look like with my cock in her mouth I didn't stick around to hear her reply. I went in search of Gabe. I found him standing by the front door, boots, hat, and coat on.

"Where are you off to?" I asked.

"Got shit to do in town."

"What kind of shit?"

My tone was accusatory and Gabe's scowl told me he didn't appreciate it but I didn't care. He was acting suspect. I didn't need my team running off in an attempt to clear out of the house to push me and Nat together.

"Oh, you know, fill up the jerry cans with diesel so we don't freeze to death and the lights stay on. I also thought I'd get some gasoline so we could fill up the side-by-side and snowmobiles. Shit like *that*."

Damn. We were running on the generator, and with the mountain already a snowy mess, we decided against having Rhode's tank filled with diesel which would necessitate us using jugs. Not ideal, but it also meant no one knew the cabin was occupied.

"Need help?"

"Nope, but Kevin's coming along for the ride. That is, if he ever gets out of the shower. Luckily, I think it's a cold one so he's not burning through the hot water tank. Someone should advise Rhode he needs an insta-hot. It takes forever for his water heater to refill."

"You trying to piss me off?"

"Yep."

"Come again?"

"Yes. I'm trying to piss you off. Most likely Kev's in a cold shower because we all heard your woman. I wanna drill that into your thick skull so you get pissed. Then you'll think

116

about why that is. And hopefully, come to the correct conclusion. Which is, you don't like much that your friend got a hard-on listening to—"

"Now you're not pissing me off, you're making me angry," I said, halting Gabe from continuing.

"Good. Angry is great. You should stay that way because I'm not gonna let up until you pull your head outta your ass."

I rolled my shoulders and prayed for patience. Gabe's biggest fault wasn't his lack of subtlety. It was his incessant need to fix everyone else's problems. He was a nosy fucker and if I didn't put a stop to it, he'd stay his course. And when he didn't make headway with me he'd turn to Natasha.

"Is this why you called me over here?"

"No. I wanted you to know we set Garrett on Nat's poker skills. It wasn't lost on any of us she was counting outs. A skill that is difficult to learn but harder to master. Myles is a damn good poker player and she outplayed him. He wasn't going easy and she didn't beat him, she bested him and did it with ease. Garrett's already looking into tables around Chicago, checking ties to Wilco Pollaski."

Gabe wasn't wrong. Myles was the best poker player out of all of us. Not only that, but he'd won huge pots in Vegas. He wasn't a high roller but he was damn good. And Nat had no trouble besting him. But it was the emotionless way she did it that told the story. When the cards were out, she didn't have a single tell and I'd paid close attention.

"Have Garrett expand that. Check underground tournaments in Vegas. And Tennessee. If Nat worked the circuit she's played in Tennessee for sure."

"I'll tell him."

"Any word from Zane?"

"Myles talked to him last night after he called Garrett. The women are locked down. None of them are happy. Which is to say, all of them are bitching. Especially Ivy, which means Zane has a burning desire to neutralize Pollaski quickly." Gabe stopped and pulled in an annoyed breath. "Garrett found more women, so Z called in Tex."

"More women?"

"Nat wasn't the first woman he sold."

"The man rents pussy," I seethed, not liking anything about Natasha's uncle, his business, or what he did to her. "It's not a stretch to sell it."

"Yeah, well, as much as I agree it's good we got the confirmation. When Garrett linked Wilco to a dozen women, he punted it to Tex. If there are more, he'll find them."

"This is gonna sound fucked but only twelve?"

"Twelve that Garrett found," Gabe confirmed. "Ash wasn't exactly lying about Nat's father selling Ashaki's mother. Everything we found indicated that was a one-off for Barny. A lesson not only to Ash's father but to all his soldiers about what happens when you try to blackmail a Pollaski. It would seem Wilco's used Barny's playbook. Twelve women who have ties to his organization. Indirect, wife, mother, sister of a man in Wilco's employ. And Autumn filled in some of the pieces."

"Was this new intel from Autumn or from what she already told us?"

Gabe gave me a disgruntled look.

"New. And Declan was not happy when Garrett called."

"I bet not."

Declan Crenshaw used to work for Z Corps. He was the team leader for the Gold Team. Former CIA and before that, he was a Marine. Autumn was an avenging angel. Straight up there was no other way to describe the woman. Having been trafficked herself, she knew firsthand what the victims went through. After her rescue, she'd set about righting wrongs. Her path had been dark and painful. When Declan and Autumn got together, Dec decided he was pulling Autumn off that path. He quit Z Corps, and he and Autumn were now free and clear of all things dark and painful. I didn't know

Declan's story but one look at the man told you it was heinous. I didn't imagine he'd take kindly to anyone calling Autumn.

"Tex is hunting them down. After we have the intel, Z will make the call. Either we'll go round them up or he knows an outfit out of Colorado. Missing women is their specialty."

"Do they understand it's not a paying job?"

"Trust me, these guys aren't in it for the money. When their team leader hears about this he'll deploy his men."

"Good men," I mumbled, wondering when I stopped being one of those.

"Good men," he confirmed. "Now you gotta date by a creek and I got shit to do."

That was Gabe's way of dismissing me and pissing me off all with a handful of words. So I let him know it.

"You're pissing me off."

Gabe flashed a smile, opened the door, and left.

I didn't have a date. I had a...*fuck*...what did I have?

"Owen?"

I turned and found Nat standing a few feet away.

Then I stood rooted and fought the pull of her. The need to close the distance, pull her into my arms, and wipe the uncertainty from her beautiful face.

When did this become my life?

When did I lose control?

And why did I want to throw caution to the wind and sweep Nat off her feet?

Naomi. I needed to spend some time in my head with my memories.

That should cure my stupidity.

CHAPTER 12

I heard.

God, my uncle was a pig.

Just when I thought I couldn't hate the man more than I already did, I was proven wrong.

The level of the Pollaski depravity shocked me. Despicable. Disgusting. It also ran through my veins.

Demonic blood, that was what I had.

"Everything okay?"

"That's what I was going to ask you," I told him.

Then I waited to see if he'd lie.

There wasn't a whole lot of truth between us. I had to admit, the scale was tipped heavily, my side being loaded down with secrets. But he hadn't been forthcoming, either. Owen knew more than he told me.

"Garrett, our IT guy, has been digging around your uncle." Owen stopped and studied me. I felt it, his gaze was seeking and deliberate. Gone was all the softness he'd looked at me with earlier. This was business. "Did you know Wilco trafficked women?"

"No," I answered immediately with the truth. "But I had my suspicions."

"Did something in particular happen?"

It was my turn to study Owen. He'd been honest with me, asked me outright what I knew. He didn't make assumptions and he didn't blow me off. He had no idea I'd heard what Gabe told him. He could've told me everything was fine but he didn't.

And after months of him taking care of me, I owed him something. No, I owed him everything. But I still couldn't tell him what he deserved to know. However, I could give him this.

"My uncle uses different businesses to clean some of his money. One of them is a family-run deli. The wife runs the counter, the daughter does the books, the son makes deliveries, and the husband runs everything else. One day I went in for lunch. Mariene wasn't working the counter. I asked about her, and Bento, that's her son, told me she was ill. A few weeks later I went back and still no Mariene. I asked again, and this time it was her husband, Pedro. He told me she'd gone back to Brazil. When I got back to the brownstone my uncle told me to mind my own business.

"Later I overheard Franco, that's my uncle's main soldier, tell my uncle that Pedro stopped making waves, but just in case he'd secured transport for Maria, that's Pedro's daughter. They never said what Pedro was making waves about but my uncle did say that he was certain Pedro had learned his lesson and wouldn't want his daughter to suffer, too."

Owen continued to take me in. His stone-cold assessment was a good reminder of what he truly thought of me. Though not enough to make me wise up and stop playing my stupid game. I needed this. I needed to be Natasha for a little while longer.

"He could've killed Mariene."

"He could've," I agreed. "As I said, it was a suspicion. Franco said transport. My uncle said suffer. I'm making assumptions though I think they're based on my uncle's behavior and what I know him to be capable of. But I fully admit I'm not privy to the business unless it directly has to do with me. And the rest of what I know is from conversations I've overheard. My uncle's sloppy when he's in the house. But not so sloppy he says too much."

"And the business as it pertains to you?" he asked.

My heart slammed into my ribs like a bullet train.

There was a saying about loose lips and if I wasn't freaking out I could probably remember it, but I was freaking out, therefore, I couldn't think about anything other than the fact I'd said too much. Way too damn much. I'd never taken Owen for stupid; he had to at least assume I'd played some sort of role in the family business. No one surrounded by gangsters and criminals was clean and innocent.

"A Pollaski has to pull their weight," I told him. "Everyone has a role."

"Poker," he mumbled.

And there it was. He'd figured it out. At least part of it.

"Gambling," I semi-corrected. "Cards."

Owen's eyes swept my face and he looked oddly relieved. I wasn't sure if he was pleased I'd told the truth or pleased I wasn't caught up in my uncle's more nefarious operations. I didn't get the chance to ask. He simply gave me a lift of his chin and walked out the door.

I didn't have to guess what he was doing. I knew he was going to find Gabe and tell him what he'd learned.

Weirdly that didn't bother me.

Weirdly *I* felt relieved.

Loose lips sink ships.

What would it be like if the USS Pollaski sank to the bottom of Lake Michigan? I'd stand at the edge of Navy Pier and cheer—maybe I'd set off some fireworks, too. I'd celebrate the death of an empire, that was for sure. But it would never happen. Wilco Pollaski would never go down, he'd built his army strong, he'd learned from my father, who was a master. My uncle had taken what my father had constructed and made it bigger. Unlike my father, my uncle had no weaknesses—not anymore. My father had killed the one person who could keep my uncle in check. It was my father's downfall—the fatal flaw in his plan.

With my mother gone, the king was overthrown. And his brother stole the crown.

* * *

WE'D WALKED TO THE CREEK IN SILENCE. OWEN SEEMED TO BE lost in thought and I left him to it. I'd already said enough for one day and had come up with an abbreviated plan. I would take in as many experiences as I could, I would speak when spoken to, but I would keep myself to myself otherwise. And before I answered questions I would carefully think over my answers.

That was my new Dreamland strategy.

Not exactly what I'd hoped for but it would be enough. I would still allow myself as much time with Owen as he'd give me.

I heard the rushing water before I could see it.

Then the trees cleared and there was nothing but beauty in front of me and I gasped.

"Wow."

I was no arborist but right then taking in the thick forest blanketed in snow, I wished I was. I wanted to know what kind of tree was sturdy enough to take the heavy load. The canopy was pure white, not a speck of green to be seen. The branches were so strong they didn't bend under the burden.

I had wished for a great many number of things in my life. One being, I'd wished I hadn't lost in the ovary lottery and I hadn't been born a Pollaski. I wished I could run away and no one would care to find me. Hundreds of wishes. But never had I wished I was a tree. But right then, looking at the tall, straight, sturdy branches I wished with everything in me I could be strong. I could spill all my secrets and trust Owen.

Who wished they were a tree? God, I was lame.

I shook the stupid thought off and glanced at Owen. He was staring at the water so I let my eyes drift over his features. He had a great profile. Hell, he had a great everything. Strong chiseled jaw, perfectly shaped brows that had to be naturally perfect—no way a man like Owen who was all *man* would have them salon-shaped. I knew under his beanie his hair had streaks of gray and being the man he was, he'd never cover that gray. Which was a good thing because it looked hot. Green eyes that weren't pale green like mine but dark green. His nose was a tad bit crooked and I'd bet it had been broken a time or two, but the slight imperfection only added to his rugged beauty.

"You've never been married."

Owen's strange statement scored through me and fear started to invade the serene atmosphere.

"No," I unnecessarily confirmed. "Have you?"

"Yep."

Whoa. Whoa. Whoa.

Owen had been married?

Then before I was done processing that tidbit of information, Owen gave me more.

"I started dating Naomi when we were seniors in high school," he said and I blinked at the name—*Naomi*—the bitch who'd done a number on him was his wife? "I left for basic a month after graduation. She stuck by me through that and A school. I went to the fleet and she stuck by me, even moved to Lemoore where I was stationed. Two and a half years later she'd stuck by me through two deployments. I thought we were solid so I asked her to marry me. Six months later we were married. It was time for me to re-enlist and she didn't like the idea, bitched but came to the unhappy realization I was serious when I told her I was going to be a lifer.

"Then an opportunity I'd been waiting for came to fruition so I took it and she was seriously not on board and bitched more, even though she knew the opportunity was what I'd been waiting for. From there, things rapidly declined until there was nothing left. She filed for divorce, unfortunately, she spent the prior eighteen months making my life hell. I thought once she'd filed she'd stop her bullshit, but she didn't. It got worse. Apparently, I was supposed to know that her filing divorce papers wasn't her wanting to end our marriage but a cry for attention. I was also supposed to magically know she wanted me to make a grand show of begging her not to leave me, tell her I was prepared to leave the military to prove I loved her. Or some such shit."

He finished his shockingly thorough rundown of his marriage. It lacked a whole lot of detail but damn if it didn't explain a lot.

He stared. I stared. Neither of us spoke.

It was uncomfortable because I had a lot of questions.

Then in a surprising turn of events, he smiled.

"Go ahead and ask before you bite through your tongue," he offered.

Thank God.

"She wanted you to leave the military?"

"Yeah. She wasn't keen on being a military wife. Naomi liked attention. Something I couldn't give her when I was out to sea for six months."

"But she stayed through two deployments."

"Yep. And she thought she could talk me out of re-enlisting. I was an aviation mechanic. A skill I could've used in the civilian marketplace and made more money. Which brings us to Naomi's second issue. She liked expensive things and didn't care we couldn't afford them. That's what credit cards were for."

"Credit cards?"

Oh, boy, this Naomi woman. Didn't sound like she was smart.

"Credit cards maxed out with no care about the interest rates or how long it was going to take to pay off. If she had five dollars she thought she should be able to spend ten. Hair, nails, clothes, shoes, purses. You name it, she wanted it and I was the asshole for not being able to provide them for her."

None of that sounded good. She sounded like a gold-digging bitch but it wasn't my place to say.

"I'm sorry she made you feel that way."

"She wasn't wrong, I couldn't afford to buy her half of what she wanted."

"So that makes you an asshole?" I asked incredulously.

"I married her, so yeah."

That made no sense.

"What's that mean?"

"It means, she came from money. I should've known she'd never be happy with what I could give her. There're certain things a woman like that expects and I was stupid for thinking she would lower her expectations and be happy with a middle-class life when she was used to more."

Unease washed over me. It seeped into my pores and made my skin crawl. Did he think of me that way? Like I was one of those women who expected *things*.

For months he'd taken care of me. Provided everything from food to clothes. I had no money and he'd paid my way.

I was worse than Naomi the gold digger.

I was a leech.

A clinger.

I wasn't accepting a helping hand, I was mooching.

"I'm sorry," I whispered and blinked back the tears. "I am so sorry, Owen."

"It was a long time ago."

"No…" My voice cracked and I clamped my mouth shut.

"No, what?"

I owed it to Owen to explain. To tell him I knew I was a clinger, a mooch, a leech, but I hadn't meant to be. I had but I hadn't. I'd known I was wrong from the beginning. I knew I was using him as a reprieve from my life but I wasn't using him in the sense that I was doing it in malice. But using was using and I'd done it.

I was so much worse than Naomi.

Worse than the women who latched onto my uncle for his money uncaring he was using them for their bodies, knowing they'd be cast aside when he grew bored with them. I was even worse than my mother who was in love with one man but married another because she was told that was the way it was going to be. And the Pollaski name and protection meant more to her than my uncle had. Perhaps I was being too hard on my mother. After all, she hadn't had much of a choice; once you were in bed with a Pollaski, you were owed by family. And being as my father had been the king he was entitled to claim his queen. Even if she already belonged to another man.

God, life sucked.

My life sucked.

"Natasha?"

It was on the tip of my tongue to end the charade, remind Owen I was Sarah. End the fantasy I'd created.

"For months I've lived with you and you've paid for everything. I'm a freeloader. I've been using you."

"What?"

"I've been using you," I repeated. "I don't have a job. I don't have money. You pay for everything while I sit in your house, eating your food, using your utilities, watching your TV—"

"Stop."

"No, there's more. A lot more. I sit around and you work. I do nothing. You pay for—"

"Babe. Seriously stop. You don't sit around and do nothing. You cook."

I cook?

"And you do the laundry," he continued. "And you clean the house."

So I was a live-in maid?

"You do any of those things before?"

"Huh?"

"At your dad's or your uncle's, did you cook, clean, or do the laundry?"

"Um…"

"Right. You didn't. You're not a freeloader, Nat. I didn't ask you to clean the house. I didn't ask you to teach yourself how to cook. And I certainly didn't ask you to do laundry. I'm a grown-ass man and can do all of that myself. You did it because you are the opposite of a freeloader and wanted to pitch in, so you found ways to do that. Which are unnecessary but appreciated. As far as everything else, my TV would be there whether you were watching it or not. The extra utilities I barely feel. The food is moot because you're the one cooking it so I don't have to eat out three meals a day so it saves me money in the long run."

Unnecessary but appreciated.

That was a nice thing to say. Actually, he thanked me a lot for cooking and doing his laundry. The cleaning he helped with as a matter of fact, Owen was extremely neat. It was me who was messy, so really I was mostly picking up after myself.

"That's not the point," I told him.

"Then what is?"

"That you pay for everything. That I live with you for free and you buy everything, down to my shampoo."

Owen's eyes got squinty, but not in a ticked-off way, more like he was assessing the situation and coming up with a new plan of attack. Owen was good at that, reading the state of affairs, gauging my mood. Sometimes I thought he could read my mind with the scary accuracy he could figure me out.

"Then when we get home, get a job."

"What?"

"When we get home get a job," he repeated.

A job? I'd never had a job, not in the legal sense. I'd never filled out an application, I didn't have a resume, and I'd never been to an interview. I had zero skills outside of being a card sharp. I knew how to hustle, that was all I was good at. That and I could set a stupid freaking table, host a party, and of course, I'd been taught the rules of fashion. What to wear, when. What not to wear. What handbag to pair with what dress. Keeping up appearances was a high priority for the Pollaskis. Perhaps I could get a job in a department store. *Right.* With no experience, Walmart or Target was more like it.

But now that Owen had mentioned working, I wanted a job. A real one. I wanted to earn a paycheck. I wanted to pay taxes. I wanted to have a schedule and complain about my boss. I wanted that nearly as badly as I wanted to live in my make-believe dreamland with Owen for eternity.

"I've never had a real job."

"I know you haven't."

God, what I would have given to know what Owen was thinking. What was *I* thinking? No, I wouldn't. I didn't want to know anything. And further, it was one thing to live in La-La-Land and pretend I could be normal, it was certainly another to give it thought. I wasn't going to get a job, because I couldn't. Zane would get fed up with my uncle's antics soon enough. Owen would never ask me to go back outright, but there was going to come a point where it would be inevitable. I should've already done it.

"Maybe we shouldn't talk about this anymore. You brought me out here to show me the creek."

"Don't." Owen's eyes held mine as he delivered his warning.

From top to toe I shivered and it had nothing to do with the cold. Owen didn't miss this, not that he missed much, which was seriously irritating.

"Say. Something," he ground out.

"What do you want me to say?"

"Anything. Just speak."

"Remember, Sarah, you don't speak unless someone asks you a question," my mother reminded me for the hundredth time. "You'll sit at your father's left during dinner. No slouching. Hands in your lap. And smile."

I nodded and my mother glared at my throat.

"Where are your pearls?" And when I didn't answer her fast enough she angrily snapped, "Speak."

Speak.

Just speak.

"I'm not a dog." I crossed my arms over my chest and tucked my gloved-covered hands under my biceps. "Don't tell me to speak."

"Seriously?"

"Yes, sreiously, Owen."

"Christ," he bit out and took a step toward me. I jerked back and he rocked to a halt. Eyes narrowed, not in contemplation but in anger. "I would never hurt you."

"You're the only one who can hurt me."

"Nat—"

"I learned a lot growing up with Barny and Wilco. The first lesson was never to let anyone close. Never care. The second lesson was love is the sword you'll die by. A weapon to be used against you. I knew it, I saw it, but I didn't truly know as one can't until it was too late. Love is a power exchange. And the person who holds that power can hurt you. Wilco cannot hurt me. He can kill me, he can sell me, he can torture me, but he cannot *hurt* me. The last person who had that power was my father. When he killed my mother, he destroyed me. But after that, his power was gone. He took the only person I cared about away from me. I had nothing left after that so there was nothing else he could do to hurt me. Lucky for me, he didn't bother to try. He didn't like me all that much and did his best to ignore me until he needed me. And Wilco never had a weapon. He took me in, did his best to make my life hell, but nothing he did hurt because I didn't care."

"I will not hurt you," he repeated.

Out of everything I told him—including that my father had killed my mother, and without actually saying it I admitted I cared about him, maybe even loved him that was what he chose to home in on. That he wouldn't hurt me. But he would. It was inevitable.

"You will. But before you do, I'll hurt myself."

"What?" Owen misunderstood and stood to his full height, shoulders back, chest out, jaw hard.

Part of me was happy to know he cared. He thought I'd hurt myself and he cared.

Scary, but I liked it.

"This is not my life," I told him.

"Funny. You're standing here so I think it is."

"No, it's not. My life is not snowy mountains, walks through the forest, beautiful creeks, and cabins. It's not chopping firewood. It's not cooking. And it's certainly not going to sleep next to you. This is my dreamland. A fantasy I'm living. I know how bad it's gonna hurt when it's gone but I'm still living it. I need it, Owen. I need something good and clean and happy because when all of it is gone—when you're gone—my real life is so dark, so bleak, so grotesque…now that I know you're real, that there's an Owen out there, I need to keep you with me. I need it. No one will ever know. It will be mine. And it will hurt so bad when it's gone, but I'm still taking this time. I'm taking everything. I know it's selfish but I'm still doing it."

"That's not selfish, baby."

I ignored how soft his voice had gone. I ignored the way he was looking at me. And I absolutely ignored his 'baby'. There was taking what I could, then there was flat-out stupidity. And allowing his sweet 'baby' to penetrate would obliterate me.

"It totally is, Owen. I'm taking more. You've given me so much, but I'm greedy and I'm taking everything. I'll keep it locked up safe. So deep, Wilco will never find it. He'll never be able to use it to hurt me. But you? You're the only one who can cause harm. You're the only one who can put a stop to my lunacy. *You* can take you away from me. And that will hurt. I know what happened this morning changes nothing between us, but I'm taking that, too. My first time where sex was a mutual exchange. Mutual pleasure. The first time I enjoyed being touched and kissed. I know it meant nothing to you but it means everything to me. It's mine and I'm not giving it back."

"*Baby.*"

That one word was tortured. It sounded as if it was pulled from the pit of his stomach and for my mental wellbeing I had to ignore what that made me feel. I had to. I was already drowning. I could barely keep my head above water and if I processed the anger and sadness in his voice I would go under.

When I could take no more I turned to look at the stream.

I concentrated on the frozen bank, the rushing water of Rapid Lightning, and wondered if that was how it got its name. I was deep into this thought, so deep I didn't hear the crunching footsteps, so deep I wasn't pulled from my thoughts until strong arms wrapped around me. Owen dropped his head and his lips brushed my cold cheek before he whispered words I'd never forget.

133

"Take what you need, Natasha. Anything you want, baby, it's yours."

My eyes drifted closed and I lost sight of the beauty before me. But in the darkness I found light. In the freezing cold, I found warmth. Owen gave it to me. With that one statement, he gave me everything.

And I was going to take it.

CHAPTER 13

I know what happened this morning changes nothing between us.

I gritted my teeth and bowed my head.

My first time where sex was a mutual exchange.

Mutual pleasure.

The first time I enjoyed being touched and kissed.

Jesus, fuck. I continued to stare at my feet, happy that after we walked back to the house, Nat had gone up to take a shower and I was alone in the cabin. Thankful she'd let me hold her for as long as she had. Grateful she'd let me hold her hand on the way back to the cabin. And pleased as all fuck she'd chatted the entire trek through the forest.

Nothing of importance was shared, but I listened to every word she'd said. She'd never been on a four-wheeler or a dirt bike. Never skied. Never sledded. Never made s'mores.

That I was going to rectify.

I pushed off the counter and slipped out onto the back patio, one of the few places I had cell reception, and called Gabe.

"'Low."

"You still in town?"

"Yep. Everything okay?"

"Yeah. I need you to grab something for me."

"Already got what you need," he returned.

"What?"

"Condoms."

"Don't—"

"Jumbo—pack that is, not size. The box should last you for the rest of our stay, unless you're planning on making her—"

"Seriously, shut the fuck up."

My first time where sex was a mutual exchange.

Fucking, hell.

"You've got a bad attitude for a man who had—"

"This afternoon she told me that what we shared was the first time it was a mutual exchange."

"Fuck."

"So you wanna keep taking shots at me, fine. But pick something else."

"You had to know—"

"Yeah, Gabe, I knew she'd likely been forced to perform sex acts against her will," I seethed. "But hearing her confirm my suspicions, it burned into my brain in a way that I will never fucking forget. So pick something else."

"Right."

"So since you're still in town grab some chocolate bars, marshmallows, and graham crackers. Also, pick up cereal— something sugary like Cocoa Puffs or Fruity Pebbles. Anything but granola, Grape-Nuts, or Cheerios. And milk."

"She's never had cereal," Gabe rightly surmised.

"She's never had cereal," I confirmed.

Gabe let out a sigh and I waited for him to tell me what was on his mind. I didn't bother bracing, I knew it was going to piss me off, probably make me angry. There was no use wasting the effort. Gabe was Gabe. He said what he wanted to say. And he did it however he wanted to do it.

"You know, you can't give her everything she's never had."

"I sure as fuck can try."

"True enough." There was another sigh and this time I braced. "Does this mean you've pulled your thumb out of your ass?"

I know it meant nothing to you but it means everything to me. It's mine and I'm not giving it back.

"It means, while we're here I'm giving her everything I can."

"You know she's not Naomi, right?"

What the fuck?

"Nat's so different from that bitch, it never even crossed my mind."

"You're a goddamn liar. I know it did, because in your mind, all women are just like your ex-wife. But I'm telling you, Nat is not Naomi."

"We're not—"

"She's not fucking Naomi!"

"We're not—"

"She's not fucking Naomi, asshole. Do you hear me?"

"How the hell can you say that, Gabe? You barely know her."

"Saw the way she smiled at you when you opened the door for her. Smiling over firewood, brother. Fucking wood. She was smiling because she did something so small that in the grand scheme of life was so fucking meaningless it's laughable. But to her, it was everything. You did that to her. She looked like you handed her the moon. Don't need nothing else. Just that smile to tell me that woman doesn't want stuff. She doesn't want your money, what you can buy her. Shit, she argued with me for thirty minutes over the jacket I bought her."

"She's feeling guilty about us buying her things."

"*No shit?* Do you hear yourself? When did Naomi feel guilt over…anything? Let me help you out with that, she didn't. Not an ounce of remorse when she overspent and got your ass in debt."

Gabe was right about that. Naomi expected *things*—a lot of them. And when I was gone, she felt it was her due getting them, not caring that we couldn't afford any of it. I went on deployment she thought that meant she deserved jewelry—expensive jewelry. And clothes, and shoes, and whatever else she wanted when she wanted. This included attention. Attention she wanted even if her husband wasn't there to give it to her—and she found a way to get that, too, frequently. By the end of our marriage, Naomi had forgotten she was married. That was my fault, too. Another misguided play to make me jealous in hopes I'd be a better husband.

"We're not talking about this. Just get what I asked."

"I'll get what you asked for when you promise me you'll think about what I said," he returned.

Now he was seriously pissing me off. Sticking his nose in shit that was none of his business. I didn't give the first fuck that was Gabe's way. I didn't care he thought his intentions were righteous.

"Mind your business."

"Owen—"

"Months. Fucking months this is all I've thought about. You don't think I see it? That I don't feel it? I damn well do. But when this is done, she's gonna be free to go on her merry way. She'll finally be clear of that asshole and she deserves the chance to explore what all that means. So, tell me, Gabe, where does that leave me? When she walks out the door—no, when she walks out *my* front door, out of *my* house, *my* life and I'm left with nothing. I know what this is."

"You don't know shit, dumbass."

And with that Gabe hung up on me.

Nosy bastard was right again. I was a dumbass. But he was also wrong, I knew Natasha deserved more than I could give her. I was still the same man I was back when I was married. I might not be in the military anymore, but I still had a job that took me out of the country for months at a time. This last stretch was the longest my team had been stateside in years. I was a nomad; I had no roots; I didn't own the house we lived in. I rented it, fully furnished. I didn't own a stick of furniture and I was okay with that. My life was all about my team—the mission. Natasha deserved better than that. I was old enough to know who I was and what I needed. Zane Lewis gave me a purpose. My work filled a need in me. My life was easy, structured, controlled.

Who the hell was I kidding?

I was paralyzed by my past. I didn't control a damn thing in my life, a ghost did. A woman who was no longer in my life controlled my emotions. Everything I thought and felt always defaulted to her. How she'd made me feel, what she'd done to me, who she said I was. And the fuck of it was, I'd believed her. I'd willingly allowed it in an effort to protect myself from ever falling for another woman. I'd given Naomi the power to destroy me.

I was a goddamn zombie.

I was everything I'd accused Natasha of being. I was walking, breathing, and going through the motions but I was not living.

My gaze went to a small stack of wood someone had piled up on the patio then moved to across the yard to the rocks Rhode had carefully stacked to form a fire pit. Tonight I'd build Nat a fire and give her s'mores. Tomorrow morning I'd give her Cocoa Puffs. Beyond that, I wasn't sure.

What I was sure about was I was done being a pussy. I was done allowing someone else to control my reactions, my emotions, my thoughts. I should've been done with it nearly twenty years ago. But instead, I'd kept that wound raw. I'd kept the blood flowing, using the pain as a reminder I was everything Naomi said I was. Needing it as proof all women were lying, cheating, grasping bitches so I'd never fall prey again.

I'd wasted years, so many years, anger flashed and burned hot. And the fuck of it was I had no one to blame but myself. I'd done it to myself. Naomi did what she did. But I'd been the asshole that had turned my life to shit.

That was going to change.

* * *

"It's on fire," Nat announced and waved her marshmallow. "What do I do now?"

"Blow it out." Big, beautiful, horror-filled eyes went from the fireball to me and I couldn't stop my smile from turning into a chuckle. "Babe, blow it out."

"You're laughing at me."

I was.

She was being cute as all get-out.

Without thought, I grabbed her wrist and guided the now scorched ball of sugary goodness in front of my face and blew out the flame. I let go and picked up a graham cracker, broke it in half, and held it out.

"Slide the marshmallow on," I told her.

Once that was done I smooshed the chocolate bar over the marshmallow, and finished by placing the other half of the graham cracker on top.

"There. It's all ready for you."

Nat looked up from the gooey mess and those beautiful eyes of hers danced. Then she took the s'more and without a shred of ladylike grace, she took a bite. A big one. Melted marshmallow oozed out the sides and over her fingers.

"This is…" she said around a mouthful of chocolate, cracker, and charred marshmallow. "The best thing I've ever eaten."

"Good, right?"

Nat chewed and swallowed before she smiled huge. "*The best.*"

"Next time, you've gotta try it with a peanut butter cup," Myles told her.

"You mean there are different kinds?"

Nat's eyes lit with excitement and all my irritation at Myles butting into my moment with Nat slid clean away. Suddenly I didn't care the guys had horned in on s'mores. Seeing Nat smile while chocolate smeared the corner of her mouth, the fire dancing in the pit, my brothers sharing in the moment, felt right.

"Pick your poison." Kevin tossed the bag of candy on the log next to Nat. "There's peanut butter cups, Snickers, Almond Joy, and Twix. Only do the Snickers if you have the patience to wait for it to melt."

Natasha bumped my arm with her shoulder and asked, "Which one do you want?"

"Just plain chocolate for me."

"Seriously? That's boring."

Her nose scrunched and her lips twisted into a disgruntled pout that looked more like a frown, and that on any other woman would've looked downright ridiculous. But she pulled it off in a way that made her look adorable. The urge to kiss her surged through me, and while I beat back the impulse, I let the desire course through me. There was no use denying it. I felt it. I wanted Natasha, and not just while we were hiding her.

I wanted her for keeps.

I wanted to stop sleeping through life and start living it.

But first I was going to free her from Wilco Pollaski.

"That's Owen," Kevin joined. "Totally boring."

"He is not," Nat defended, and the tingle that worked its way up my back made me jolt in surprise.

Unfortunately, Gabe didn't miss this, and when I looked over at him, his dirty look said it all.

CHAPTER 14

It had been two days since my first s'mores experience. Two days of everything being the same but completely different. The vibe in the house had totally shifted, Owen seemed at ease therefore the rest of the guys followed. They cut up more, made jokes, poked fun at one another. We ate meals together, sat around the fire together, and the guys had even loosened up and told a few stories.

I now knew when Owen was in the Navy he'd been EOD —I'd learned that was explosive ordnance disposal. That was bomb disposal, I'd learned that, too. Further, I'd figured out that was the opportunity Owen had been waiting for that his ex-wife had bitched about. I could see how a woman would be leery of the man she loved defusing bombs for a living, but I didn't think that was her issue. I hadn't broached the topic of Naomi even though I had a thousand questions about her. I was too scared to ask.

I also found out that Kevin and Gabe both served in the Navy. Myles was the odd man out and had served in the Army. When this conversation had come about there was some weird rivalry that led to Kevin saying, "Go Navy, Beat Army." That outburst earned Kevin Myles's middle finger and muttered curses. Owen had smiled and told me he'd explain later though he hadn't done that yet.

I'd eaten sugary cereal that I decided I didn't like. Cocoa Puffs was okay, only if eaten by the handful without milk. Fruity Pebbles were disgusting. Gabe was an excellent cook, and the only thing Kevin could do was use the grill; otherwise, he sucked in the kitchen and burnt grilled cheese, which sucked because I'd found I loved them and could eat one a day. That was if they weren't burnt. I'd yet to find Myles in the kitchen. Come to think of it, Myles spent a lot of time holed up in his room alone. Or he was pacing the backyard on his phone. He wasn't mean about it but he was the most closed-off.

Owen on the other hand was no longer guarded. He hadn't shared his deepest, darkest secrets but he was noticeably more relaxed. He hadn't asked any more about my past. He hadn't brought up our morning of orgasms and he hadn't touched me, kissed me, or even given me a longing look that would suggest he wanted a repeat performance. Which was a shame because I absolutely did.

So now, on the third morning in a row I'd woken up in bed next to him, I was fidgety. I knew what his hands and mouth felt like. I knew he was giving me this time. S'mores, cereal, walks around the property, more wood chopping— which by the way I was getting the hang of and totally loved. Easy, calm nights around the fire pit. But I was still disappointed. Selfishly I wanted more.

"Babe."

Owen's sleep-rough voice curled around me and I smiled. "Sorry."

I didn't bother playing dumb. We were well beyond coy. He knew, I knew why he made his low warning.

It was early, the sun was barely peeking through the windows but I was wide awake. I rolled to my side then sat up. But before I could throw my legs over the side of the bed,

Owen hooked me around the middle and hauled me across the mattress to the middle of the bed. He rolled me to my side, maneuvered his body behind mine, jerked me closer still, then he pressed his chest against my back, and settled his arm around me.

Through all of this, I stop breathing.

"Sleep, baby."

Baby?

I felt my muscles get tight and my heart started pounding so hard it was a wonder my body wasn't rocking with the beat.

A few moments later, I was still thinking about Owen's muttered 'baby' when he spoke again, "What's on your mind?"

A million and one things.

"Nothing," I lied.

"Babe, you're strung tight and you're holding your breath."

I exhaled and tried to relax. I knew it wasn't going to work, not with Owen close. Not with his arm around me and his thumb gently stroking my forearm. Not with his crotch pressed against my ass. Now I was awake for a different reason, one that had nothing to do with all the thoughts racing through my mind.

"Nat," he prompted.

"What does go Navy, beat Army mean?" I blurted out, then tucked my chin and closed my eyes in an effort to block out how stupid I sounded.

"That's what you're thinking about?"

"One of the things, yes."

"Football rivalry," he started.

"The military plays football? I mean, like on teams?"

"No, baby, the service academies do. The rivalry is between West Point and the Naval Academy. It's said, though I've never been to West Point, that there are Beat Navy signs up all over post and the cadets yell "Beat Navy" after their meals. They take this shit seriously. And during the season, Kevin and Myles take it to an extreme."

"Do you guys go to games?"

"I've been to one, years ago. Great game, until Army won and took home the Commander-in-Chief trophy. I thought Kevin was going to have a heart attack and I swear I saw actual tears in his eyes. I lost five hundred dollars on that game. I wasn't happy, but Kevin's a third-generation Naval Academy graduate—I swear he bleeds blue and gold. After that miserable experience driving home from Philly to Annapolis, I swore I'd never go to another game with them."

I couldn't imagine big, buff Kevin crying over anything. But I could totally see him complaining about his team losing and doing that in such a way it would make Owen miserable.

"Do they still go?"

"We haven't been stateside for football season in the last five years. The Army-Navy game is sometime in December so if we're…" Owen paused then he abandoned his thought. "I'm sure they'll get tickets for this year."

"What were you going to say?"

There was a stretch of silence and I didn't think he was going to answer me. The old Owen, the one I'd lived with in Annapolis, was reserved. He had an uncanny way of being open and closed off at the same time. He'd tell me things but it always felt like he was holding back big chunks of information. Something that never bothered me before because I was doing the same. And as much as I'd been curious and wanted to know more about him, I never asked. Mainly because I was afraid if I did, he'd ask me questions and the delicate line we were skirting would be ruined. I hadn't wanted to out-and-out lie to him, I'd just wanted to hide who I was and what my family did.

"I was going to say if we're still stateside, they'll probably go."

If?

Owen was leaving?

Why hadn't I thought of that?

Because I'm a selfish twit.

"Breathe, baby," he whispered and tangled our legs together.

I didn't breathe.

I didn't move.

"How soon would you leave?" The question was out of my mouth before I could think better of it.

I didn't want to know but I *had* to know.

I had to know how much time I had left with him.

"Not sure. Zane's been restructuring. Our team specializing in maritime security, the last two contracts that came up, Zane passed up."

My curiosity got the better of me and I couldn't hold back my rapid-fire questions. "Maritime security? Like Captain Phillips? Why did Zane pass up contracts? What's restructuring mean?"

Owen gave me a squeeze and I quieted even though there was more I wanted to ask.

"Yes, like Captain Phillips, but you can only believe ten percent of the headlines and even less about the movie. All that shit is sensationalized. Zane passed on the contracts because they were too dangerous. There's risk, then there's stupid. We don't do stupid. We take calculated risks. And that's part of what Zane's restructuring. He also wants to avoid burnout by rotating teams. Blue has been out to sea more than we've been home. That takes a toll. He wants to avoid that so he'll send out a new team to take our place and move us into something different."

"What's Blue?"

"My team. We're Blue. Thad, Brooks, Kyle, Max, and Dec are Gold. Leo, Jasmin, Linc, Colin, Jaxon, and Zane are Red."

I desperately wanted to know what 'something different'

meant but I didn't ask. I changed my mind—I didn't want to know when he was going to leave. Just the mere thought of it hurt. But it was a good reminder our time was limited. There was an expiration date and I needed to soak in as much as I could. There was no time to waste.

It was on that thought, I squirmed closer to Owen. If this was all he was willing to give I was taking it and I was memorizing how warm I felt with him behind me. How safe I felt tucked close.

"Sleep, baby," he repeated and kissed the top of my head.

I committed that to memory, too.

It took a while but cocooned in Owen's embrace, I fell back asleep.

* * *

My eyes came open and sleep slowly receded but when it did, I realized I was alone in bed. The room was bright and I was cold. So freaking cold I shivered. I tried to push my forlorn thoughts away but they kept flooding my mind. I had to tell Owen the truth. It was time. Well-past time.

There was a lot he needed to know. Things that would fill in the blanks and make his job easier. I should've told him months ago.

Before I could lose my courage I got out of bed, not bothering to shower because that would give me too much time to second-guess what I was about to do. I didn't even take the time to brush my teeth or put on clothes. I was going to do this in my pjs. I was too weak to do it any other way. Too cowardly. If I didn't do it right this minute I'd chicken out.

I rushed down the stairs and when I hit the living room, Gabe, Kevin, and Myles all turned to look at me. Their matching stares of concern hit me like a ton of bricks, a blow to my stomach, a slap in my face. In one way or another, they all cared, I could see it plain. They were worried about why I'd run down the stairs like a crazy woman.

"Where's Owen?" I asked.

Gabe's eyes narrowed and he lifted himself off the couch. "You okay?"

"Where's Owen?" I repeated.

"Right here." Owen stepped into the room and his eyes did a full-body sweep before he moved my way. "What's wrong?"

"I'm ready," I announced.

"Come again?" Owen asked but didn't stop walking my way.

"I'm ready to tell you."

"Tell me what?"

"Why Wilco wants me back."

Owen jerked to a stop and I thought that was the best thing. I didn't want him too close when I told him. Hell, after he knew, he might never want to be close to me again. This was counterproductive to me living in my dreamland but he deserved to know the truth. Know who Sarah Pollaski truly was. Know who he was sleeping next to.

Oh, God, I was going to throw up.

I was going to ruin everything.

"Baby."

Owen's soft voice spurred me on. He had to know. He couldn't call me 'baby' and not know.

There was only one way to do this. I had to purge it all at once.

Everything.

I needed it out.

"My first living memory was my father slapping my mother. I don't know what for. But he slapped her and she apologized to him. I remember it clearly. She didn't even cry. She just stood in the foyer with my father's handprint on her face and said she was sorry. Father didn't say anything but he saw me. Then he walked back into his study and my mother calmly went into the bathroom."

"Nat—"

"That happened a lot. My father slapping my mother. On occasion, it would escalate to more and she'd have a black eye or a swelled lip. She never said anything. She never did anything. She would just take it and apologize to him."

"Baby, stop."

I didn't stop. I couldn't. I needed to get it out.

My gaze lifted and my eyes locked onto Owen's and once again I used his strength.

"When I was fifteen, I saw my father kill my mother. It was their anniversary and she was drunk. Thinking back, since I could remember they never celebrated that day but my mother would get drunk and spend the day crying. It was the only day of the year she showed any emotion and it was profound sadness. I never understood until that day. She was drunk and yelling at my father." I stopped and took in a breath and when I let it out I finished. "My mother was in love with Wilco and Wilco loved her. The two of them had been together when my father decided he was going to be the one to marry her. My uncle being the dutiful brother, stepped aside but never stopped loving her. She hated my father and hated my uncle for not protecting her. Loved and hated Wilco at the same time, that is. She just hated my father. It became clear that day why she didn't love me. How could she? I was the product of a forced marriage, a life she didn't want. And my uncle hates me for much of the same reason, I'm the reminder my father had the woman he loved. My very existence disgusts Wilco."

"Your mother was reported missing by her sister." Kevin told me something I knew.

"Yep. My aunt hated my father. She wasn't allowed to come to the house. But my mother still kept in touch. Funny things happen when you buy police loyalty. A week after my mother's death she made a call from the grave to the police chief and told him she was fine and had left my father, was seeking a divorce, and was happily living in New York. The police reported this to my aunt and the case was closed. As I'm sure you know, my father legally divorced a dead woman and according to her tax filings, she's still alive living in Massena, New York. She owns a home, pays her bills, and files taxes. Though my aunt is dead, she had a horrible car accident."

"How do you know that?" Owen asked.

"Know what, that my dead mother draws a paycheck from a dummy corporation my father owned, that Wilco now owns and all of her bills are paid on time?" I didn't give Owen time to confirm that was what he was inquiring about and continued. "Because *I* paid her bills. Because I set up her direct deposit. My father was a criminal but he wasn't stupid enough to let a death go to waste. Yet another avenue to clean his dirty money."

Something flashed in Owen's eyes but I pushed aside the pain it caused and continued. There was more he needed to know.

"I learned to play cards when I was little. The only time my father had any interest in me was when he was teaching me to play. By the time I was a teenager I could count cards. He started setting up games with his soldiers. They thought it was amusing having me at the table until I took their money. Then they kept coming back in an effort to win some back. When I was eighteen my father started having me sit at bigger tables, not with his soldiers but real players. Two years later he had me at high stakes games and that's when I started earning my keep."

"Natasha," Myles cut in but I didn't allow him to stop me from getting the rest out.

I was numb, totally emotionless, it felt like I was telling a story that was not my life. How I'd been forced to do things I didn't want to do. But there was more, so much more it would take days, but they had to know the highlights. They needed all the information so they could decide if they really wanted to help me or not. My guess was, they'd be done with me. Pack up their stuff, drive us down the mountain, and leave me at the airport to find my own way. And back to hell I would go.

"I was ten the first time I met one of the women from my father's stable of prostitutes. She came by the house—this was at my father's request so he could fuck her. She was his favorite, said she was clean. That also happened frequently. My father didn't care if my mother was in the house or if I was. He'd call over his hooker, fuck her in his office, do this loudly, and send her on her way. Through all of this, I stayed silent. I learned what happened if I spoke. I wasn't as strong as my mother, when I felt the sting of my father's palm on my face I cried. That would earn me another slap, and more and more until I stopped whimpering. Crying is for pussies. Crying is a weakness and Pollaskis are not weak. Women do not speak out of turn, they shut the fuck up and take what they're given. Pollaskis are to prove their loyalty. And I knew one of the ways my mother proved she was a Pollaski was by spreading her legs for the family. My father whored her out —she brought in top dollar. If you wanted to fuck The Boss's woman you paid. And men paid, but Wilco was not allowed to buy my mother's time. Another way my father taunted my uncle. Then he killed the one person that kept Wilco in check. The only thing my uncle cared about was finding a way to get my mother back. My dad used to say, pussy is the downfall of man. He was right. He killed my mother, and Wilco plotted for ten years, turned my father's soldiers against him, took his business, and finally dethroned him.

"I know where the girls are. I know where the client lists are kept. I know how the payouts are made, what accounts they come from, and who is on my uncle's payroll. I know my mother is dead. I know what my father did to Amie's family and I know why. I also know why my uncle was happy to sell me. Like my father, Wilco doesn't miss an opportunity to make a problem go away and do that making a buck. Though, in my case, it was a bad deal. I made him a lot of money at the tables, much more than he sold me for. But he had to get rid of me, so he did."

"Why'd he have to get rid of you?" Kevin asked softly.

"Two reasons. I saw him kill an FBI agent and that same night I saw a cop dismember the body."

I said it.

I thought I'd feel better, I thought it would feel good to finally tell the truth. But it didn't. I felt sick to my stomach. The guilt I felt didn't magically vanish. I witnessed a man being tortured and brutally murdered and I'd done nothing. I didn't attempt to stop it, which would've been futile and I would've ended up dead as well, but at least I would've died with some morality.

"Do you know his name?" Owen asked and my heart broke.

No, it shattered.

Gone was the tenderness I'd heard over the last few days. Gone was the Owen who had been open and kind. I couldn't even say he reverted back to the man I'd met because I'd never seen him look at me with such revulsion.

"That night my uncle called him Agent Conor but I knew him as Steel. He'd worked with Wilco for ages, maybe two years. He ran the girls. And when Wilco added heroin to his menu of drugs offered, Steel was the one who ordered the shipments. Most of them came out of San Antonio. Steel had a contact there, Axel, who got the heroin straight from Mexico."

"Undercover," Myles muttered.

"Yes, Wilco found out he was an undercover FBI agent and he killed him in the house, in front of me. Though he didn't know he was doing that last part. I wasn't supposed to be home. Wilco had sent me out to work, I was done sooner than he thought."

"Work?" Owen spat.

I had nothing else to hide. He now knew without a shadow of a doubt I was as filthy as the rest of my family. I may've never killed anyone but I still had blood on my hands —wet, sticky, warm blood that wouldn't wash away. I was trash like the rest of them.

"A new client needed to be vetted. I took him to dinner but didn't need much time to figure out I wasn't going to approve him. Not only did his financials show he couldn't afford more than a few appointments but he had a drug habit. Clients only got to partake in one or the other; they either bought drugs, or women, never both. I concluded my dinner and went home early and walked in on Wilco killing Agent Conor."

The room was silent, but I didn't need words to feel the electricity snapping through the air. I felt every zap painfully pulse through me. I was acutely aware that every man in the room was staring at me but I didn't take my gaze off Owen. He was the only one who mattered to me. I didn't know if I was looking for forgiveness or if I wanted him to hate me as much as I hated myself.

"I need to go call Zane," Owen broke the quiet.

I watched as he walked across the room. I kept watching until I lost sight of him when the back door closed behind him. Only then did I allow my shoulders to hunch and my lids to lower, blocking out the room but not the pain.

There it was, it was done.

I'd said my piece and now it was over.

They all knew who I was. Owen knew the truth. I could pretend all I wanted but I wasn't Natasha. I was Sarah and I'd never shed her no matter how hard I tried.

CHAPTER 15

Fuck me.

Fuck everything straight to hell.

I wasn't sure which part of the goddamn scene I hated more, the fact that while Natasha spoke she'd done it with no hint of emotion, not a speck of inflection in her voice. Totally dead and void. Or if it was the way she'd stared at me, her face bleached of color, eyes dull and hollow, looking at me as if she were waiting for my wrath. Waiting for me to turn into the fucking monster her father was and strike her down—physically or emotionally she'd been prepared for the blows. *Fuck me.* She actually looked like she hoped I would. No, the part I hated the most was the fact that was her life. Had been her life. *Had* been, past tense. That would no longer be the case.

Never fucking again would she vet a motherfucking John for Wilco. She'd never play another hand of cards. She'd never pay her dead mother's bills, witness another murder. She'd never even breathe that piece of shit's air. And she would never fucking again be forced to prove her loyalty by selling her body.

Fuck that.

Fuck him.

Never again.

My gut clenched at the thought of Nat being used. The knots that were already formed in my stomach tightened and I had to breathe through the anger.

There was knowing then there was *knowing*.

We'd known some of what Natasha had told us. For instance, we'd known her mother was not living in the house in Massena, we knew the corporation that issued her paychecks was bullshit. We'd known her father had called a hit on her aunt and the woman's death was not an accident. And finally, we knew the cop that had taken the mysterious call from a dead woman was on the take and he wasn't good at hiding it.

However, we hadn't known Nat knew as much as she did. We hadn't known, though we'd assumed she'd played some sort of role in the family business. I still had questions but they'd have to wait until I was in the right frame of mind to ask. Additionally, a dead FBI agent put a new spin on the situation. Zane had to be informed. So that was what I was going to concentrate on instead of my overwhelming desire to kill Wilco Pollaski. Not only from the crimes he'd committed but for the dead, cold, empty look he'd put in Nat's eyes. For the hurt he'd caused her. Then there was that goddamn hopeful look that I'd lash out and shred her.

What the fuck was that?

Blood roared in my ears as I pulled my phone out. It took every ounce of willpower I had to stay outside and make the call I needed to make and not rush back into the house and demand everyone leave so I could drill Natasha for answers.

I didn't remember dialing Zane's number. I barely took in his greeting before I launched in and laid it out. Not until I was done did I realize Zane hadn't said a word. Hadn't even grunted. Which was very unlike Zane Lewis. He always had something to say.

"You get all that?" I asked.

Still nothing.

"Z?" I called out.

"Give me a minute," he returned. I gave him the minute he requested and I did it silently.

Each second that ticked by infuriated me. I was impatient to get back to Natasha. Anxiety gnawed at my insides. I had to get back to Nat and just when I was ready to tell Zane to hurry the hell up or call me back he spoke.

"I think I know how we're gonna take down Pollaski—"

"Take out," I corrected.

"Same thing."

"Not even close, Z, you say take *down*, like we'll be turning him over to the authorities. I say take out, as in, *out* of breath, dead, put to ground."

"You let me handle Pollaski. You take care of your girl."

"Zane—"

"Listen up, Owen, this isn't my first rodeo, it isn't even my fifth. I know how this goes. You got your head so full of Natasha you're not thinking about anything else. This is the part in this game where you'll get all touchy-feely and shit and threaten me with bodily harm if I don't pull out all the stops to protect your woman. Save it. One, you're in the middle of Idaho, nowhere near me so you can't do shit but flap your gums. I got this under control. You know I do, Myles knows I do. I always have shit under control unless it's my woman getting kidnapped. Then I get cranky and lose my shit, but that's only happened once, so there is that. However, this merry-go-round we're on, I've been here before so I know how this is gonna play out. Keep your shit, see to your woman, and leave the rest to me and your team. Whether or not Wilco is breathing at the end of this does not matter as long as he's neutralized for good."

"It goddamn matters to me."

"Christ Almighty, baby Jesus, I figured you'd be further

along than you are. You haven't pulled your head out of your ass yet. Let me help you with that."

"Don't—"

"When your dumb ass is lucky enough to get a taste of sweet, you taste it. When you're lucky enough for all that sweet to look like Natasha, you better figure out a way to keep it. But more than that, when you get a woman who's been through hell and still gives you that sweet, you find a way to smooth all those sharp edges. You bust your ass to give her good, show her how life should be. You do not do that by killing her uncle and landing your ass behind bars."

"I'm sorry, I'm confused, does this 'smoothing the sharp edges' also include sawing off a man's dick—"

"Yeah, yeah, that was in the heat of the moment. In hindsight, I should've shoved it down the fucker's throat. He had my woman goddamn near-naked, threatening to do vile things to her. When that happens to Natasha, I give you my permission to saw off a dick. But until that happens—"

"That shit is never gonna happen," I ground out. "Not fucking ever."

"Right, and since it's never gonna happen, you take care of your woman. You don't plot revenge. You don't make a move unless I tell you to make it and certainly not until I tell you to. We're in a holding pattern, but this new intel is about to catapult us straight to lightning speed.

"I know someone who's gonna take an interest in this new intel, and from what I know about him, Cruz doesn't fuck around, not with dead undercover FBI agents and not just because he nearly died when he was undercover and so did his woman, but because he's FBI and he'll be rabid to take down a man who killed one of his own. It's also known far and wide Cruz has a personal mission to staunch the flow of drugs. His hatred goes beyond the normal—his ex-wife got caught up with drugs and he was forced to watch a woman he cared about spiral out of control. So, my guess, Cruz will be all over this. Bonus is he lives in San Antonio so he might already know some of the players or know of them. Either way, I'm calling Tex and Cruz and we're setting shit in motion."

All of that sounded good, except for the takedown part. I wasn't pleased with the prospect of Wilco not being buried.

"I still think Wilco needs to find himself in the dirt."

"Christ," Zane sighed. "My two-year-old pays better attention than you do."

"Your son's not two."

"Whatever, don't tell my wife I don't know how old my son is, she'll take exception to that. My point is, you're not paying attention."

It couldn't be said that Zane wasn't highly intelligent—it was part of what made him so dangerous—but he was annoying as fuck.

"I goddamn am."

"No, brother, you're not. Sarah Pollaski knows nothing but loss. She was born into shit and did what she could to survive. I'm not happy she's sat on this information for as long as she has, but I get it. She couldn't trust any of us. She still doesn't trust *us* but she trusts *you*. Now you need to take on the gargantuan task of proving to her she made the right call. And you need to start by giving her and only her all of your attention because it's the only way she'll be able to prove to *you* that you can trust *her*. Until then you've got nothing but spent condoms...you are using condoms, right?"

"This conversation's over."

"You have no sense of humor. I can already see you're not going to be any fun. Myles will be a blast and Kevin, he's easy to get riled up. I bet they'll appreciate my condom speech."

"I find that to be doubtful."

"Yeah, you're right, no one thinks it's funny until it happens to the next guy, then y'all get it. In the meantime, trust me, glove up, and use this time to convince Natasha she loves you."

Loves me?

Love?

Who the hell said anything about love?

"Oh, and tell Myles I emailed him the report he wanted. Talk soon."

Zane disconnected and I growled in frustration before I shoved my phone in my back pocket.

"He hang up on you?" Gabe asked.

Sneaky bastard.

"Yep. Asshole always gets in the last word."

And that was the God's honest truth. I'd never ended a conversation with Zane another way. He always snuck in some wisecrack then hung up before you could respond. Something else that was annoying about my boss.

"What he'd say?"

I filled Gabe in on the important parts and left out the rest. I didn't need Gabe horning in on the condom topic—he was being irritating enough as it was. And I was never going to say the word love in front of him.

"All of that sounds good but I'm sensing you're not happy," Gabe noted when I was done.

"Not a damn thing to be happy about."

"Right."

"Gotta get back inside to see to Natasha."

"Wasn't lost on you," Gabe mumbled and I stopped staring out over the view and looked at Gabe.

"None of it was lost on me. Never seen a woman shut down and go blank like that. It was like she was reading that shit from a script and it was not her life."

All of that was worrisome, but it was the look she gave me—the pleading in her eyes for me to punish her that turned my stomach.

"Shocked she said as much as she did."

I was, too. I'd waited a long time for her to come clean and now that she had, I wished she hadn't.

"Brace, brother," Gabe continued. "There's a fuckton more she's hiding. I suspect she gave us what she thought we needed to help further the investigation, but the rest, the real hurt, she's still got buried. You better learn cool and do it quick if you want her to give you the rest."

"Learn cool?"

Gabe didn't make me wait before he laid it out.

"Twice she's opened up and twice I've seen you lose your cool. Which is not like you. Never known you not to have a tight hold on your control. I give you the first time, total sneak attack thanking you for buying her her first pair of sneakers then laying it out and calling herself pussy and further hammering it home that her father was a piece of shit and so is her uncle. I get why you stormed off needing a minute. Fuck, man, I wanted to let my anger loose, but you didn't see her after you left. She doesn't understand why a man, especially one that cares about her, would lose his mind hearing that shit. And she doesn't understand because no one has ever cared about her. Period. No man, no woman, no one. She's cither silent as a mouse scared to death to speak or she's blurting out the most jacked-up shit and she does it unknowing that it will set you off.

"My guess—this morning she woke up and for whatever reason decided today was the day she was going to open up. No warning. No slow lead-in. No head's up. She just let that shit fly and when she did you didn't hide your reaction. Not only did your expression scream fury, that room was filled with your anger."

Goddamn right, I needed a minute after Nat had referred to herself as Pollaski pussy. Not until I left this earth would I forget her pretty mouth uttering the words, 'pussy was to accept whatever form of appreciation offered, be it lewd comment, invitation to dinner, or a fuck in the coatroom.' So, fuck, yeah, I'd left the room so she wouldn't see how angry I'd been that she'd been used and abused. I reckoned she'd seen enough ugly in her life and she didn't need to see mine, not when I couldn't lock it down, not when I couldn't get the image of my beautiful Natasha dressed like Call Girl Barbie dripping in Pollaski diamonds while getting fucked in a goddamn coatroom. That alone had me seeing red, all the rest of it, whacked. Her not being allowed to dress the way she wanted, forced to live a life she didn't want. She'd been sold and bought and been treated worse than a dog.

There was no way to play that cool. There was no chance I'd be able to hide my fury from her.

No one has ever cared about her.

There was my answer.

"I need to talk to Nat."

"Think you should take another minute before you go inside. You're breathing fire, brother. You don't even have a loose hold on control, you flat out got none."

"Nope," I agreed then warned, "She doesn't need control, she needs to know straight to her soul I care. The only way I get that across is by showing her. Me locking my anger down doesn't show her I care, it shows her the opposite. She doesn't understand I'm shielding her. She sees it as me shutting her out. I don't need a minute, she really doesn't need any more time in her head without me there to pull her out. She needs me breathing fire. She needs to see I will scorch the earth for her. She needs to know I'm the man who will take her back and feel her pain. And that's damn well what she's gonna get and she's getting it starting now."

"Righteous."

"Glad you approve, Gabe, but here's a warning—no more pushing. My head has been successfully extradited from my ass, now you let me play it my way."

"Got it."

Use this time to convince Natasha she loves you.

Jesus, fuck. I was going to do this.

Natasha was not Naomi. She wasn't other women. Not even close.

She was mine.

I knew it the moment I laid eyes on her in Alaska.

I might be slow on the uptake but I would not be slow to win.

CHAPTER 16

"You hungry, babe?" Kevin asked.

My torso jerked and while I couldn't be a hundred percent sure since I'd never done it before, I think I had my first ever nervous tic. At least that was what I thought it was. I mean, I did feel my head twitch to the side and at the same time my shoulder came up, and while that was going on the rest of my body jolted. If that wasn't a nervous tic then it was the beginning stages of a full-fledged nervous breakdown. Tic sounded better. Tic meant I wasn't completely coming undone.

"Um…you okay?" Kevin was staring at me like I was crazy.

Damn.

Maybe I was closer to a breakdown than tic.

"Negative," I told him.

"Negative?"

"Yeah, negative. As in, no, I'm not okay. Not even a little bit."

"You will be."

That was highly unlikely.

"Did you not just see me have a mini seizure? I think that's the first sign of not-okay."

"Yeah, I saw. You kinda looked like Myles the time Gabe hit him with the taser."

Great. Perfect. Awesome.

"Why did Gabe shock Myles with a taser?"

"Well, Gabe says it was for research purposes. He was testing the effectiveness. But truthfully, Gabe did it to see if Myles would piss himself."

I narrowed my eyes in skepticism and asked, "Are you pulling my leg *and* making fun of me?"

Kevin didn't notice or ignored my narrowed gaze. Probably the latter, none of these men missed much, which meant Kevin didn't care I was giving him my best glare. I was uncertain how I felt about this. Actually, I was unsure about the whole situation. Surprisingly, I'd found that once I'd started to blab it was easy to continue. As long as I stayed detached, that was the key. I could give the facts and details, I just couldn't think about how I felt about—then or now. I'd had lots of practice disconnecting from my feelings. I was a dab hand at pushing my emotions aside. But now that it was over I was struggling. Owen had fled like the hounds of hell were nipping at his heels. Moments later, Myles wordlessly left out the front door. One of the two places there was cell service up here, though the backyard was the better of the two. Gabe had given me a smile and nod which I'd decided to take as a sign of support before he left out the back. That meant I was left alone in the living room with Kevin.

The absurdity of the moment hit.

I couldn't say I'd laid myself bare but I had delivered some ugly truths as they pertained to my life. Things I was very ashamed of, crimes I'd committed, horrible deeds I'd done. And now after all of that Kevin's response was to ask me if I was hungry, as if I hadn't just said what I'd said. Then he went on to tell me that Gabe had tased Myles to see if he'd piss his pants, as if I hadn't had a mini-nervous-freak-out that may or may not have been a borderline psychotic episode.

Totally ludicrous.

Absolutely absurd.

"Shit, you're really not okay," Kevin muttered. But he didn't sound concerned, he sounded like he was going to laugh.

In an effort to cope with the madness that was my life, because it was either laugh or cry, there was no other way around it—I'd gone around the bend straight to schizophrenic and I laughed.

I roared with it. Totally lost my mind and descended into insanity and laughed. And once it bubbled to the surface I couldn't control it. I laughed at my horrible life. I laughed about how deeply I loved Owen. I laughed because I'd never have him. I laughed at the way Kevin was backing away from me, proving I was crazier than I thought. Then I laughed at the thought of Gabe tasing Myles. I laughed at the ridiculousness of me telling the guys I'd witnessed my father killing my mother, my uncle killing an undercover FBI agent, and Kevin offering to make me breakfast.

I laughed and laughed and did it until my stomach hurt and tears were running down my face.

"What's funny?" Owen asked as he sauntered into the room.

There was nothing funny about it but I laughed harder.

"Dude, she's cracked, brother," Kevin said, still staring at me.

"Babe?"

"Wh...wh...what?" I stammered.

"You okay?" Owen asked, but he was looking at Kevin who now had his hands up in surrender.

"Don't look at me. All I did was ask her if she was hungry. Then this started." One of Kevin's hands pointed at me.

"What's funny?" Owen repeated.

There wasn't a damn thing funny and that was what was funny.

It made no sense, not even to me and I was the one laughing.

"Nothing."

"Then why are you bustin' a gut?"

That was a really great question.

"Because I'm nervous."

I wasn't sure that was the whole truth but I was going with it.

"You often laugh when you're nervous?"

I didn't need to think about my answer and this time I spoke the whole truth when I admitted, "I have no idea, I've never been this nervous, not in my entire life."

"Why are you nervous, baby?"

Was he cuckoo?

My gaze moved through the room, stopping on Kevin long enough to ascertain he looked uncertain, then my eyes went to Gabe who also looked uncertain but weirdly proud. I was unsure how I felt about that. He'd told me to open up, to give Owen more. But he'd warned me to go gentle. Which I hadn't done. I'd woken up, come downstairs, and just started talking. I hadn't considered my words. I'd simply blurted them all out as quickly as I could.

Then I remembered something else Gabe had said, something bigger, something that was totally contradictory to me opening up—*but a man who cares about a woman really doesn't want to hear that fucked up shit happened to her.* Now I was more confused.

When my eyes went back to Owen he was staring directly at me. No, he wasn't staring, he was watching me with laser focus therefore I had all of his attention. I fought the good fight, or at least I tried to battle the urge to fidget. In the end,

I lost and I knew it because Owen didn't miss me wringing my hands together.

What could I say? I *was* nervous.

"I'm sorry."

Owen's brows pulled together at my apology. "What the hell do you have to be sorry for?"

"I shouldn't've…or I should've warned you all I wanted to talk and not sprung it on you like an idiot."

Gabe grunted something unintelligible. Kevin remained silent. And Owen stood frozen. My nerves skyrocketed and I took Owen's silence as him needing more of an explanation.

"I'm sorry for the way I did it, but I needed to get it all out and—"

"We knew most of what you told us," Owen cut me off. "Only parts you filled in were that you saw Barny kill your mother and why he did, which, baby, I have to say, I'm sorry you witnessed that. There are no words for how jacked-up that is. We knew there had to be a good reason Wilco wanted you gone, we just didn't know what that reason was. We knew you were involved in your family's business, just not all the ways. And, baby, the way you play poker we'd figured that out, too. We also know you're holding back more and when the time's right you'll share that. Breaking that down for you, you got no reason to apologize and no reason to be nervous."

"But, I was involved—"

"Did you volunteer for that shit?" Owen spoke over me.

"No, of course not."

"Did you ask for a position in the Pollaski organization?"

"No."

"Right, so why the hell are you apologizing for something you didn't want to do? You got not one fucking thing to be sorry for."

That was where Owen was very wrong. I had loads to be sorry for.

"Yes, I do," I whispered.

"Babe, you don't."

"I should've been stronger. I should've told. I should've turned snitch and stopped them."

"Yeah, and you'd be dead right now."

"And maybe Agent Conor wouldn't be," I returned. "Maybe a mother, sister, daughter, wouldn't be turning a John right now at this very moment, taking it any way the *client* demanded. Maybe one of my uncle's soldiers wouldn't be on the street pushing drugs. Maybe my life isn't worth them suffering so I can breathe."

"Do not start *that* shit again, Natasha," Owen growled and a shiver went up my spine. It went other places, too, places that I didn't want to think about while we were talking about my filthy family. "There's no maybe about it when I say, you got nothing to be sorry for. Not a fucking thing. All of it, every last damn thing is on Barny and Wilco. And, babe, check this—for the last time, *you*, *your* life, is worth everything."

I loved that Owen thought that but I didn't agree. And I was positive Agent Conor's family, whoever they were, wouldn't agree either.

"We'll have to agree to disagree about that," I muttered.

"Yeah, we will. For now. But one day, we'll hash that out, and when we do you'll come around to my way of thinking."

I didn't know what 'hash out' meant and right then I was freaked out enough so I decided I wasn't going to ask for clarification. Which he'd give me and that would freak me way the hell out. That meant I was keeping my trap shut—no more talking—period.

Though I nearly caved under his silent contemplation. Thankfully, before I could speak again and continue down a scary road I wasn't prepared to travel, Kevin broke the quiet.

"Alrighty then, now that we've settled that, who's hungry?"

And just like the first time he'd brought up food, my body jerked in surprise, though this time I controlled the head-to-shoulder tic—but just barely.

"Jesus," Gabe grunted. "Is there ever a time you're not worried about food?"

I couldn't say for certain because I was no longer paying attention but I think Kevin answered. Then I heard more low, rumbling voices but the words didn't make sense. I was too busy fighting the pull of Owen, fighting my need to close the distance and go to him, fighting all that was him and my desire to go to him and beg him to fix my life so I could stay with him forever.

It seemed I was always at war, always fighting an unwinnable battle. I was over it. Over my life, over my family, over everything.

I just wanted one thing, just one—my life to be my own.

I wanted choices.

If I did, if I were allowed, I'd choose Owen.

CHAPTER 17

Mere feet separated me and Nat. A very wary Nat. The longer I took her in the faster the pieces clicked together until the puzzle was solved and the picture was complete. A picture I liked a fuckuva lot, therefore, I was done ignoring what was growing between us.

It was a damn miracle I'd managed it as long as I had. But the day had come, and there would be no more denying what I knew. Natasha was mine—I knew it, I felt it, and I allowed that feeling to take hold and settle deep.

It was time.

No more fucking around.

"Come 'ere, Nat," I called.

Our gazes remained glued as she made her way to me, and when she was within reach I hooked her around her middle and pulled her closer. She let out a squeak and her hands landed on my chest to brace her fall. I waited a moment and let the rightness of her pressed close wash over me. This, right here, was where she was meant to be. In my arms, out in the open, and I needed her to know that.

"What's wrong?"

Those beautiful green eyes tipped up, and since the decision had been made to move forward I no longer had to keep myself in check so I didn't. I lifted my hand, cupped her cheek, let my thumb glide over the corner of her mouth.

"Nothing's wrong."

"What's happening?"

"You know what's happening."

For someone who was a master at poker, when she wasn't at a table she was shit at hiding her reactions. A hundred emotions played across her beautiful face until she decided on uncertainty.

"I don't think I do," she whispered.

"Things have changed."

Natasha's hands fisted my tee and her gaze dropped to my throat. I waited a beat for her to gather herself, then my thumb did another glide, this time over her lips and I couldn't wait for another opportunity to have my mouth on hers. This time not in a frenzy, I'd take my time and enjoy every inch of her.

"Owen." I heard the wobble in her voice and when she lifted her eyes they were watery, open, vulnerable.

Beautiful.

Straight-up unmasked beauty.

"Trust me."

"But—"

"Baby, trust me."

I heard the guys moving around the room preparing their exit. I'd made my statement, I'd done it in front of them so there was no mistaking my intentions. I wanted to give that to Nat. She needed to know what we'd started wasn't a secret. We were not going to continue to sneak around, and unwittingly that was what I'd been doing. I'd been a coward and a fool.

No more.

I waited for the back door to click shut before I dropped my lips to her forehead and repeated, "Baby, trust me."

"I don't know what to say."

"Do you know what you feel?"

Nat nodded, the motion causing the wetness that had gathered to spill over. I watched the tears leak from the corners of her eyes and it dawned on me—throughout the months I'd seen her cry once. Not when she was tied to a chair, beaten and bloody. But not after I took her home and cleaned her up. Not when Wilco found her and she was scared out of her head. Only when the woman she thought was her best friend died in front of her did she shed a tear. Other than that, not once, no matter what life had thrown at her, had I seen her cry.

But she was crying now.

"How about for now, you just go with what you feel and trust me with the rest."

Her tiny fists tightened and stretched the material as she held on. That was all I needed, for her to hold on and trust me.

"I'm too scared."

"Take what you need, Nat. Take it and trust me to protect it."

"Don't." That one syllable sounded ragged, painful, like she'd spoken it through shards of glass.

"Baby, that dreamland you're living in, it isn't a fantasy. It's your life. Straight-up you told me you needed it, you wanted it, and you were taking it. Something else—I was wrong. What happened the other day, it changed everything between us. Every. Thing. And don't twist that into this being about sex, what changed has nothing to do with me finally getting my mouth between your legs and everything to do with me having to acknowledge I cannot control what I feel for you. I tried, Nat, I held back for months. Every day I fought the allure of you. The best and worst part of my day was coming home to you. Knowing you'd be there to greet me, knowing I couldn't have you."

Her forehead hit my chest and she shook her head.

"You can hide all you want but you can't deny the truth."

"You don't know what the truth is," she mumbled against my chest.

"I do know and I'm done pretending we don't—"

"You do not know the truth." Nat punctuated her statement by jerking my tee and pressing her forehead deeper.

"Then tell me, what's the truth?"

Slowly Nat's hands unwrapped but she didn't take them off my chest when her head came up a fraction. She rolled up to her toes and her lips grazed my neck before she stopped to whisper in my ear, "The truth is, I fell in love with you when you carried me to an SUV."

I felt the muscles in my neck get tight. Then I found I was struggling to breathe.

"The truth is," she continued, still whispering, "I fell more every day. And every day I wondered if I was falling in love with the man who saved my life or just plain falling. Then I realized I wasn't falling, I was there, in love with a man who *happened* to save my life, a good man who deserves more than I could ever give him."

Jesus Christ.

"The truth is, I want to trust you. I want it so bad I can taste it. But the fact remains you deserve better than me."

Nat started to move away but before she could get far my fingers dove into her hair and I guided her face to my neck and held her there. Her body was tense, mine frozen solid but I still felt it. Nat's choppy breath fanning over my skin, the rapid beat of her heart pounding against my chest, the slight tremor of her frame. I felt it all, liked what I felt, and let it cut through the residual fear. Nat wasn't Naomi, she wasn't anyone but herself. She was strong and fragile. Hardened by life but still soft.

"How about you let me decide what I deserve?" I suggested.

"Owen—"

"You love me?"

If it was possible Nat's body strung tighter.

"Yes."

I closed my eyes and let that sink in, enjoying the feel of her in my arms even if she was stiff.

"Then trust me. That's all you have to do. No more shielding. No more hiding. No more pretending. I swear, baby, I'll guard your heart. I will not hurt you. Live this with me, live it real, and let's see where it goes."

Natasha nodded and my hand slid out of her hair down to the back of her neck and I gave her a squeeze.

"Is that a yes?" I asked.

"Yeah."

Thank fuck.

Before I could express my gratitude I heard a throat clear and my eyes snapped open to find Myles standing across the room.

"Sorry to interrupt but I got Tex and Cruz on the line and they have some questions."

It must be said my boss didn't fuck around. Normally this was a quality I admired, but right then with my woman in my arms after she'd admitted she loved me and had since we'd met and she'd agreed to take a chance on us, I wasn't in the mood to appreciate anything about Zane Lewis. I was in the mood to take my woman upstairs and show her exactly how happy she'd made me.

Now that was going to be delayed but what's more, Nat had gone positively wired. She wasn't trembling, she was shaking.

"Nat, baby, look at me." She shook her head and burrowed closer. "You have nothing to be afraid of."

"I knew."

"Say again?"

"I knew. I didn't come forward. That makes me an accessory."

Fuck.

My eyes shot to Myles and he gave me a sharp shake of his head.

"You're covered, Nat. You've got nothing to worry about."

She didn't move, not a muscle. Didn't take a breath. Didn't twitch. Didn't act like she'd heard me at all.

"Baby, I need you to trust me about this, too. We've got your back. You're covered, I promise."

That did it. She pulled her face from my neck and lifted her red-rimmed eyes to mine.

Good goddamn, I wasn't sure if I was elated she was staring at me with unashamed love or if I wanted to turn away from the blatant fear. And how in the fuck could both of those shine so bright?

"Natasha." That was all I got out before my throat clogged. I didn't give the first fuck if Myles heard it, didn't care if he saw. I dropped my forehead to hers. "Swear it, promise. You and me we got this, baby. Just stick with me, yeah?"

"Yeah."

Christ.

Strong.

"Okay." I lifted my head, straightened, and tucked Nat to my side, giving her no choice but to wrap her arm around me or have it smooshed between us. She did just that and hooked her fingers into a belt loop.

I let that wash over me, too. Only then did I turn us to face Myles.

He took in our position and dipped his chin.

"Got it," he mumbled, knowing exactly what I was communicating.

My shit was fully sorted. Everything had changed. Natasha wasn't a job, she wasn't the woman I was harboring,

OWEN (SPECIAL FORCES: OPERATION ALPHA)

she wasn't the woman we were trying to get clear of the Pollaski filth. She was simply mine. And because of that, she was theirs and the protection they'd offered had now shifted into something more.

Myles bent his head, swiped his finger over the screen of his phone, then said, "Tex? Cruz? I'm back."

Both men gave muttered "here" before Tex asked, "You got Owen with you?"

"Yeah, I'm here."

"Is Sarah with you?"

I heard Nat's swift inhale and I pulled her closer.

"Natasha," I corrected. "For all intents and purposes, Sarah Pollaski is dead."

"Copy that," Tex returned then amended, "Natasha there?"

When she remained quiet I gave her a squeeze and she squeaked, "I'm here."

"Mind if we ask you some questions?"

A beat of silence ensued and I reckoned Nat was gathering up her courage. I knew she'd best the feat, she always did, so I remained still and let her work through what she needed and a second later I felt her straighten.

"No, I don't mind. I'll help any way I can." Nat's voice rang out sure and strong.

Indeed, Sarah Pollaski was dead.

CHAPTER 18

Owen had moved me across the room and helped me sit before he took his place beside me.

I'm not sure how he maneuvered us. I had no recollection of walking to the couch. Too much had happened in a short period of time. All of it heavy, all of it weighing on my chest, making it hard to draw in enough oxygen. It was a good thing I was now sitting because I was afraid I was going to pass out at any moment. The only reason I hadn't was because Owen was beside me, our joined hands resting on his knee, a knee that was pressed against mine. As a matter of fact, there wasn't an inch of space between us.

I was grateful for the support. So far the man called Tex hadn't asked me anything, he'd just recounted what I'd told the guys earlier.

"Do I have that correct?" Tex asked.

"Yes."

"And you're sure it was Agent Conor?"

"Um…" I glanced at Owen, looking for guidance but instead, I found soft eyes that made me melt. More support but no help. "The best I can be sure. That's what my uncle called him. But before that, I knew him as Steel."

"Natasha, I'm Cruz Livingston with the San Antonio FBI. Can you describe the man, Steel?"

I would rather not. The guy had been creepy as all get-out and he'd scared the crap out of me any time he was at the house.

I clutched Owen's hand and allowed myself to remember one of the many times I'd been in Steel's presence.

"He was tall, really tall, not overweight but beefy. He... um...had brown hair, longish, didn't hit his shoulders but almost. Arms full of tattoos. He always looked dirty, like he needed a shower. Brown eyes. Mean looking. He played the part well, the...um...undercover part I mean. He scared me, I didn't like being around him. Now I feel bad because he was probably a good guy just playing a part and he was really, really good at it. I would've never guessed he was FBI by the way he looked at me."

At the time I'd thought the stares he'd aimed my way were salacious, like he wanted to get me alone in a room and not take no for an answer. But now I wondered if he was acting, or maybe trying to ascertain my part in my uncle's business.

"Tattoos?" Cruz asked. "Can you describe them?"

I could, or at least I could vividly remember one of them.

"He had a naked pinup girl on his right arm. Some sort of vine or barbed wire, I never got close enough to study it but he had one on his back. It was huge. Shoulder to shoulder." I felt the tremor slide through me, remembering the time I saw Steel without a shirt on.

"If you don't mind me asking, Natasha, how'd you come to see the tattoo on his back?" Cruz asked.

I tried to pull my hand free but Owen held strong.

I looked down at our combined hands, thinking I loved the way Owen's engulfed mine. I loved how something as simple as holding my hand could give me courage. But I needed him to let me go.

"I can't do this unless I turn it off," I whispered, not taking my eyes off our hands.

"What does that mean?" Owen asked.

"It means you have to let me go. I can't go where I need to go while you're touching me. I can't let the filth touch you."

"Baby—"

"I can't, Owen. I have to go into my head and pretend this isn't my life, this isn't real. I can't be *her* and touch you. This…" I tightened my hand under his. "Is us. This is clean. I need it to stay that way, so while I'm talking about this, I can't touch you."

"That's whacked, Nat."

"It's what I need."

I knew it cost him. I felt the tension rolling off him in angry waves when he loosened his grip and allowed me to slide my hand free. And the second I did, I wasted no time. The faster I got it out the better. And just like earlier I slipped into a place where I felt nothing. All emotions shut down. And Sarah Pollaski was resurrected. She hadn't been gone long so it was easy. So easy I hoped one day she'd be gone forever and I'd never be able to find her. The shield I'd once clung to now felt ice-cold. The burden was so heavy I wanted to shed it immediately and find Natasha.

This had to be the last time. I had to give them everything so I could forget.

"My uncle was generous with freebies," I started. "The caveat was he got to watch."

"Freebies?" Myles asked.

I ignored the disgust in his tone, mainly because it was disgusting but also because I had to rush through this.

"Yes, his soldiers, suppliers, sometimes even a new client got a taste for free. My uncle called it a teaser. But he got to watch. And freebies were always done in his home office and recorded. Of course, the men didn't know they were being recorded."

"Blackmail," Kevin interjected and I startled at his voice, not knowing he'd come back inside.

I ignored that, too.

"Yes, blackmail. If the teaser was being given to someone important the girl would be...um...young."

The vibe in the room changed. Try as I might, I couldn't disregard the oppressive fury that filled the space.

"Maybe—"

"Go on," Tex encouraged. But his voice had gone hard and menacing, too.

"So, yes, blackmail."

I'd totally lost my train of thought and couldn't remember why I'd brought up the freebies in the first place.

"The tattoo," Cruz prompted.

Right. Steel's back tattoo.

"I saw Steel in my uncle's office getting his freebie. His shirt was off and his back was to me and he was pumping away into one of my uncle's girls." Owen grunted beside me and I wondered why in the world I'd given that useless tidbit. "The tattoo covered his whole back. There was a gun in one hand and a severed head in the other. Oh, and the head had a blindfold on. And Loyalty to One was written over the head. I think there were some other letters on the motorcycle guy's vest but I couldn't see what it said."

When I stopped talking no one said anything. The air was still thick, and my heart was pounding at an alarming rate.

"Does that help?" I asked.

"Steel wasn't an FBI agent," Cruz said.

"But, my uncle called him Agent Conor."

"Have you ever heard the name, Chico Malo?" Cruz went on.

"Yeah. He's a supplier from Mexico, mostly heroin."

"*Was* a supplier. He's dead."

I didn't know what to say about that, so I said nothing. It didn't seem like a bad thing to me. a man who ran drugs was dead but for some reason, I got the feeling it was important to Cruz though he didn't expand on why that was when he continued.

"And you know a man named Axel?"

"I've heard the name, yes. Axel was the middleman," I explained.

"He didn't hide his business from you," Tex weirdly commented.

I felt Owen shift next to me and I tried my best to stay in character even though I desperately wanted to reach over and touch him. But I had to finish this. And not the twenty questions that we were playing, drawing the conversation out. I needed to lay it out and be done with it. Done with the Pollaskis. Done with Sarah. Just *done*.

"They trained me well," I told Tex. "First my father taught me all I needed to know. As far back as I can remember I knew my place. His lessons were painful, so I learned quick. After my uncle killed my father I thought I'd finally be free. My uncle hates me, I'd hoped he'd be happy to set me out. The fallen princess, penniless and homeless. I wasn't so lucky. Wilco had plans for me and his training wasn't painful —it was brutal. So I learned again and did it fast. I played his game and kept my mouth shut but I sure as hell made it so I won."

"Won?" Tex asked.

Without lifting my gaze off the coffee table I scooted away from Owen. I was serious, I couldn't let the obscenity of my former life touch him. I needed physical distance. I heard Owen's disapproving grunt but didn't stop my slide until I was as far from him as the small couch would allow.

"Yes, won. He'd send me out on a delivery, and the package would be light. Not much, but enough that the buyer knew and would complain. This happened three times and each time Wilco flew into a rage and used his fists to communicate how unhappy he was. After the third time, he never sent me on that kind of errand again. He'd send me to entertain a client and I wouldn't perform to the client's satisfaction. That happened twice and both times Wilco expressed his displeasure. I knew I would have to contribute to the family. But I would not run his drugs and I would not ever be rented pussy. So I made that so. I know I'm justifying my actions and I don't mean to, but out of all my uncle's business dealings, the gambling was the least disgusting. It was something I could live with. It was illegal, it was wrong, but it wasn't morally repulsive. That was what I won—I didn't have to spread my legs or deliver poison. I vetted clients but I didn't have to screw them.

"Wilco knew he had me cowed. He knew I'd never run. He knew I'd never be doing what I'm doing right now so he conducted business in front of me. I'm sure there's a lot I don't know. He has warehouses and an office where he spent a lot of time. But at home, he spoke freely, he screwed his women, he watched his men screw them, he didn't care I knew he killed my father. But for some reason, he cared I saw him kill Steel. He was wired after that—kept me in the house, no more client dinners, no more games, no more talking. Then he sold me and now he wants me back."

"Not gonna fuckin' happen," Owen seethed from beside me and I didn't need to be touching him to know he was irate.

"Steel wasn't an FBI agent. He was a confidential informant. Steel Conor belonged to a motorcycle club here in San Antonio," Cruz told me. "I spent months undercover with them. They were scum, all of them, through and through, worst of the worst. Facing some serious charges Steel flipped and offered up Wilco Pollaski for a lighter sentence. FBI and DEA jumped at the chance to take down the untouchable. From the report I read, Steel was getting close. Axel is a different story, one I'm not at liberty to discuss, but between those two they were working to bring down the empire.

When Steel didn't check in and went MIA, my colleagues thought he'd run and have been searching a good long while to bring him in."

Worst of the worst.

For some reason that made me feel better. It shouldn't have, a life was still taken but I couldn't deny I felt a smidgen of relief that a good man hadn't died in front of me. A death I hadn't reported.

"You didn't have him chipped?" Myles asked in disbelief.

"We did. Last place it was active was a strip club. The theory was Steel cut it out and took off. Once he got the goods on Pollaski, Steel was facing a lengthy sentence, figured he had time to rethink his deal. Like I said, Steel was close, we had a time frame and location of the next shipment of drugs. All we were waiting on was the exact date. Steel went missing two weeks before that was supposed to happen."

Two weeks? I thought back to the time after Steel died and tried to remember what business my uncle had been conducting.

"There was no shipment," I told Cruz. "Not two weeks later, more like two days. And it wasn't drugs. Wilco rotates his stable. Girls from New York were coming in and the girls from Chicago were going to New York. Franco would've overseen the exchange."

"Franco Dalto?"

"Yes," I answered Tex. "Franco is my uncle's right-hand man."

"Set up, or was Steel a dumbass and got it wrong?" Gabe joined the conversation and I looked up at him.

"Set up," I answered.

"My uncle tests loyalty and does it often. He gives misinformation and watches. If he told Steel a shipment of drugs was coming in and gave a location, I guarantee he was

RILEY EDWARDS

watching. If he saw something unusual happening he'd know he had a leak."

"Shit," Cruz cursed. "Our people moved in on the location to set up surveillance."

"Then Wilco knew Steel was a leak," I told him. "Two reasons for my uncle to get his hands dirty. One is to teach a lesson to a soldier and he delivers those lessons personally. And the second, he disposes of rats. He calls himself the exterminator."

"Do you have anything else for us?"

I thought about Tex's question, and being as this was the last time I wanted to talk about my uncle I thought on it hard. Owen admitted they'd dug into Wilco's business, they likely knew more than I did. But they didn't know him. Whatever they'd read about his crimes didn't do the man justice. They couldn't know how deep his depravity ran. No sane person could imagine.

"Do not trust anyone in Chicago," I started. "You might think you know who he has on his payroll but you don't. There are people he hasn't activated yet. He waits until he needs them, then approaches them with what he has on them. And everyone has secrets they don't want told. Everyone. Something as simple as a married man getting a lap dance to a man of the cloth getting a blow job. I am not joking. Every person has dirt in their closet and Wilco has a way of finding it.

"Franco will die for my uncle. He will kill for him. Wilco knows where Franco's family is and being as Franco wants his sisters and mother safe he will do anything for Wilco, and I mean anything. Do not underestimate Franco."

I paused, needing to gather my thoughts. This was harder, and as much as I tried to push Natasha aside and keep my cold detachment in place I couldn't. No matter how hard I'd tried over the months to keep my emotions at bay and not get attached to the people who had shown me kindness, I couldn't do it.

Eva had taken me under her wing and had done everything she could to connect with me. She'd gone as far as enlisting her friends—Tatiana, Emerson, and Anaya. All four women had been generous with their time. They'd come to the house to keep me company. They'd brought me books and magazines. Eva had bought me cosmetics and nail polish. Anaya being the closest to my size had brought me a ton of clothes after she'd gone through her closet.

So many people had reached out to me and offered their friendship. And they didn't stop doing it even after I'd repeatedly rebuffed their efforts.

I could not live with more guilt. If something happened to one of them because of me I couldn't live, period. I would rather die than have one of them harmed. And that wasn't me having a death wish like Owen had accused. That wasn't me thinking my life was worthless. It was the plain truth.

Before Owen and Eva, I had never known kindness. Not ever. But loyalty had been ingrained into my soul from the moment my father could teach me. Unfortunately, I'd been forced to show my loyalty to the wrong people. Owen and his friends were not the wrong people, they were good and kind and clean and they deserved my undying gratitude.

I owed it to all of them.

Even if Owen didn't like it, I would give it to them.

"One last thing." I stopped and cleared the lump in my throat and fought the sick feeling in my belly. "Wilco will carry out everything he threatened."

"Nat—"

"Everything. Do not ignore his threats. Don't think he will not take out every woman on that list. He will not hesitate and he won't do it fast. Women are nothing to him, meaningless pussy. He is so disgusting there are no words to express how bad he is. Pure evil down to his soul. And he is uncontrollable. He values nothing but his throne. He cares for no one. He has no weakness because he doesn't have a single emotional tie to anyone or anything. Take his stable, he will not care other than the money he's losing while he rebuilds. Cut off a supply chain, he'll find a new one. I disobeyed a direct order. There will be hell to pay. Please understand that, someone will pay the price for my disobedience. And that person should be me."

"Are you shitting me?" Owen roared and I jumped. "No one is paying for jack shit, Natasha."

He was wrong. Way wrong. Someone would. I knew it as fact.

"What I'm saying is, I cannot live with someone getting hurt because of me. I can barely breathe as it is knowing what I did, what my father did, what Wilco does."

I stopped so I could shift in my seat and face Owen. And once I did I realized my mistake. I never should've looked at him. The sheer magnitude of his emotions was on display. Nothing hidden. And before I could recover from that hit his next words plowed into me and stole the oxygen straight from my lungs.

"Baby, hear this and hear it good. There is no way those women will be touched. None. You think Wilco Pollaski is the devil, but I can assure you he is no match for Zane and the army he has at his back. What Barny and Wilco have done, will do, could do, might do, none of that is on you. What those motherfuckers forced you to do isn't on you. I know you don't believe me right now, but you will. There will come a time when you're clear of this and you've had time to heal when you'll reflect. And when you do, you'll understand what I'm telling you is the truth. You don't blame the victim for the actions they took to survive. And you might not like that but there's no way around it. You were a victim in their fucked-up, whacked—"

"But I—" I tried to interrupt Owen but he interrupted me right back.

"Straight-up, Nat," Owen snapped. His voice was colder than I'd ever heard it. "You enjoy taking cock for money?"

"What?" I breathed then tried to suck in air but I couldn't.

Owen's question burned through me, leaving pain in its wake.

"Wilco pimped you out. Did you enjoy taking cock for money?"

"Absolutely not!"

"Right. So you did what you had to do to survive. Lived through that nightmare, then after you had to endure that, you took a fucking beating so you wouldn't have to do it again. So tell me, are you responsible for that?"

"No."

"Right. What'd you do with the drugs when your packages were light? Did you sell it on the side? Inject it? Give it away?"

"No, of course not. I flushed it."

"Yeah, you flushed it and took a goddamned *beating*."

Okay, I was beginning to understand what he was saying, but I still held guilt. I should've found a way out.

"I see you're getting it," Owen continued. "So let me help you out some more. There was no one for you to go to. No one you could've gone to for help. They made sure of it. They kept you where they wanted you. *They* pay. Not you. Not Ivy, Eva, Emmy, Anaya, Vi, or anyone else. Wilco's time is up. He fucked up, Nat. He made threats he cannot follow through on. He touches any one of those women hellfire will rain down on him. He attempts to get his filthy hands on you and I will personally rip his throat out. No joke. I will kill him."

Something strange happened and it happened so quickly I didn't understand what it was and I didn't get a chance to process it before I was up off the couch and cradled in

Owen's arms. He was carrying me across the room when he said, "No more questions. Nat's out. This shit ends for her now." And that was when I realized I was sobbing. Big, wracking body-shaking sobs.

I shoved my face in Owen's neck. And stopped fighting the memories. Horrid, appalling, revolting, unspeakable moments filtered through my head. My whole life was one hideous waste. Once they started I couldn't stop them until my world exploded and pain engulfed my entire being.

"I hate him," I croaked.

"I know you do, baby."

"I want her to die."

"Who, baby?"

"Sarah. I want her to die. I don't want to be her. I don't want to remember. I don't want to—"

"She's gone, Natasha."

"Not yet."

"Then let's get the rest of her out."

That was what Owen told me. His voice sounded sure. He made it seem so simple that I believed him. I believed that together we could let Sarah go. And it worked.

Then it didn't. And when the time came, I learned a new lesson.

I didn't have the first clue what real pain felt like.

I never should've believed.

CHAPTER 19

Only after hours and hours later, after Natasha had finally worn herself out, did I get up and leave her in bed. So many fucking tears—buckets of them had leaked from her eyes until my tee was soaked through. I didn't know a woman could shed so many tears. And I could've gone my whole goddamn life not knowing and been happy.

I paused at the bedroom door and looked back at a sleeping Natasha. She was curled on her side hugging a pillow, one I would replace when I slid back in bed with her and wrapped her back around me. But for now, the pillow would have to do. I had to go downstairs and talk to the guys. Plans needed to be made.

By the time I hit the bottom step I hadn't checked my anger—not that I tried. At this point, it was an impossibility. Through the tears, Nat had talked. Every word she spoke broke me.

"How is she?" Gabe asked from the couch.

I stared at my teammate, a man who had been a friend for a long time, a good man, one I trusted with my life. And as I locked eyes with him I didn't bother to hide how goddamn ridiculous his question was, therefore, he didn't miss precisely how ludicrous I thought it was. So when he muttered, "Right," it was not surprising.

"What did Tex say?" I asked on my way to the kitchen.

"Not much," Gabe told me. "You know him, he takes it all in, does his magic, and comes back with what we need. Now Cruz, he had a lot to say."

I grabbed a protein bar and jerked my chin, silently demanding Gabe to continue.

"Steel Conor was a mean motherfucker. Cruz met him when he was undercover with the Red Brothers MC. Wilco did the world a favor taking Steel out but Cruz still wants to nail Wilco for his murder. Tex is doing his thing with that but it's unlikely a body will turn up. And get this shit— Axel was running his game from an FBI safe house. I don't know how that was pulled off but somehow they managed it. Steel negotiated a lighter sentence but Cruz had piled so much shit on Axel no one would give him time off his sentence. But Axel bargained for a move. Too many enemies in Texas."

"Why'd they keep Axel locked up?"

"Too many ties to Mexico."

I nodded and chewed the rest of my bar.

"Tex is calling in a favor. He wants more coverage in Maryland."

It was good Gabe had brought that up. That was what I wanted to talk to him about.

"When are we going back?"

"We're not. Tex made his calls and Wolf, Abe, Cookie, Mozart, Benny, and Dude all agreed to help. They're flying to Maryland."

I didn't like this plan, and not because I didn't believe the men Tex had called in weren't good at what they did. They were. I'd known Faulkner 'Dude' Cooper a long time. He was an explosives expert and had taught me a lot over the years. The rest of the guys were solid, smart, and no doubt could handle the situation. The issue was, I wanted to be the one who handled this particular problem.

"Owen," Gabe started then wisely snapped his mouth closed.

"I need you to take care of Nat."

"No, brother."

What the fuck?

"No?"

"No. You're staying here and *you're* taking care of *your* woman."

I clenched my jaw, and through gritted teeth, I told him, "I will be taking care of my woman."

"Not the way she needs."

Now he was pissing me off.

"Fuck—"

"Tell me, how's Nat?"

I snapped my mouth closed and my body went solid.

"Yeah, that's what I thought," my friend who was about to get punched in the throat snickered. "You okay with me being the one holding your woman when she's crying her man left her?"

"I'm not leaving her. Not like that and you know it, asshole. This has to end for her."

"And it will."

"Not the way I want it to."

"Are you listening to yourself? Not the way *you* want it to? Selfish much? We're all up here taking her back and you know why we're doing it without complaint? Because we knew what she meant to you long before you had the balls to admit it. So here we are, Owen, up in the mountains freezing our asses off taking her back—which means we're taking *your* back. Zane's busting his ass to get her out of that fucked-up mess. And shit's not going the way *you* want?"

Jesus, when Gabe put it like that I had to admit, I was being a dick. Everyone was chipping in, doing more than their fair share. Which was to say, doing anything at all. Natasha's issues weren't theirs. Wilco Pollaski wasn't a paying job. And now Zane was forced to call in markers and pay out of pocket to make a point—that no one threatened his woman, his men, his business, or any of the women under his care. And the point would be made—loud and clear. Just not how I wanted to drive it home.

But as selfish as it was Gabe didn't understand.

"You don't get it," I told him.

"Get what?"

"How it feels to hold the woman you've fallen in love with while she relives the nightmare she endured. A nightmare that is so dark, so traumatic, she shook so violently her teeth clattered. I hope to God she got all that shit out because I am not lying when I tell you that if there's more I do not want to know. You've been at my side a long time, Gabe, so you know, you lived it with me. We've seen some gnarly shit, we know what lurks in the dredges of society. But still, Nat knows better than us. She lived it. *Lived. It.* You heard it, she was pimped out, but you didn't hear what that did to her. You got the cold, emotionless story. You didn't hold her while those memories flooded. He sold her virginity."

I watched Gabe flinch and it sucked, me telling him that, but he needed to understand. "Yeah, brother, Wilco Pollaski sold her virginity. Now, I'm not a woman and I don't think I have to be to know straight to my soul that shit is beyond fucked. Something that was precious for her to give was bought. So, as selfish as it is, and I admit, I'm being a selfish bastard, I need this to end for her. And the way it needs to end is permanently. Not with the looming threat of that motherfucker going to trial and getting off. Or with him rotting in prison but still calling shots, meaning that threat is still there."

"I get that," Gabe conceded. "But, Owen, you're not gonna be the one to end it. Your priorities have to shift. You *have* to trust your team to handle this. If you don't and you leave her here, you'll lose her. She won't understand. I heard everything you said, but I don't think you heard yourself. Nat gave that to you—not to me, not to Kevin, not to Myles. You. You're her lifeline, you're the one she trusts. Don't break that trust, brother."

Goddamn, Gabe was right.

I didn't want him to be right. I wanted... what the hell did I want? I wanted Pollaski dead. I wanted Natasha safe. I wanted her in my life and in my bed when we went home. I wanted to live my dream. The life I thought I'd have before things went bad with Naomi. I wanted to be happy and the only way I got any of that was if I trusted my team. They'd handle Pollaski and I'd handle the rest.

"You're right," I begrudgingly admitted.

"Of course I am."

Smug bastard.

"Don't be stupid," I returned and Gabe smiled.

"Right. Just to finish this up. Zane sent the plane to pick up Wolf and his team. Benny needed a few extra hours to help Jessika at the bar and Abe had something going on with his kids but they'll be in Maryland by tonight."

Guilt infested my insides. Those men all had wives and responsibilities, yet they were dropping everything to help a woman they'd never met.

Fucking, hell. My head dropped forward as the knowledge rushed through me.

"You know they'd do anything for Tex," Gabe said.

He was talking about Wolf, Abe, Mozart, Cookie, Dude, and Benny. And Gabe was right about that, too. Tex and the other six retired SEALs were brothers—closer than blood. But other than knowing Dude on a professional level none of them knew me and they certainly didn't know Nat.

"And Mozart and Cruz have a connection," Gabe went on. "The way Cruz tells it, part of the reason he went into law enforcement was because of Mozart's sister, Avery. She was murdered and that tragedy struck Cruz deep. He's never forgotten Avery Reed, and because of that, Mozart and Cruz have a bond. Mozart's all in. Cruz for his own reasons, one of which is the drugs Pollaski puts on the streets means Cruz is all in. As in, *all in*, brother. Cruz is getting a team together and cashing markers. So what I'm saying is, they're all happy to do it. For you, for Natasha, and with that comes the added benefit of taking a drug-dealing pimp off the streets."

"Right," I mumbled, still staring at the floor.

"I get it's a hard pill to swallow but I know you're gonna do it."

It was damn hard but I was going to choke it down and take what was being offered. But fuck if it didn't taste bitter.

I heard footsteps and my head shot up to find Nat coming down the stairs. That bitterness started to evaporate, and when she walked directly to me and plastered herself to my side, I hitched my arm up to make room for her and suddenly I tasted nothing but sweet. The guilt settled and so did my soul.

"I woke up and you were gone," she whispered.

I tightened my arm around her and kissed the top of her head before I said, "I was coming right back up."

She nodded against my chest and shoved her face deeper. *Christ*.

That felt sweeter.

It also felt a lot like she was trying to melt into me and disappear.

I looked up and caught Gabe staring at Nat, the muscles in his neck tight, his body held stiff. Yeah, he saw it—it wasn't sweet at all. And it wouldn't be until she could breathe easy.

* * *

OWEN (SPECIAL FORCES: OPERATION ALPHA)

"I LOVE THIS!" NAT SHOUTED OVER THE WHINE OF THE ENGINE.

We were on one of Rhode's four-wheelers. Nat was behind me with her arms wrapped tight around my stomach and her chin resting on my shoulder. After I'd coaxed her to eat something I'd taken her up the mountain to a spot I'd discovered the first time I'd visited. We weren't at the peak but we were damn high and the sight before us was out of this world.

I shut down the ATV and patted Nat's thigh.

"Hop off, baby."

She reluctantly did as I asked but she did it excitedly babbling, "This is so beautiful. I've never seen anything like this before."

Nat's boots crunched in the snow as she made her way to the edge of the bluff. The valley below and the tree-covered mountains in the distance did make for a spectacular sight. But I only had eyes for the woman with her head tipped back taking in the warm rays of the sun. It was a perfect day; a cloudless blue sky, sun high, taking some of the bite out of the crisp air, but not enough to make a dent in the compacted snow.

All of that beautiful.

Natasha soaking it in, more so.

Amazing.

Every inch of her. Top to toe. Inside and out.

I took in her smile and couldn't fathom how after the morning she'd had she could look so happy. After she ate lunch she'd gone upstairs to get dressed and had come back down in another pair of fleece-lined Carhartt pants these ones tan. The color may've been different from the others but they fit her the same as the first, which was to say perfectly. Her long honey-blonde hair was in two braids— one on either side of her head. And right then with her wool beanie pulled down, the brim covering her eyebrows, those braids hanging out the sides pulled to the front, the rubber

199

bands brushing mid-chest, she looked hot as fuck. Fresh-faced, eyes no longer red and puffy from crying, and rosy cheeks—she looked like a high-class mountain woman, which normally wouldn't go together, but Nat made it work.

And she looked happy smiling up at the blue sky.

I walked up behind her and wrapped my arms around her middle, fitted myself to her back, and held on tight.

"How ya doin', baby?" I asked and braced.

I figured I knew how she was doing but that smile threw me for a loop. So had her happy skip to the edge of the clearing. When we'd left the house Nat was still quiet. She'd readily agreed to go for an ATV ride, but there was no spark, no shine in her eyes. Now it seemed she had some life in her after our long ride.

"I'm...good," she whispered.

"Nat—"

She shuffled and wiggled until there was no space between us. Her hands came up, hooked onto my forearms, and her head dropped back to my shoulder.

"I'm good."

Still not mollified, I asked, "What does *good* mean?"

"I just had my first four-wheeler ride."

"Okay," I said slowly.

"And it was awesome. I want you to teach me how to ride."

I wasn't sure what that had to do with her being good but I went with it.

"I can do that."

"I know you can," she murmured. Then just as quietly she continued, "This morning wasn't good."

That was an understatement. This morning and the aftermath that followed was something I'd never forget.

"But you made it better."

Fuck me.

200

"You took me for a ride and brought me here. You gave me all this beauty. But before that, you gave me everything."

Jesus. Fuck me.

Overcome with emotion, I buried my face in her neck and breathed in. Pine, cold, and Nat's flowery shampoo. I could live the rest of my life happy smelling that shampoo—go to sleep, wake up, with the scent of jasmine and lemon. Go to work and tick off the minutes until I could go home and see her smile.

Hell, yeah, I could live the rest of my life happy.

"Baby—"

"You don't understand."

"I think I do."

"No, Owen, you don't." Nat dropped her hands and twisted in my arms so she was facing me. She tipped her head back, placed her palms on my chest, and her eyes locked onto mine. "You gave me this." I opened my mouth to speak but her hands pressed deeper and she shook her head. "You made my fantasy a reality. All my life I was alone. No one ever made me feel safe until you. No one has ever cradled me in their arms, carried me to bed, held me while I cried. I've never been safe—period. I've never gone to sleep not worried about what the next day would bring. I've never woken up happy. I've never been excited for what the day would bring. I've never loved anyone. You gave me all of that and more. I'm okay because you made it that way. You gave me a safe place to get it out—all the ugly, disgusting, painful parts of my life, and the whole time I was doing it you never let *me* go. You held me in your arms and I let *her* go. She's gone. I don't want to be Sarah Pollaski, I want to be Natasha, I want to be *yours*."

The cool air in my lungs burned as I exhaled.

There it was—Nat was ready. She believed.

"I fell in love with you the night you burned boxed mac and cheese. You were adorably disgruntled, banging around in the kitchen, ranting about how the directions on the box weren't right. Then something struck you funny and you smiled. Just a hint, a ghost of a grin but that was all I needed."

"That was only a few days after I got to your house," she told me something I very well knew.

To be precise it was the third night she'd been there. I'd taken a shower and when I came out prepared to call and order takeout, I found her trying to cook. It was a disaster— the macaroni was burnt beyond edible, and had to be scraped off the bottom of the pan. She didn't have the first clue what to do in a kitchen but she'd tried. However, it was the ranting that had caught my attention. In those early days, Natasha barely spoke, so hearing her raving about burnt food and wanting to do something nice for me had hit me square in the chest. But when she smiled, I felt that blow down to my bones. That was the first time I'd ever seen her full lips tip up into a grin.

It was at that moment I saw her as a beautiful woman. A woman I wanted to see smile every day and I wanted to be the man that put that smile on her face. Then I promptly shoved my feelings aside and refused to acknowledge I fell in love with a woman I knew nothing about. A woman who was painfully sad. A woman who was so goddamn strong she'd survived hell.

Jesus, I was a jackass. I'd wasted so much time.

"Yep, so now do you understand what I meant when I told you every day it was torture coming home, having you in my house, sleeping in another room, and not being able to be with you the way I wanted? Not being able to touch you, kiss you, hold you. I'd rush home after work to see you, knowing the woman I wanted more than anything was waiting for me. But when I got there I couldn't *have* you— and more, I couldn't give you me. I couldn't make you happy the way I wanted. And that fuckin' killed."

"But now you have me," she muttered. She rolled to her toes and her cold lips brushed feather-light across mine.

"Now I have you," I confirmed and pulled Nat tight against me, keeping our lips connected, thinking now that I had her, there was nothing holding me back from kissing her. So that was what I did, not wasting another moment, not hiding, or keeping myself in check. I kept the kiss gentle —slow glides, our tongues teasing. Not a get-to-know-you kiss, but a welcome home.

This went on a good long while, standing on the top of the bluff, surrounded by the best Mother Nature had to offer, pristine splendor as far as the eye could see—not that I was looking but I knew it was there. And still, the woman in my arms was far more pretty.

Nat slanted her head and took our kiss from slow and sweet to scorching hot. Not only did the kiss deepen but her hands went to my neck and she held tight. At the same time, she pressed closer and wiggled. My already-hard cock started to throb, and as painful as it was going to be it was time to end the festivities.

Natasha had other ideas. Not wanting the kiss to end, she held on and pressed deeper. All of that felt great, but it was the moan that vibrated from her chest, up her throat, and coated my tongue, that nearly did me in.

I wrenched my mouth from hers. Still breathing heavy I warned, "Natasha."

"Don't stop."

"Baby—"

"Please don't stop. We're out here all alone."

"Nat—"

"I need you," she pleaded and I swear to God it was by sheer force of will I didn't rip her clothes off and take her right then and there in the snow.

But that was not going to happen. Not with Nat. Not

now. My hands slid down her back and cupped her ass at the same time I thrust my hips forward.

"That need goes both ways," I told her. "But the first time you take a man, the first time you take *me* it will not be with your pants around your ankles bent over an ATV. You want that adventure later, I'll gladly arrange it, but not now. The first time will be in our bed where I can take my time, worship you."

"Owen—"

"And make no mistake, baby, I *am* your first. There is more to sex than the physical, more than two bodies coming together, more than want and desire and hunger. When you feel that need and it goes both ways, when it's shrouded in care and concern and love, sex becomes more—two people connecting spiritually. And while I'm all about communing out in the open, in God's country, surrounded by all this beauty, the first time I'm taking my time so you know you are loved."

"Owen," she breathed and I liked the sound of that so much I decided I wanted to hear it again while I was moving inside her.

I dropped a hard quick kiss on her lips and pulled back and asked, "Understood?"

"Yes."

"Good. Now, you wanna drive back or you wanna sit bitch and wrap your arms around me?"

Nat's response was instant—it was blinding, it was beautiful, and it stole my breath. If I wasn't already in love, her wide, pretty smile would've made me jump headfirst into the emotion.

"I want you to teach me how to drive."

I knew that would be her answer.

"Then hop on and let me teach you."

She didn't move away but her hand went from my neck to my face and her thumb glided over my jaw.

"You're the most handsome man I've ever seen, Owen."

Before I could return the sentiment, she was out of my arms, skipping to the ATV.

Nat was good.

How she could recover as fast as she had, I'd never understand.

I also wasn't giving the thought any more headspace.

She was good, and by tonight, she'd be better—and every day from then on I'd work to keep her happy and whole.

If I had known then what I know now, I would've understood there would be no such thing as *whole*, not for Natasha and not for me.

CHAPTER 20

"Owen," I panted and squirmed.

Slow hands continued to glide down my ribs, while his mouth blazed another trail of kisses between my breasts. This wasn't the first time his lips had made the trip south so I knew where they'd stop and it wasn't where I wanted them. Right before he got to the good spot Owen would reverse course and nip his way over my stomach.

He was driving me insane.

Had been the whole night. After dinner, he told Kevin he was in charge of KP duty, then announced we were going to bed. After that, he didn't delay. Or he did, depending on how you looked at it. He'd promptly taken me upstairs, but instead of jumping straight into bed, he brought me up to the room, set me on the bed—yes, *he* set *me*—literally he picked me up and plopped my tush on the bed and told me he'd be right back. He disappeared into the bathroom and a few minutes later he came out and carried me into the bathroom. Undressed me and helped me into a bubble bath. I was going to protest this unnecessary detour but when his clothes hit the floor and he got in behind me, my objection died.

Owen had washed my hair, conditioned it, ran his soapy

hands over my shoulders, arms, and chest. He toyed with my nipples until I was shivering, then his hand went between my legs and he played there until I was trembling and my heart was full to bursting. What he had not done during our bath was let me climax. He'd taken me to the edge and backed off. Each time he'd done this I'd groaned my displeasure and he'd kissed me silly.

Now I was on the bed naked, Owen was naked, and he was taking his sweet time.

I was done with slow about an hour ago. I wanted more. I wanted to feel him inside me. I was primed, ready to go, and frustrated.

"Honey," I moaned as his tongue swirled around my nipple. "You're killing me."

"You feel it yet?" Owen asked. But as soon as he got the words out he was using his mouth for something far better than talking.

His lips latched onto my nipple, my back arched off the bed, and my hands dove into his hair, holding him to my breast. One of his hands was still roaming my side. The other was roaming, too, but it seemed intent on its destination, and when I felt Owen tap my thigh I opened my legs wider. Two thick fingers pushed inside, my hips bucked, and my eyes closed as pleasure ricocheted.

Owen tore his mouth free and his rough, sexy voice called my name. I ignored his summons but not the coarse, lust-filled tone—*that* made my hips surge again.

"Natasha," he rasped again, and it was crazy but just the sound of his voice made my pussy convulse. "*Christ.* Answer me."

Answer him?

Had he asked a question? If, and it was a pretty big *if* since I was damn near mindless, I was close to recalling what he wanted me to answer, I lost the thought when Owen twisted his fingers inside me and started rubbing. The new sensation took the near out of mindless and swept me away. Something new was building, something I'd never felt. Bigger than a normal orgasm. It made my toes curl, my thighs quiver, and I fought the urge to close my legs.

"What's—"

"Tell me, baby, you feel it yet?"

Oh, yeah, I felt it. My body sang with it, his heat, his weight, what he was doing between my legs, my nipples still tingled from all the attention he'd laved.

"I feel it," I moaned and dragged my hands down his back, loving the way his muscles bunched under my palms.

Sleek, smooth, hot skin. There was so much to explore, so many places I wanted to touch, kiss, lick, all of them available to me when Owen had me pinned under him. So my hands moved to the one place I could reach and I dug my nails into the hard muscle of his ass and silently begged for more.

However, Owen wasn't silent. Not that he was begging, but he had a lot to say, all of it good, all of it rocked my world. All of it a dream come true and not just because he was naked on top of me with his fingers working magic. It started when his face went to my neck and he started kissing me there, and it didn't stop until he nipped and licked his way up to my ear. That was when he commenced his life-changing soliloquy.

"I don't think you do, Natasha. I don't think you *feel* it yet. How much it means to me." Owen stopped to run his tongue over the shell of my ear. "How good you taste." He paused again and roughly thrust his fingers deeper. "How good you feel. Sweet fucking torture, you squirming under me, trusting your body to me, trusting I'll take care of you. And I will, promise, Nat, your body, your heart, you can trust I'll give you everything you need."

"I feel it," I whispered and he must've believed me because his fingers slipped out and he reached beyond me and slid his hand under the pillow.

I would've complained at the loss of his fingers but he was using his teeth to rip open a condom wrapper and relief swept through me.

Finally.

Owen went up to his knees and I watched as he rolled the latex down his thick shaft. At the last minute I remembered Owen was naked, my eyes had barely had the chance to take in the rest of his muscled abs, defined ridges, and valleys that I wanted to run my hands over but I was too late. Owen dropped back down and balanced on an elbow, holding most of his weight off of me.

His free hand glided from my hip, over the outside of my thigh. His touch was gentle, reverent, but his voice held an edge when he said, "Guide me in, baby."

It took a moment for me to understand what he was asking for but when I got it, I wasted no time reaching between us and wrapping my fist around him. I was pulling him toward me when he grunted, "Eyes."

My gaze snapped to his and I froze.

Hard but soft.

The green orbs darker than normal, so dark they looked black. Deep grooves formed around the corners of his eyes and his brows were pinched. A mask of control. It was costing him, holding himself back, going slow for my sake, and I loved him all the more for it. I loved the way he was looking at me, waiting for me to guide him inside. Not taking but waiting for me to give it to him.

My choice.

My body.

My choice.

Owen got it, he understood more than I did how important it was I had control.

"I *feel* it," I whispered. "I know what you're giving me. Straight to my soul, honey, I feel it."

And because I had control but I wouldn't for much longer

I gave Owen's hard length a long, firm stroke and watched his jaw clench. Oh, yeah, he was holding back—big time. But he didn't need to. I tugged his erection closer until I had the tip where I wanted, then I removed my hand and smoothed my palm over his jaw, and rested it on his cheek.

"I trust you," I told him and his eyes flared. "It's mine to give, Owen, now it's yours. Honey, take it."

His hand on my thigh stilled and I felt the muscle under my palm jump. What he didn't do was take it.

"I've waited for you all my life, honey. All I ever wanted was to love and to be loved and be free to feel. I choose you. Now, please, Owen—take what I'm *giving*."

Slowly, so slowly, achingly, beautifully slowly he pushed in. His eyes didn't leave mine as he filled me. His face didn't relax, if possible his frame grew tenser. Brittle, like he'd shatter if I touched him.

"Jesus," he bit out.

I shivered under him and my need to touch him won out over my fear he'd fly apart. I left my hand cradling his face where it was and picked my other one off the bed and just as gently as he'd touched me, I let my fingertips trail down his back and watched his eyes narrow. Normally this would worry me, scare me even, but I knew I had nothing to fear— not from Owen. He'd take care of me, body and heart, he'd promised.

Inch by inch he was stretching me, then he pulled back and started all over again. Slowly gliding.

It was beautiful what he was giving me, but I wanted more.

"Owen."

"Yeah, baby?"

"Do you feel it?"

"Yeah, Nat, I feel it."

"Then let go."

His head dropped forward and I lost his eyes.

"Can't."

I loved he thought that, loved he wanted me in charge, but I needed him to be him.

"I need you to. I'm not broken."

Owen's head snapped up and he pinned me with an angry gaze.

"Not a fucking thing broken about you."

"Then let go and give me what I need."

With that he slammed in so hard, filling me full my spine arched and my breath whooshed out.

"Look at me," he demanded.

"I am."

"No, baby, look at me."

I was looking at him, right into his glistening eyes, his tight face. He said nothing but I didn't need him to. I didn't need words to understand what he was communicating but he gave them to me anyway.

"Means everything, you giving me this."

"I know."

"Everything, baby."

"I know."

He shook his head like I didn't know but thankfully let the conversation die and went on to get to the good stuff.

"I do something you don't like, something that doesn't feel right, or something that doesn't feel good, you tell me and we'll switch it up."

"Okay."

"You don't keep that bottled up, you say it immediately."

"Okay."

Owen shifted and his cock slipped in deeper and I couldn't stop the mew that slipped out.

"Jesus," he growled. "Wrap your legs around me and hold on tight."

I did as he asked and hitched both my legs high, then wrapped them around his hips and locked my ankles.

"Fuck, you feel good," he said and pulled out only to push back in. "I want your hands on me the whole time, Nat, I want you touching me."

I could do that, hell, I wanted that. So what was I waiting for? I moved my hand from his face, slid both arms around him, and my hands started touching. They glided from his shoulders to where my heels rested on the small of his back. Up and down they went and as they did I watched his face start to relax.

"If I'm too rough—"

"You won't be. Please, Owen, fuck me."

"No," he grunted. His hand moved lightning fast and he fisted my hair to keep me still, then he lowered his face down and continued, "No matter how I take you, rough, hard, slow, gentle, bent over the couch, sliding up your ass, however adventurous we get, however dirty we want to play, I will never *fuck* you. You are not a place to stick my cock. When I'm inside of you, any way I can be, I am not ever fucking you."

Okay, I really loved that.

"Okay, honey."

I didn't get to say more— not that I was going to say more —but if I were, Owen was done talking and he shared this by slamming his mouth down on mine. But once his tongue swept my lips and I happily opened for him, he didn't take the kiss wild. He kept it sweet. It was wet and deep but not wild. He controlled everything about the kiss—teasing, light touches of our tongues. It was in direct contrast to how hard he was driving inside of me. That was measured, too, but it was hard. A slow, hard pounding that drove my need through the roof.

I felt every wide inch of him stretching my inner muscles as I clung to him with all four limbs. I touched everywhere I could, lifted my hips to meet his thrusts, my body in tune with his every move, but more—so much more, my thundering heart was fully engaged. I felt everything.

This was the dream.

More than any fantasy I could conjure up. Owen covering me, connected to me, tying me tighter to him with every swipe of his tongue, every thrust of his cock. I felt so much, it would take a year to fully understand all I was feeling. But there was one thing I didn't need time to think about. I might have fallen in love with Owen months ago, but never had I loved him more than I did in that moment. And it wasn't because my body was on the verge of a monumental orgasm the likes of which no human in the history of humanity had ever had. No, I loved him more because he had given me back something I'd lost. Myself, *my* control, *my* ability to give.

Mine.

And because I had it I could give it to Owen.

And I freaking loved that.

On a downward glide, Owen twisted his hips and grinded the root of his cock against my clit. My head jerked back, unfortunately breaking our kiss.

"Ohmigod," I groaned.

"Christ," he returned.

His groan sounded so good it sent a tremor through me and my legs started to loosen.

"Tighter," Owen commanded.

I complied instantly, used my heels as leverage, and rocked up.

"Harder," I begged.

"*Jesus*, fuck," he groaned and my pussy shuddered.

"So close," I warned.

Owen took me harder. So hard I had to hold on to his shoulders while his driving thrusts took me straight to the edge.

"Need to see you."

I righted my head and when I did, my body locked.

"Honey," I breathed.

"Yeah, you *finally* feel it."

I did. Though I'd felt it before, the love that shone in his stare couldn't be missed. I could've been blind and I still would've felt it, it radiated from him out of every pore.

"Do you feel it?" I asked.

"Straight to my soul."

"No, what I'm feeling, do you know?"

"Straight to my soul," he repeated. "Gonna take you there."

Though I should've been the one warning him I was already there. But I didn't need to because he knew.

Owen buried his face in my neck and breathed in so deeply I not only felt it but I heard it.

"I love the way you smell," he started. "Love the way you taste, your skin, your mouth, your pussy." Owen nipped my neck, bringing me closer. "Need you to come, baby."

"I'm gonna..." I trailed off because my climax was starting to wash over me.

"No, baby, now. I need you to come right fucking now." He punctuated his demand by sliding his hand under my ass and lifting me, then drove down, grinding hard.

It was partly the friction on my clit that threw me over the edge, but mostly his gruff voice full of sexy gravel that did it.

And just as I'd expected, it was monumental. I felt it everywhere, womb, nipples, clit, every muscle in my body caught fire and singed.

"Fucking, hell," Owen cursed. "So fucking tight. Gonna take it now, baby, hold tight."

My sex-muddled, blissed-out mind had no idea what Owen was going to take. But I readily agreed.

"Take what you need."

Faster. Harder. Rougher. Deeper.

Owen's mouth worked my neck, his cock between my

legs, the light smattering of chest hair abraded my nipples and it built again—fast and furious. My body seized and Owen bit down on the sensitive tendon, planted himself to the hilt, and groaned long and deep.

I was still pulsing around him, my second orgasm sizzling my nerve endings, when Owen lifted his head and I righted mine. The second I did our eyes locked and he started a slow, gentle glide.

"Un-*fucking*-believable," Owen moaned and I whimpered my agreement.

"Beautiful," he continued.

I was still holding on, Owen was still sliding, and all of the earlier tension had faded. I wasn't sure if that was because he was mellow from his orgasm or if he was relieved I hadn't...no, I wasn't going to go there and ruin the moment. My past wasn't going to creep in and invade the perfection of the moment.

"Thank you," I whispered.

"Nat—"

"No, honey, don't interrupt me. Thank you for giving me that. All of it. Straight to my soul," I parroted his earlier statement.

Everything about Owen changed. He was too manly to be described as playful or cute—he was sexy, handsome, down-right hot—but the way he was staring down at me with a glint in his eyes and the ghost of a smirk, put him as close to playful as I suspected he could get.

"Not a hardship taking my woman there, baby."

Yeah, he was being playful.

Unfortunately, I wasn't. There was something he needed to know and it sucked because it would mean bringing my past into our perfect moment but I had to do it all the same.

I unhooked one of my hands from his shoulder and brought it around so I could reach his face. I took a second to trace his jaw and feel the stubble there. Then my mind wandered to how outrageously hot he'd look with a beard. When I was done visualizing that spectacularly sexy image, I moved my fingertips over his lips, the side of his nose, between his brows, brushed his hair off his forehead, then raked my nails over his scalp.

"I feel clean," I murmured quietly but I knew Owen heard. "I've never in my life felt clean. You gave me that. I've never been touched with love. You gave me that. I've never known care. You gave me that. I've never felt comfortable being me because there was no part of me that was clean and good to feel comfortable with. You gave that to me. Thank you," I finished on a whisper.

"Natasha—"

I had more to say so I said it.

"I figure if a man like you, a good man—brave, honest, bold—can love me then maybe there's something to love. Maybe I'm not as dirty—"

I shouldn't have pressed my luck and I knew this when Owen lowered his face to mine, nose to nose, and said, "Again, baby, there is not one motherfucking thing dirty about you." And since he was close I felt, heard, and again *felt* the colossal shift in his mood. "I cannot tell you how pleased I am that you think I gave all of that to you. So don't mistake me when I tell you I don't ever want to hear you thank me again." I didn't have time to recover from the hurt he delivered rejecting my gratitude, something I felt deeply about when he explained why. "You don't need to thank me for loving you."

"Owen—"

Apparently, it was his turn to talk because he kept on saying what he needed to say.

"With that love comes the rest and I don't need you to thank me for it. What I need for you to get is you are always safe to be who you are with me. Say what you want, act how you want to act, be who you want to be. You trusting me is everything." Owen gave me more of his heavy weight and finished with, "It *says* everything."

Okay, so he'd taken the sting out of not wanting me to thank him.

"So, I can say what I want to say just as long as it's not thank you."

Owen narrowed his eyes and since I was now in the mood to be playful because he'd given me two awesome orgasms and made it clear he loved me, I set out to take us back to light and easy. "May I thank you for dinner?" Owen grunted. "May I thank you if you do something nice for me?" That earned me another grunt. "May I thank you for orgasms?"

"Yeah, baby, you can thank me for all of that," he agreed.

"Great," I wheezed. "Maybe now you can get off of me so I can breathe?"

"I'm getting off all right, but I'm not sure if you'll be breathing when I'm done," he said and lifted some of his weight off me.

"So your plan is to kill me."

"No, baby, my plan is to give you so much to be thankful for you'll be breathless."

"And what about you, will you be breathless?"

"Been that way since the moment I saw you. You stole the air straight from my lungs and I haven't caught my breath since, hope to God I never do."

I knew the tears brimming in my eyes started to spill down my cheeks, and as tired as I was of crying I didn't attempt to stop them. Owen gave me a moment to compose myself before he muttered.

"Gonna get rid of this condom. When I get back I want your ass at the edge of the bed, soles of your feet on the mattress, and your knees spread wide."

That statement took me from emotional to turned on in a nanosecond.

Owen pressed a hard open-mouth kiss against my lips and I felt him smile there.

"Love you, Nat."

Yeah, my heart was full to bursting.

"I love you, Owen."

His tipped up lips brushed mine once more before he got out of bed to get rid of the condom. By the time he got back, I was in the position he'd semi-asked but mostly demanded I be in.

Then he commenced making me the most thankful woman in the world and he succeeded spectacularly. By the time Owen was done I'd lost count of how many orgasms he'd given me, we'd gone through three more condoms, and the only reason Owen didn't go for another round was because something that sounded a lot like a shoe banged against the wall followed by Gabe's loud complaint.

I should've been embarrassed but I absolutely was not.

CHAPTER 21

"Tip your ass, Natasha."

"God," she moaned and did as I asked, giving my fingers better access to play between her legs.

Nat was facing away from me, hands to the tile wall. Hot water pounded on my back, steam roiled around us, my rock-hard erection trapped against her now tipped-back ass, two fingers in her drenched pussy.

Not even five minutes ago I'd blown down her throat. That was after she'd sucked me off in what had to be the best blow job I'd ever had. What she lacked in experience and skill she made up for in eagerness. The woman worked my cock like it was her sole mission in life to bring me to my knees. And every sexy noise moaned around my cock, every lick, every bob of her head had been so hot, she accomplished her mission in record time.

In the last three days, I'd had Natasha in a variety of ways, countless orgasms given and nearly as many taken. That was, I'd been giving them and when she looked happy and satisfied I'd taken mine. From the first time we'd made love to when she'd dropped to her knees ten minutes ago and given me world-class head there hadn't been a moment of hesitation. She trusted me—simple as that. And I took great pains to make sure she knew no matter how hard I took her, how dirty the words were I whispered in her ear, I knew her body was a gift and it was a gift I cherished.

But just to say, my girl liked dirty. The filthier I talked the harder she came.

But this morning Nat had woken up in a certain mood. She'd felt like giving, and I'd gladly taken her up on what she was offering and got off in a huge way. Now it was my turn to return the favor.

"Soaked," I told her as I pulled my fingers from her pussy and dragged them up to her clit. "Tell me, baby, what has your pussy so wet? My fingers? Or was it my cock in your mouth?"

"You in my mouth," she moaned and I circled her clit harder.

"Mm," I hummed against the back of her neck. "You like sucking my cock?"

She nodded and said, "I liked you watching me while I was sucking your cock."

Sweet fuck.

I dipped my knees, lined my cock up, and drilled inside. Nat's head flew back against my shoulder and she pushed back to take my pounding.

"Harder," Nat gasped. She slid her hands wider and locked her elbows.

"So fucking sweet, baby."

"Harder, Owen."

"Not yet, Nat."

"Need you harder."

I dropped my face to her neck and breathed deep. The smell of jasmine and lemon filled my nostrils, a scent I never would've had a mind to pay attention to, a scent that now turned me on to such a degree I lost my mind at the barest hint of it. I let my teeth graze the spot under her ear that I knew she liked, and just as I knew she would, a low keening moan echoed.

"You want my mark on your neck, Nat?"

"You know I do."

Yeah, I knew she did. Every time I was inside of her she offered me her neck, and the one time I hadn't sunk my teeth into her tendon there, she'd pouted the rest of the night. Fuck, yeah, my girl liked my teeth, but more, liked seeing the mark. I knew because I caught her staring at herself in the mirror touching it. But I also knew because Nat straight out told me she liked it. She couldn't explain why, but she liked knowing I gave it to her. And like with everything else, I gave Nat what she wanted.

"Earn it, baby."

She righted her head and tilted it to the side until she caught my eyes and slowly smiled.

"Earn it?" she asked like she liked the idea.

Sweet, Jesus.

"Yeah, baby, I want you to earn it."

Her beautiful smile which told me she was happy, really fucking happy, turned deliciously wicked.

Oh, yeah.

Fuck, yeah.

Natasha got off on playing. Which got me off in a big way. So big I was a hell of a lot closer than she was. And that was a problem but one I could easily rectify.

I slowed my thrusts, moved my hand from the hip I was gripping, and cupped her full breast, rolling her nipple between my fingers, pinching until I heard Nat's groan.

"You play dirty," she complained.

"You like it dirty."

"You do, too." And before I could confirm I did indeed like sex dirty she'd removed a hand off the wall, bent forward, reached between us, and cupped my balls.

"Baby," I growled and pulled her nipple.

"You wanna play, honey?" she asked in a mock sweet voice. "Then we'll play," she finished.

Not verbally but physically.

After that, I was a fucking goner. She tipped her ass higher, slammed back into me harder, and at the same time massaged my balls. Natasha was not gentle in her ministrations. She tugged and rolled and the tighter she cupped me the harder I drove in.

Jesus, fuck she was magnificent.

"Gonna blow, Nat, move your hand."

"Do it."

"Move your hand."

"Earning," she puffed out. "My mark."

Christ.

I lowered my mouth back to her neck and gave her the edge of my teeth and her pussy convulsed.

Thank Christ.

"Do you know how good your pussy feels, Nat?" She shook her head and I smiled against her skin. "You're tight and warm and smooth inside."

"Oh, God," she panted and reared back reaching for her orgasm.

There it was. My girl, she liked dirty. I'd never tested it but I would as soon as we were home—I was certain I could get her off just by talking to her.

"Love the way your pussy clenches my cock. Fucking love how you feel bare, sleek, and hot and so fucking wet. Love watching my cock dip in and come out coated in you."

"Owen," she cried out right before she lost her hold on my balls. Her rhythm turned wild, and her body locked.

"Fucking hell, baby."

I slammed in deep, closed my eyes, my teeth sunk into Nat's neck, and blinding, white-hot pleasure exploded. The sound of Nat whimpering pulled me from my trance and I immediately released my teeth.

"Fucking shit, baby."

"Yeah, you can say that again," she muttered and reached up to hold my arm across her chest, anchoring her close.

I slowly glided, letting the phenomenal orgasm wane while contemplating the fact that after Nat had drained me dry twice in back-to-back sessions my cock was still rock-hard and ready to go again, something that had not happened ever in my life. Not the back-to-back sessions, but my cock not softening a touch before I wanted more.

Such was Natasha. I'd always wanted more, but since she'd opened up that feeling was relentless.

Top to toe beautiful, and wild as all fuck in bed—out of bed it was amazing to watch her come into herself. Now that she wasn't hiding and the real her was on full display, she had Kevin, Gabe, and Myles eating out of the palm of her hand. She had me wrapped around her finger. She was funny and had no issue making fun of herself. She was giving to the point she was spoiling my teammates. She was smart, and in the days since she'd laid it out first to us then to Tex and Cruz, at her request she'd talked to Zane and given him the locations of Wilco's stable.

Something else notable was she had not called Wilco Pollaski her uncle. She called him by his first name. The change was blatant, she'd made the decision to completely separate herself. Once she'd fully committed to putting Sarah behind her she'd blossomed.

It was beautiful.

All of it.

And as much as I wanted to take her again, we needed to get out of the rapidly cooling shower and get on with our day.

"Baby?"

"Hm," Nat hummed and I smiled.

"Got stuff on today," I reminded her. "We need to get out."

"'Kay."

"You good?"

"No. I'm great," she sighed and her languid body sagged more.

I slowly pulled out, savoring the last drag of my cock through her wet, tight heat. Once I was free I turned her in my arms and her chin tipped up and I caught her eyes.

"Beautiful," I murmured before I dropped my lips to hers.

"Funny, I was going to say the same thing," she said against my lips. "Don't know how I got so lucky, just know that I am."

Fuck, she was killing me. This was something new, too—in the last few days she'd stopped hiding. In other words, she found every available opportunity to tell me how she felt about me, about us being together, and about our future. Not only with words, though she was using them abundantly now, but in everything she did. And every time she did it scored a path of fire through my chest. A burn I lived for.

"I think I'm the lucky one."

I felt her lips smile against mine, then she pulled back and looked up at me. *Happy.* That was all I could think, she looked happy.

"That's part of what makes me so lucky. That and you're totally hot, you're sweet, you let me be me, you're protective and bossy, and you get growly which *totally* turns me on, you're great in bed, and you take care of me. You're so-so in the kitchen, but I figure if that's your only flaw I can live with that."

"You think I'm great in bed?" Natasha's brow raised in the perfect 'don't be a dumbass' look. What she didn't do was answer. "You think I'm hot?"

"You know you're all that," she sassed.

"What about the chips? Am I all that *and* a bag of chips?"

Her lips twisted into an adorable smirk before she returned, "Hm…I don't know about the chips."

"You don't know?"

Nat shrugged. The exaggerated movement meant her bare, wet tits brushed my chest and my cock twitched between us.

That got me an eye flare and smile.

"You think my cooking's so-so?" I moved on.

"Unlike your other skills, honey, your cooking leaves something to be desired."

"Right." I chuckled.

"Though if I had to choose, I'd pick your overcooked soft noodles over the alternative."

"Right," I snickered.

"I love you, Owen," she whispered.

My heart thudded in my chest and that burn started. I buried my face in her neck and rubbed my lips over my mark.

"Love you, baby."

* * *

"This lasts much longer I'm getting a hotel," Gabe groused.

I hid my smile by taking a long pull from my bottle of water.

"Not even ten minutes of hot water left," he continued.

I bet there wasn't.

"I see you're amused."

I lowered the bottle and stopped hiding my grin.

"Yep."

"Bastard," he mumbled and walked away.

The shake of my friend's head and his smile took the heat out of his insult.

Kevin walked in from outside, his face like thunder, and I braced.

"It fucks me to say this," Kevin started.

"Say it," I invited.

The front door swung open and Myles came bounding in with a deep scowl.

"You tell him?" Myles barked.

I looked back at Kevin and caught him shaking his head.

"Tell me what?"

"Gabe!" Myles bellowed.

"Fucking, hell, what's going on?"

"What the fuck?" Gabe clipped as he came back into the living room.

I heard the footsteps coming down the stairs and looked over just in time to see a pale-faced Natasha jump over the last two steps. Her panic-filled eyes hit mine and I wanted to throat punch Myles for scaring her.

Then Myles laid it out and he didn't go gentle, each word he spoke sliced through me but what's more, it shredded Natasha.

"Eva's been in an accident. Elijah's been flown to Shock Trauma, Liam's in the back of an ambulance, and Eva's being transported behind him."

"Fuck," Gabe snarled. "The others?"

"On lockdown. Zane's moving them to a secure location as we speak," Kevin announced.

"Where was the team? I thought they all had guards?" I asked.

Myles's scowl deepened and his face turned a frightening shade of red when he said, "Someone hit the office, Thad's house, and Leo's house at the same time. Leo caught the guy, Jaxon went to Leo's to assist. Linc, Zane, and Wolf went to the office. Kyle and Abe went to Thad's. Cookie was covering Brooks, Mozart was covering Kyle's, Benny went to Linc's. And Dude was heading to Eva."

"Where the fuck was Max?" I growled.

"Out of town..." Myles let that hang.

I knew what that meant. Max was a cold motherfucker. If Zane was sending a one-man army to Chicago to get intel,

Max was his best play. Mean and cold when he wanted to be, he'd fit right in with the dredges of society.

"She didn't have cover?" Gabe asked disbelievingly. "No fucking way Max would leave without knowing someone was covering his wife twenty-four-seven."

"Don't have the specifics on that but she and the kids were staying with Brooks and Anaya. All hell broke loose and Eva took off. She was supposed to wait for Dude. From what I got Elijah was at a sleepover. Zane thinks she got impatient, wanted her boy home, and didn't feel like waiting for a bodyguard."

"Thinks?"

Gabe asked the question I didn't have the balls to ask.

"She was unconscious and had not come to when Zane called."

"Unconscious?" Nat squeaked and my gaze sliced to her.

Motherfucking hell.

"Baby—" My words died a slow painful death in my throat when she blinked rapidly and tears started rolling down her bleached cheeks.

"I knew this would happen!" she shrieked. "I knew it."

"Nat—"

"I knew it. I told everyone he would do this. Now…now… oh my God! Now…"

Natasha didn't finish what she was saying because the second I got close she threw herself in my arms and buried her face in my chest. Loud, body-shaking sobs tore through her. And there I stood torn. Max was a good friend, and his wife Eva and his boys were injured. Another friend, Thad, and his wife Emerson had a daughter. I was torn because I wanted to get my ass on a plane and jump in the mix. I wanted to end this. But I couldn't for the life of me stop myself from wanting to take Natasha and run. Take her and disappear so Wilco Pollaski would never find us.

CHAPTER 22

I knew what I was about to do was wrong.

I should've turned around—but I wasn't going to.

No, not wrong. It was the right thing to do, but Owen was going to be unbelievably pissed and he'd probably never forgive me.

For the last thirty minutes, I'd been on auto-pilot. I couldn't think about what I'd done. It had been easy. No, it had been the hardest thing I'd ever done in my life. But I was right to do it. The closer I got to the airport the tighter my stomach cramped. As soon as I made it off the mountain without running off the road killing myself, I started making calls.

God, Owen was going to be so pissed.

The first call I made was to Wilco. The conversation was curt and quick. I informed him I was coming home, he told me there would be a plane ticket waiting at the Spokane airport. He already knew where I was. I knew better, he'd always known.

Once that was done, I called Tex.

To say the man was furious was an understatement. The anger I heard in his voice was almost enough to scare me into turning around and going back to Owen—which was what Tex was demanding I do. By the time I ended the call, I couldn't say Tex was any less angry with me but I'd given him everything I had on my father, Wilco, the Pollaski organization, shell companies, addresses, all the names I could remember on Wilco's long, extensive list of high-powered people he blackmailed. Every detail I could remember. And I told him where I thought my mother was buried. Not that it really mattered—my father killed her and he was dead, but I still gave Tex the intel. I also told him I would keep Owen's cell phone, which I'd swiped out of our room, powered up and on my person for as long as I could. I figured once I was collected from O'Hare I'd be going to Wilco's brownstone, but to be on the safe side, until the phone was taken from me, Tex could track me. He also made me promise to memorize his number, Zane's number, and Myles's. Since I'd stolen Owen's phone Myles would be the fastest way for me to get to Owen.

Not that he'd ever want to talk to me after this.

The shrill of Owen's phone ringing made me jump in my seat. I was still on 90 West, my exit was coming up, and I needed to pay attention but I still answered.

"Hello?"

"Natasha." Owen's furious growl filled the SUV and I knew I'd been wrong.

Owen wasn't angry, he was breathing-fire, singe-the-earth mad.

Oh, shit.

"I have to do this," I rushed out.

"No. You. Don't."

"Please, honey, listen to me. I have to. I told you I can't live with it and now I know how right I was. Those two boys are hurt and in the hospital because of me. Eva is hurt. The—"

"Do not do this, Nat."

"I have—"

"Baby, please, do not do this," he whispered and my heart shattered. "Don't do this to me, to us, baby. I'm fucking begging you to come home."

I saw the exit and for a nanosecond, I thought about not taking it. I thought how easy it would be to chicken out and pull off the road and let Owen and the guys find me. They'd figure out a way to pick me up. They'd have to get another car since I'd stolen the SUV, but they'd do it. Especially Owen.

He'd come.

I knew it.

Actually, that was what I was counting on.

I took the exit.

Then I did something I never thought I'd have to do again. I pulled on my Sarah Pollaski façade.

"I called Tex, he knows everything—"

"Baby, please."

"I told him everything I remember. He can help—"

"Jesus, fuck, Natasha!" Owen shouted and I jerked the car. My fake persona slipped and wet pooled in my eyes.

I had to be stronger than this if I was going to stay alive. I had to find the old Sarah. She could endure anything. I had to be strong.

"I'm sorry, Owen. I'm so, so sorry. I love you but—"

"If you fucking loved me your ass wouldn't have snuck out of the house the second my goddamn back was turned. If you loved me, you'd fucking trust me to take care of this."

Oh, God.

I had to get off the phone. I couldn't listen to him any longer. I was too weak. I wouldn't do what I had to do.

"I trust you with my life," I told him.

"Mark this, Natasha, I'm coming for you. And fair warning, baby, when I do I'm gonna be fucking pissed."

"I'm counting on it, honey."

"Jesus fuck."

"I love you, Owen. Straight to my soul, I love you. No matter how this ends I need you to know you gave me everything. I'm happy. I'm clean. Now I need to do this so I can be free. So no one else is hurt. I'll buy you time. But, honey, please hurry. I don't know how long I can last."

"Fucking hell!" he roared and I pulled the phone from my ear. "Don't do this, baby, please, Nat. Just—"

"I love you," I sobbed. "I'll be waiting for you."

I stabbed blindly at the screen until I finally disconnected.

Owen called five more times.

I didn't answer.

I parked in long-term parking, texted Tex where I left the SUV. Then I made my way to the ticket counter and that was where my plan was shot to shit.

"Good to see you, Sarah," Franco sneered. His hand wrapped around my bicep and I was assaulted with a whiff of his overbearing cologne. "After all this shit you've caused, you're lucky you wised up. Saved me the trouble of collecting you. Now stay smart and don't make a scene."

What in the world was happening? What had I made easy and how had Franco made it to Idaho so quickly?

We were outside almost to a silver Cadillac Escalade when Franco said, "Your uncle's a smart man." A man I recognized as one of Wilco's soldiers opened the rear passenger door when we got close.

Franco shoved me in, the door slammed, and moments later we were driving out of the airport.

I was fucked.

CHAPTER 23

"What does that mean exactly?" I heard Myles ask Tex.

He'd been talking to the man for the last ten minutes. But he hadn't put the call on speaker, the way I was feeling and the incredulous expression Myles was sporting, it was probably a good thing I couldn't hear what they were discussing.

Natasha had been gone ten hours. She was not on a flight to Chicago. No ticket had been purchased in her name. I would've been impressed Tex could hack into the Spokane airport's security feed as quickly as he had if my goddamn woman hadn't gone rogue.

I might've been concerned how Wilco had found us if I wasn't so motherfucking pissed I couldn't see straight.

Max had done his thing in Chicago. He dug up what he needed and let it slip to the right people that we had the intel we needed to take Wilco down. Word had traveled faster than Max thought and Wilco had a few extra hours to make his play.

The fuck of it was, Eva's accident was just that—a goddamned accident. Someone had blown a red light and T-boned her. A sixty-two-year-old physician, who had dozed off behind the wheel after being on call in the ER.

A goddamn accident that had nothing to do with Wilco.

Yet, Natasha hadn't waited for the facts and details. She'd heard Eva, Elijah, and Liam were injured and had taken off like a shot.

Now she was well and truly missing.

Franco Dalto had met her at the airport, then she'd walked out with him, climbed into the back of a luxury SUV, and they'd driven straight back into Idaho and vanished. One of the reasons Rhode had built his cabin in Sandpoint was because Idaho was not a state that intruded on the privacy of its citizens. It was not common but it wasn't rare, at least not in Northern Idaho to see men and women walking down the street with a sidearm strapped to their belts. There weren't cameras on every telephone pole like in big cities, thus Tex didn't know where Franco took Natasha.

Outside of him crossing back into Idaho, she was a ghost.

We'd taken Rhode's Jeep down to Coeur d'Alene and now we were on standby. Ghost, Abe, and Mozart were headed our way. Cookie, Benny, and Dude were staying in Maryland and they'd head to Chicago with Thad, Kyle, and Brooks if Nat made her way there.

Cruz had put together a team and he was headed to Chicago. The FBI was taking no chances using local resources. I was fairly certain that was going to ruffle feathers. I was a hundred percent certain I didn't give a fuck.

I wanted Wilco shut down. However that came to be I no longer cared.

My priority was getting Natasha back.

And when I did I was handcuffing her to my bed where she'd stay until she saw the error of her ways.

"And you're positive?" Myles's question pulled me from my thoughts. "Garrett on that, too?" There was a pause then, "Copy that. I'll call you back."

Myles tossed his phone on the hotel dresser and kept his eyes adverted when he said, "Pissed as fuck at your woman."

I felt my neck tighten. I clenched my jaw and tried to clamp onto my patience.

I failed.

"Don't—"

"Pissed as all fuck," he interrupted me and turned his head to look at me. "Worst part is I wanna be more pissed than I am but the problem is I understand why she bolted. Not only that, I respect it."

What the hell?

"Say again?"

"She called Tex on her way," he told me something I very well knew. And he knew I knew it because Tex had already called in this information.

"Right. She called him on her way to the fucking airport where her plan was to get on a fucking plane and fly her ass straight back to the nightmare we'd all been trying to clear her of. A plan that was shot to shit. Now she's in the wind with a man who we know has no conscience, no issues hurting women, and not a shred of decency in his body. A man who will not hesitate to hurt her, violate her, or *kill* her. What she didn't do was fucking trust me to handle it. So with all of that, how can you stand here and tell me you respect her decision to bolt?"

In true Myles fashion, he said what he had to say and he said it straight. No punches pulled, no thought, he just laid it out.

"Naomi fucked your shit up."

"Why are we talking about her?"

"She fucked you up so bad, years after you got shot of her ass, she was still dragging you down, and I know that as fact because when I met you that bitch had been gone a good number of years and those wounds were still fresh. A man who is over his ex-wife unlocks that ball and chain and throws it away. He doesn't throw another padlock on and wear it around his neck. Whatever she broke in you was wide open, had been for as long as I've known you. But those gashes started to close, then they stopped bleeding, and the longer Natasha was around the more they started to heal. I know what Naomi did to you, and it wasn't her overspending, her being a bitch to you, and it wasn't her cheating. That shit, a man can get over. She castrated your ass, and she did it in a way that made you believe *you* were the asshole in that relationship. She made you believe you were a shit husband who couldn't take care of his wife. I cannot imagine why you allowed that, but you did, and since then you have kept believing it."

Fuck, that hit way below the belt. But as true as what Myles said was the case, I didn't understand why he was talking about my ex-wife.

"Do you have a point to this?"

"Yeah, I do. Nat isn't Naomi."

Fuck me, I'd heard that before. Not only that but I'd come to that realization all on my own and didn't need another goddamn lecture about it.

"I'm very aware of that."

"I don't think you are. You don't trust her—"

"Come again?" I grunted and crossed my arms over my chest so I wouldn't reach out and strangle my friend. "I don't trust her? She fucking left."

"She did, and she had reasons. None of those reasons were because she didn't trust you. The opposite actually. She trusts you with her life. She went back because she knew you'd come and get her. She trusts you'll end this for her, but in the meantime, she's protecting people she barely knows. And she's doing that not because she's a good person, but because the people she's protecting mean something to you. They're your people. That I can respect. Her plan was shit, but she had no idea Wilco had hired a bounty hunter to find her, and she didn't know because we didn't even know. Wilco did that on the DL, made the arrangements personally, and didn't bring in his right-hand man until it was time for Franco to come and get her. And we know that's the case because the men Max managed to flip, had no clue Franco was out of town and had not heard Wilco was still looking for his niece. As far as everyone was concerned they all thought he'd written her off."

I trust you with my life.

Fuck.

My head dropped forward and I took in the carpet.

I love you, Owen. Straight to my soul, I love you. No matter how this ends I need you to know you gave me everything. I'm happy. I'm clean. Now I need to do this so I can be free. So no one else is hurt. I'll buy you time. But, honey, please hurry. I don't know how long I can last.

"Jesus, fuck," I spat.

I trust you with my life.

She was buying us time. She'd delivered herself to hell so no one else would get hurt.

Nat didn't know the accident wasn't because of Wilco. She just reacted and sacrificed herself for people she didn't know very well but knew I cared about.

Fuck me.

Fuck me.

Fuck me.

I understood she thought she was doing the right thing, but she absolutely hadn't. I understood because she'd spelled it out for me and I still thought she was wrong.

"I begged Natasha to come home," I told Myles. "Fucking begged. I've never begged for anything, not when the woman I'd spent years with told me she was leaving me if I reenlisted, and not when she served me with papers. I didn't beg to save my marriage but I sure as fuck begged Nat not to leave me. Yet she did."

"Owen, brother, I get you're pissed, I'm fucking pissed,

too. She went off half-cocked and seriously screwed up but she did it for all the right reasons," Myles pushed.

Therefore I pushed back. "Is there a point to any of this?"

"Yeah, Owen, there is. Tex and Garrett found her."

"Then why the fuck are we still standing here?" I roared.

An old habit, one I'd conquered when I learned control, clicked back into place and my hands slid into my hair and I tugged until I registered the pain. Something I hadn't done in well over a decade, something I stopped doing when I started controlling every aspect of my life. I kept everything in order so I would never feel this.

"We're talking about this now, so when we get to her you won't—"

"I won't what?" I bit out. "Be pissed? Brother, I am beyond fucking pissed, and don't tell me you understand because you don't. The woman you love isn't at the mercy of a monster so you don't know jack. You think I'm pissed she left? I'm goddamn scared out of my mind that by the time we get to her, the woman who rolled out of our bed this morning will be gone. She's lived through enough, and I'm terrified if Franco touches her, violates her, she will not be Natasha. You've seen her—when she goes inside her head and has to remember who she had to be she shuts down. The switch flips and she's off. I'm afraid when I get her back I won't be able to *get her back*. Now stop wasting time and tell me where she is."

"Outside of Missoula, Montana."

Christ, that was under three hours away.

Ten hours she'd been gone and she was under three hours away.

Fucking, fucking, hell.

"Why are we still standing here?"

"Two reasons...no, three. We're waiting for Kevin and Gabe to get back from picking up Abe, Wolf, and Mozart, we're waiting on Tex and Garrett to finish gathering their intel which includes a brief from Cruz. And last, I needed to see where your head was at."

I rocked back on my heels and opened my mouth, but before I could say anything Myles got there first. "Check your temper, brother. You know why we needed to have that conversation."

Myles's phone clattered on the dresser and we both looked at it before he snatched it up and answered.

"Garrett?"

"Update. Cruz checked in and confirmed Wilco Pollaski is not in Chicago. He and his team couldn't gain entry. Cruz made the call to keep this under wraps, as in need to know only. They called Dude and he agreed to go up there and help them. He's on his way there now."

"Dude?" I inquired.

"You and Brooks are our demo experts. Brooks is tied up and you're there. Dude volunteered to handle Cruz's situation."

"Are you saying Pollaski's brownstone is rigged?"

"Rigged to blow sky high. Cruz called it at the last second. His team was going to breach and a wire caught his attention. He inspected the best he could and called it into Tex. Tex called Dude."

Close calls were never good. A close call with an explosive device was ass-clenchingly too close.

"Anyway, since the company jet is on its way to Idaho, Zane called in a marker. Dude's flying there in luxury. Cruz has his warrant, so as soon as Dude works his magic, they'll be in."

Dude would have that place cleared in no time. The man not only knew how to disarm any IED he also had excellent instincts. He'd taught me a lot, most of it had nothing to do with making and disposing of ordnance. He'd taught me to trust my gut, use more than my eyes and ears to assess a situation. A lesson that had proven invaluable over the years.

"Last thing," Garrett said and I froze at the tone of his voice. "Don't kill the messenger but Wilco ran. He knows he's fucked, and a man like him does not run, he stays and fights for his kingdom."

Which meant Wilco knew his kingdom was crumbling and he'd be livid thus he'd take that anger out on the person he felt responsible for his demise.

Natasha.

My throat clogged and bile rose.

"The game's changed," Myles muttered.

"It has. Cruz wants your body cams on, capture if possible."

"Garrett—"

Garrett didn't wait for Myles to continue his statement. "If possible. Cruz isn't stupid—that's why he wants the body cam footage. Shit happens, he knows this. The FBI wants Pollaski, if you can deliver him breathing that's the first option. If you can't, well, shit happens."

"Copy that. We should be on the road in the next half hour."

"I'll have everything you need before you get there."

Myles disconnected the call and held my gaze.

"Promise me you got your shit together."

I didn't bother opening my mouth to speak. I couldn't make that promise and I wouldn't lie to my friend.

"Fuck."

Yep, *fuck* about summed it up.

"Owen—"

"Don't make me promise you something you know will be bullshit, Myles. What I will tell you is, Natasha is my first priority. I will get her out by any means necessary but I will not actively hunt Wilco. That said, he or Franco stand between me and my woman, I will not hesitate to take either of them out."

"I can live with that."

242

It was good he could because that was the way it was going to be.

I'm coming for you. And fair warning, baby, when I do I'm gonna be fucking pissed.

I'm counting on it, honey.

Ten hours ago I'd burned through my pissed.

Now fear coated my skin. It had burrowed deep, it had infused my bones, and it had taken over my mind. All I could think about was that Natasha was in the hands of the Devil.

CHAPTER 24

I heard the front door open, I heard his voice, and I stood.

Then there he was.

The Devil himself in a fifteen-thousand-dollar suit.

I'd spent so many months pushing him from my mind I'd almost forgotten what he looked like. The Devil of my nightmares was ugly and fanged, he was not the good-looking man that stood before me. In a cruel twist, Wilco Pollaski was handsome. As cliché as it was, and it was supremely so, my uncle looked a lot like Ray Liotta. That was a well-aged Ray before his supposed plastic surgery. A compliment Wilco received a lot, one that stroked his over-inflated ego. He loved that women compared him to who he thought was the ultimate movie gangster.

There was a reason why he landed what he called high-class pussy. It was more than his money and expensive suits, unfortunately, he was just that good-looking. Women flocked and when they needed a nudge toward the bedroom he knew how to charm their Weitzman pumps in the direction he wanted.

He was disgusting.

The Devil.

But the Devil's greatest lie was fooling the world that he didn't exist and Wilco had a way of fooling women into believing he wasn't evil.

It had been hours since Franco had brought me to the retreat and I'd stupidly thought I wouldn't have to face Wilco until I got back to Chicago. I'd been sitting in the parlor for so long I become hopeful. Stupid, *stupid* me.

"You've caused me a great deal of trouble, Sarah," Wilco said as he rounded the oval pedestal table in the center of the foyer, coming to a stop a few feet away from me.

Sarah.

God, when would she finally die?

I said nothing. Not that there was anything to say. Wilco didn't expect me to answer. As a matter of fact, he hadn't asked a question, thus, I wasn't permitted to speak.

His pale blue eyes narrowed in disgust as he took me in.

"My God, look at you," he sneered. "Disgraceful."

I knew what he saw. Owen and I had planned on taking the ATV out so I'd dressed accordingly. Though even if we hadn't, I no longer owned a stitch of clothing that would be acceptable under Wilco's scrutiny. *Thank God for that*. The thought made me grin.

"Is something amusing?"

I shook my head no and schooled my features. I had to be on my game if I was going to survive long enough for Owen to find me. I couldn't be Owen's Natasha, not in front of Wilco.

The silence in the room should've been comforting. There was a time when the quiet was my only friend. Quiet meant I wasn't being given orders, I didn't have to speak, I didn't have to listen. Silence meant my ears weren't burning with the muffled sounds of nasty sex. My stomach was clenching in fear of what Wilco might say.

But now, it was deafening. Now, I was used to Owen, Myles, Kevin, and Gabe. There was always chatter around the cabin and before that when it was just me and Owen at his house I couldn't wait for him to come home so I could hear him talk.

Wilco hadn't stopped his angry perusal and when his mouth twisted in a furious grimace and his glare turned malicious, I knew I was in trouble.

Big trouble.

"What is that?" he seethed and stomped closer.

What was what?

"Answer. Me."

His beady eyes were aimed at my neck, and fear, real fear trickled down my spine.

I'd made a huge mistake. Or, I made another huge mistake. I'd taken my jacket off in the Escalade. Then when Franco had been distracted I balled it up and slipped it under the seat. I knew I'd be patted down as soon as I entered the house and Franco would find Owen's phone. I'd told Tex I'd leave it on for as long as I could so he could track my whereabouts. Now I wished I had that jacket. My white thermal left too much of my neck exposed.

I knew what Wilco saw.

My hand automatically lifted to cover Owen's mark. Not out of shame. I wanted to protect it. That mark was mine and only mine. Wilco didn't get to distort it, mock it, he didn't get to *look* at it.

"I always knew you had it in you. Same as your mother—a lying whore."

I didn't even flinch at him calling my dead mother a whore. I'd heard it all my life. I was numb to it. Not only that but the uncomfortable truth was—she was a whore. A high-priced Pollaski whore. That was what they'd made her. My father and my uncle, they'd fought over her, they'd degraded her, then my father pimped her out mostly to piss his brother off, but also because my mother brought in top-dollar.

Disgusting.

"The difference is her pussy was worth more than that." Wilco swept his hand up and down indicating my clothes. "Thought you were a dead fish, that was what the clients reported, said you were so bad in the sack only good thing about you was that you were fresh. Now I see all you needed was a little training. I should've put the effort in. Lucky for me, I no longer need to, seeing as you took it upon yourself."

Wilco smacked my hand away from my neck and stared at my mark.

"Fucking whore," he scoffed.

When his hand made contact with my face the shock of pain didn't register. Not right away. The first thing I cataloged was the sound. Crisp, loud, it bounced around the foyer until it slammed into me. Then the pain blossomed.

This...I was used to this. This was what I needed. I needed the pain to remind me I couldn't be Owen's, not here. Not in front of Wilco. He'd smell my weakness.

I didn't move a muscle, I didn't so much as twitch when my cheek throbbed from Wilco's slap.

More would come.

I knew it.

And it would be worse than an open-handed smack across the face. Wilco liked to use his fists. Those would come soon.

"Franco?" Wilco snapped, and like the good little soldier he was, Franco appeared at Wilco's side in a flash.

"Yeah, Boss?"

Boss. Gag. Franco sounded like an eager puppy ready to sit, roll over, or play dead. A far cry from how he behaved when Wilco wasn't around.

I didn't hide my smirk. Franco didn't miss it. And he didn't bother masking his response.

Not so tough now that your master's yanking your chain.

Franco's face turned a deep shade of red.

Oh, yeah, he could read my mind.

"How much longer until the plane's ready?" Wilco asked and I was pretty sure all the blood had drained from my face.

Pretty sure became positive when Franco smiled and replied, "Less than an hour, sir."

"What?"

Wilco's head snapped back in my direction and his hand whipped brutally across my face.

"Shut the fuck up." *Same cheek, he always went for the same cheek.* "You seemed to have forgotten your place. Pussy stays quiet until it's ready to be used."

God, he was gross.

"Are we clear?"

I pinched my lips and nodded.

"Something for you to think about, Sarah. You'll be paying for all the trouble you caused. And I mean all of it. No more of your bullshit. I was too soft on you, I see that now. I've got clients lined up in Canada. Clients who are eager for fresh. I suggest you take the next hour and catch up on sleep because, from the time we land until you pay me back every dollar I've lost because of you, you're working. Due to your reputation, I had to get creative, so there are no rules. The client gets what the client wants—whatever he wants. Rest up, dear niece, you're going to need it." Wilco's gaze sliced back to Franco and he ordered, "Get this bitch out of my sight."

Franco didn't delay. He stepped close and grabbed my bicep harder than he needed to—way harder, so hard my control slipped and I cried out.

Wilco smiled.

Disgusting pig.

"And, Franco, for your trouble, you don't have to be gentle."

Oh, God.

Oh, no.

"Freebie?" Franco asked hopefully and I whimpered.

"Soon, friend, soon. She's got some work to do first."
Wilco held my eyes and my loathing built to an all-time high.

I'd hated my uncle all my life. I'd never had a shred of
respect for him. I'd never felt anything but revulsion. But
right then with his handprint stinging my cheek and his
depravity unbridled I hated him more than I ever had in my
life. More than any human had ever hated another person.

I had less than an hour to find a way out of this mess. Less
than an hour to figure out a way to kill my uncle.

I was not getting on a plane. I wasn't going to be whored
out. And I wasn't waiting for Owen.

"Move," Franco grunted and yanked on my arm.

I was going to kill him, too.

And as he dragged me up the stairs I plotted. By the time
he shoved me into a bedroom, I didn't have a good plan. That
seemed to be the reoccurring theme with me, none of my
plans worked and I got an in-your-face reminder when
Franco slammed my back against the wall. I was still reeling
from my head cracking against the drywall when his hand
snaked between us and grabbed my breast with such vicious-
ness I screamed in pain.

Without letting go he lowered his face to mine and his
bad breath overpowered his bad cologne. My mind was still
fuzzy but I had the wherewithal to struggle. The problem
was Franco was stronger than I was and the more I struggled
the tighter he gripped my breast.

"Keep fighting, bitch," Franco sneered. "Nothin' gets my
dick harder than a bitch fighting."

Oh. My. God.

I forced my body to still. I forced the bile not to rise. I
forced the air out of my lungs because I was getting
lightheaded.

"Soon, Sarah," Franco growled.

It wasn't sexy like Owen's gravelly, rough voice.

It was predatory in a way that made me feel dirty. Franco

was a filthy, disgusting rapist. An animal who needed to be put down.

His hand on my breast loosened and he slowly dragged his palm back and forth.

No. Hell no.

I could stomach him manhandling me, but something inside of me broke when he *touched* me.

"Get your hands off me," I demanded.

"What did you just say to me?"

"Get your hands off me, you fucking pig—"

I said no more.

My breath came out in a whoosh when his fist connected to my solar plexus.

"What'd you call me?"

"Fucking pig," I repeated. "Piece of—"

Whoosh.

My breath was gone again.

"You either gotta be stupid pussy or this is you begging for my dick. Which is it, Sarah? You a stupid pussy or you—"

That time it was Franco who didn't finish his sentence when my knee came up and smashed his balls. Unfortunately, Franco had turned and deflected most of my upward knee thrust but I knew I clipped him. Which was really, really bad for me proving just how stupid I was.

It could've been five minutes, a half-hour, five seconds. I wouldn't know because by Franco's third strike blackness was swimming in my peripheral vision. By his fourth punch I went to a place so deep in my head I could no longer feel the pain of his blows, and sometime after that, I lost consciousness.

At least I knew he wouldn't touch me. After all, he liked his women struggling, and I had no fight left in me.

However, sometime later when my eyes opened my first thought was I was going to kill Franco then I was going to kill Wilco. I just needed to find something—anything—in the room that would do the job. If I could just search the desk drawers. The thought was fleeting because the pain was so unbearable I once again gave in to the darkness.

Mark this, Natasha, I'm coming for you.

God, please hurry, Owen.

CHAPTER 25

"You're sure she's still there?" I asked.

"Best I can be with no eyes," Tex's voice boomed from Myles's cell. "As I've explained, your phone's GPS signal is still at that location. Either they found it and left it behind when they moved, or they haven't moved. My gut says she did what she said she was going to do and found a way to hide the phone. And I know that Pollaski owns the retreat. It was under one of the shell companies she gave me that I hadn't found."

"Losing your touch, old man?" Wolf taunted.

"Hardly. The company's owned by Wilco's first wife's cousin. I hadn't run the wives yet. Cruz needed intel on the drugs and women for his warrant, and before that, Zane needed his vulnerabilities so he could move in. I wasn't looking for properties."

Abe chuckled and even if I wasn't in the mood to find anything funny, not even in my state could I miss Tex's affronted huff.

"Bet Cruz is happy to tie up that loose end," Mozart noted. "Been a long time, since his run-in with the Red Brothers. He'll be happy to put it behind him."

Kevin caught my attention and slowly dipped his chin, his silent demand for me to keep my cool.

"Garrett's calling in, Tex, gotta take this," Myles said.

"I'll be in touch."

Myles slid his finger over the phone and switched to the other call.

"Garrett?"

"It's go-time," Garrett announced. "Wilco's jet is being refueled."

"Flight plan?" Gabe inquired.

"Nothing filed."

Jesus Christ. If Wilco got her on that plane she'd be gone.

"Do you...can we...fuck..." I stammered, unable to articulate my question.

"I can track the plane," Garrett answered my disjointed inquiry. "Problem is when it lands. If I don't know where it's headed can't get men on the ground."

I tried my best but I couldn't seem to swallow the boulder-sized lump in my throat. I thought the closer I got to Natasha some of the tension would ease. I would feel better knowing I was making strides in getting her back. I'd been wrong, so fucking wrong. The closer we got to Missoula the harder my heart thumped in my chest.

Now we were in a pay-by-the-hour motel about fifteen miles from where the retreat was and my insides were cold-soaked. We were supposed to check in, drop off Abe, Mozart, Gabe, and Kevin. But before Wolf, Myles, and I could head out and scout Pollaski's compound Tex called, then Garrett, and now we were moving on to plan B—going in blind. Definitely not our best option but if Pollaski's jet was being fueled up, I wasn't waiting. I'd be going in full Winchester with no backup before I'd allow Nat to get on a plane.

"Owen?" Wolf called and I lifted my gaze to find him studying me. "You good?"

No, I was not fucking good. But I didn't bother to

vocalize my thoughts, not that I needed to. Wolf knew damn good and well I wasn't close to being *good*. Wolf was a smart man, he was also a man who understood better than most what a man feels when his woman is in danger. Everyone knew his story. It was no secret his wife, Caroline, had been kidnapped and almost died.

But he'd saved her.

Caroline was alive and well. I tried to hold on to that, not the ugly feeling that was choking me. I needed to believe Nat and I would get our happy ending, too. I had to *believe*. The alternative was incomprehensible.

"It's not gonna be pretty," Abe told me.

My eyes sliced to Wolf's teammate and I couldn't hide my flinch. Abe spoke the truth—hell, the man always spoke the truth. He was famous for his honesty but right then I didn't want the fucking truth, I wanted to load out and get on the road.

"We've got twenty acres to cover," I said, ignoring Abe. "Tex said five of Pollaski's soldiers are unaccounted for besides Franco. We know at least one, the driver of the Escalade is here. Franco, the driver, Pollaski, and possibly four others."

"Brother—" Gabe cut in but wisely shut his mouth when I crossed my arms over my chest.

"No more goddamn lectures, no more sermons, no more speeches. I'm not good and won't be until Nat's safe. You wanna help me with that, let's go. You wanna preach about how I need to check myself and lock down my anger, save it. I'm not locking down shit. I'm going in and getting my woman. And any one of those motherfuckers who tries to stop me will be on the receiving end of my goddamn *anger*."

I paused and looked through the three men who had taken time away from their wives and families to help. "'Preciate you three stepping up. But something you should know. This is gonna get messy. If you don't—"

"We're well acquainted with messy," Mozart stopped me. "We go in, you don't leave my side."

"I don't need a babysitter."

"Yeah, you do," he corrected and I ground my molars in an effort not to lash out. "You got your mission and we've got ours. Your head is so full of your woman, you won't have a mind to what's going on around you. My job is to keep you safe when you execute your objective. Your brothers have your back, my team has your back, but you do not make a move without me at your side, yeah?"

Since he'd ended on a question I answered, "Copy that."

I grabbed my vest off the bed and watched as the other men followed suit. The three of them had been retired a while, but like anything borne from years of routine and training, they slipped into their roles easily. *Once a man is dangerous, he's always dangerous.* And Wolf, Abe, and Mozart were dangerous men.

Mozart was done first and at the door ready. Hard and impassable, a far cry from the man who an hour before had taken a call from his wife, Summer. My heart had seized when he ended the call sweetly telling her he loved her.

Fucking hell, I wanted to tell Nat I loved her. Something I hadn't done the last time she'd called. She'd told me, but I'd been too busy begging her to come back to me. Too out of my mind with fear to formulate the words. I should've told her.

What if that was the last time I spoke to her and I didn't—

"Owen!" Kevin snapped and I blinked.

Shit, goddamn. I couldn't go there. It could be the last time I heard her voice.

"Head. In. The. Motherfucking. Game," Kevin ground out, punctuating each word.

Right. Head in the motherfucking game. I had blood to spill and a woman to rescue. And not in that order.

Nat was first.

She was always first.

* * *

"FORGOT HOW FUN THIS WAS," ABE'S VOICE BOOMED IN MY EAR.

I scanned the area in front of me. Pollaski's house sat off in the distance and I now understood why this place was called 'the retreat'. It would've been cool as fuck if I didn't know the horrors that had likely occurred within its brick walls. The structure looked like a castle. The satellite images didn't do it justice—the blueprints only showed the layout, nothing could convey that opulence.

"The prospect of taking down bad guys?" Gabe returned over the radio.

"Nope," Abe answered. "Though that has always been the plus-side of our job."

Every light was on in the house, a beacon in the dark, sitting in a canyon at the base of Franklin Trails. Thankfully, there were no other houses around, the retreat was isolated smack in the middle of the twenty acres and in the dead of night, no one would be on the trail. There wasn't a car or person in sight when Mozart and I had dropped Abe and Kevin off at what was known as the back nine. It was the start of the eight-mile Franklin loop. They'd quickly exited the Jeep and disappeared into the dark.

"You gonna tell us or leave us hanging in suspense?" Gabe asked.

I fought to keep my temper in check. Normally I'd participate in the banter, use the mindless chatter to cut through the tension. But that night, knowing my woman was so close yet so goddamn far away, locked behind the wall of the fortress in front of me, I was in no mood to listen to bullshit. Anything could be happening to Natasha.

Any.

Thing.

"The adrenaline rush of roping down a sheer drop down."

"Don't break a hip, old man." Wolf chuckled and my jaw ached as my molars ground down.

"Please, God, don't break a hip. We promised Alabama we'd bring you home unbroken," Mozart joined in.

I snapped. There was no other way to explain it. My chest burned with anxiety and the stranglehold I had on my fear broke loose.

"Gabe, what's your twenty?" I pushed out.

"Same place it was two minutes ago. Escalade is disabled and I'm in position."

Right. In position, Gabe was waiting for Abe and Kevin to come in from the back. Wolf and Myles had taken the newly rented SUV and were coming in from the east.

Newly rented because Nat had stolen the other one.

Sweet Jesus, she'd been gone so long it felt like weeks when in reality it had been fourteen hours. Fourteen, long, excruciating hours.

A hand landed on my shoulder and with a bone-jarring shake, Mozart snapped me back into the present.

"Keep your head, brother," he murmured.

"In place," Wolf radioed.

Thank fuck.

"Got eyes on four," Gabe came back, all-business. "No sign of Nat or Pollaski."

"In place," Kevin called in and my heart rate spiked.

Almost.

Mozart and I made our way through the sparse litter of trees, keeping to the shadows. A few more yards and we'd be ready.

"Gabe, you got anything else?" Myles asked.

"Heavily armed. No curtains or blinds on the windows. Pool is lit, no go on the back entrance. So far, no outside patrol." Gabe paused then a ragged curse, and ice water ran through my veins. "Something happened. Two guards are running up the stairs."

I felt my body go solid and that ice water pumping through me turned to ice.

There was nothing left but cold, calculated intent.

"Get the fuck in there, now," Gabe barked. "I'm hitting the side door."

Mozart took off in a sprint and I followed. I could hear labored breathing echoing in my ear. But all I could feel was my gun in my hand, the weight of the vest I'd strapped on, and the fury I'd locked down rage out of control.

I love you, Owen. Straight to my soul, I love you.

I let her avow wash over me and I leveled my firearm, prepared to bring my woman home.

CHAPTER 26

I had no idea blood was so warm.

I'd seen it, I'd felt it leak from my nose, I'd tasted it, but I'd never known how warm and sticky it was when it poured out.

When it puddled.

Now I knew.

I looked down at my hands and they were still covered in blood.

So much blood the coppery smell filled the room, it coated the floor, I could see the smears my knees left, my handprints from where I'd crawled through it.

Crawled, but not far.

"I hate you," I whispered.

Wilco didn't answer.

He'd never answer again. The letter opener I'd used to stab him was still lodged deep in his mangled throat. It wasn't as easy as the movies made it look. It took force to jab a pointed instrument into flesh. It took more than one attempt to hit the right spot. Add in a man double my size, fighting, it was a lot harder than I'd thought it would be.

And so much more blood.

It sprayed, it flowed, it pooled.

The room looked like a crime scene. It *was* a crime scene now.

I heard footsteps pounding up the stairs and I scrambled to stand, my bare feet not finding purchase in the slippery wet all around me.

The door flung open and it was too late.

Franco took in the scene. His nasty, hate-filled eyes came to me, then he smiled when he saw my very dead uncle on his back, his eyes still open and a look of shock still on his face.

Shocked I'd fought back. Shocked I'd spoken. Shocked I had it in me to hit him back when he slapped the shit out of me—*again*. But more than anything he was shocked when I reached under the pillow for the letter opener I'd found only minutes before he'd opened the door and I stabbed him in his stomach before I took the letter opener to his throat.

Over and over I stuck him as hard as I could until he collapsed and I fell on top of him. Utterly exhausted from the exertion.

So tired.

So much blood.

So very dead.

"For a dumb bitch, you made this next part easier." Franco barked a laugh. "One less thing to do before we leave."

"I'm not going anywhere with you."

"What'd you say?"

"I said," I cleared my throat and wished I could get to my feet but I knew it was useless. I'd have to crawl to the dresser to hoist myself up and there was no way I was crawling anywhere in front of Franco. "I'm not going anywhere with you."

"I see you think you have a say, bitch, but you don't. What was Wilco's is now mine. You're mine. Everything he had is mine. Now get the fuck up, we're leaving."

"No," I said with all the bravado I could muster.

I was in trouble, big trouble. By killing Wilco I'd handed Franco the keys to the kingdom. I had no fight left in me, but I wasn't going with him. Not anywhere. I was staying in this room until Owen found me. It was my only hope.

I'd planned on taking out Franco first, but as per my normal luck—which was to say, no luck whatsoever—Wilco had come up to collect me. The plane was ready. An aircraft I was not getting on. I would die in this room before I was whored out. I would kill before I was forced to live another second of the life I'd escaped.

"Sarah—"

"My goddamn name is Natasha," I spat. "And listen to me, Franco, I'm not going anywhere with you. Your best chance at surviving is to get gone and do it quickly."

"Get gone? You think because you did me a favor and took out the old man, I'm not claiming my prize, then you're fucking stupider than your uncle said you were."

Of course Wilco thought I was stupid. All women were stupid. *Pussy was stupid.*

Fuck him and fuck Franco.

"I'm not a prize and I'm sure as hell not yours."

"I see you think that asshole's coming for you, but your uncle made sure when he and his friends got to Chicago…" Franco paused, smiled, and winked. "*Kaboom.*"

Kaboom?

What did that mean?

"There would be nothing left of him but ash."

Would Owen go to Chicago to look for me? That was where I told him I was going, where I told Tex. No, no way. Tex would know. I left the phone on, he'd trace it and tell Owen.

He was coming. I knew he was.

Time. I just needed to give Owen more time.

We've got your back, you're covered, I promise. Owen had said that to me once. He also promised he was coming for me.

He'd come. I knew it.

"Franco!" someone shouted from the hallway. "We've got company."

My heart rate spiked and hope bloomed.

Please let it be Owen and the guys. Please let it be Owen. Unfortunately, as I was chanting my mantra I wasn't paying enough attention to Franco. He was across the room fast, his hand wrapped around my bicep faster. I dug my heels in and leaned back, making it so Franco was dragging me through the blood. His feet slipped but he quickly recovered and continued to yank.

I couldn't let him take me out of this room. I knew once he got me to my feet he'd use me as a shield.

I needed Franco off-balance, it was the only way. With every last bit of energy I had, I lobbed my body to the side. Franco pitched, and when I had my chance I twisted and kicked the back of his knees, making them buckle. From there everything was a haze of fury.

I attacked.

I punched, kicked, struggled, and together we rolled in the blood. This was unlike the movies, too. Two minutes of fighting for your life felt like an eternity. My muscles screamed in protest. My body ached and I felt every blow Franco landed.

I'd done my best.

I'd fought hard.

But I was no match for a two-hundred-pound man. He easily pinned me under him.

"Fucking cunt," he rasped and I was happy to see I'd at least tore a gash in his lip. "I'm gonna fucking kill you."

"You might. But I'd rather die than—"

I didn't get to finish my badass declaration because

Franco was gone. As in gone—up off of me and sailing in the air until I heard a loud bang then a second crash.

Then all my words simply died because Owen was standing there. Face like thunder. Eyes not on me but the blood in the room. And when his gaze came to mine it was glacial.

"Jesus, fuck!" he roared.

"I'm okay," I squeaked.

"Jesus, fucking Christ."

An artic chill washed over me. Perhaps he didn't hear me.

"I'm okay, Owen. None of it's mine."

"Owen?"

I jolted and scrambled back when I heard a voice I didn't know.

"It's all good, Natasha. All good," the man said.

I didn't spare a glance at the man speaking. I only had eyes for the man stalking toward me. Owen bent down and scooped me into his arms. And try as I might, I couldn't hold back the cry of pain as Owen straightened.

He said nothing, but he didn't need to. The hard set of his jaw said more than a million words.

He walked down the stairs, through the foyer, and out the front door. Gabe met us there, took me in, and his eyes flashed with something so scary I buried my head in Owen's neck. I knew what he saw. I knew because I could taste Wilco's blood—I'd rolled in it. I had it all over me.

Always dirty.

My body bucked and that hurt, too. And as the tears fell, tiny rivers of blood washed down my cheeks.

"Baby."

The tortured sound from Owen only made me sob harder.

Not because I'd killed Wilco. Not because I was covered in a warm, sticky mess. Not because I was right then, quite literally covered in Pollaski stench.

I didn't care about any of that.

All I could think about was this was the third time Owen had rescued me. The first time he'd carried me in Alaska, saving me from a lifetime of misery, I had a bloody gash on my forehead. The second time he'd carried me out of a building after untying me from a chair, my childhood friend dead on the floor, my face battered, after saving my life. This time he carried me to safety after I'd killed a man. All three times he'd done it gently. All three times he'd risked his life to save mine.

"I'm free," I mumbled.

Owen grunted and kept walking.

"Straight to my soul," I said louder.

"Fucking Christ."

His words were harsh but his squeeze was gentle.

I smiled against his neck.

He was mad at me but I knew he loved me straight to his soul, too.

I didn't need him to say it. I was in his arms surrounded by it.

I was free to live my dream.

CHAPTER 27

"Nat."

The groan felt like it originated in my gut and slithered its way up my chest. The sound was low and deep and even to my own ears, it sounded foreign.

Natasha lifted her head and the first thing I caught was her feisty smile. Thankfully, I'd seen a lot of those smiles over the last six weeks since we'd been home.

The first week had been hell. Natasha had woken up every night with nightmares. Not of her killing Wilco—of her going to jail. She'd been petrified someone was going to come arrest her. Then she got official word from Cruz that the FBI had been in constant contact with the Montana authorities and Wilco's death had been ruled justifiable homicide or death by self-defense.

After Cruz had given her the good news she relaxed, but she was still keyed up. That was until Tex had worked his magic and a brand-new driver's license and birth certificate came in the mail.

She was officially Natasha Cullen.

When Nat saw her new identity she laughed her ass off.

I didn't.

All I could focus on was how much I liked her having my last name, and how that came about, no matter how much I liked it, left a hole in my heart. I wanted her to take my last name because she was my wife not because Tex was being a funny guy. Though I figured the man knew what he was doing because it'd lit a fire under my ass.

The next day I went out and bought a ring. Nat didn't know it yet, but one day soon she'd become Natasha Cullen for real.

After that, we fell back into our routine. I went to work and she did her thing. The only thing that had changed was when I came home from work I got to pull her into my arms and kiss her breathless. And after we ate dinner, watched TV, or alternately went out to dinner or hung with the guys, we always ended up in my bed and I left Nat another kind of breathless.

She'd told me while we were in Idaho she was living in a dreamland. Now, back in Maryland, I was living my own version of the fantasy. Only mine was better because it was real. Day in and day out I was with Nat. Every day I learned something new. Every day I fell more in love.

"Owen," she whined. "I liked what I was doing."

My hands on her hips tightened, then they started to wander up her waist, over her ribs, and finally, they reached their destination. Nat's back arched as I weighed her full breasts in my palms. Thanking the universe it hadn't taken her long to heal. Not for me, for her. She had to live with those fourteen hours and I hated she bore the bruises. But they'd all faded. Though those hours were seared into my memory; I chose not to let them infest our life.

She was alive.

She was safe.

She was here.

She was mine.

The here and now. That was where we lived and I took great pains to make sure she didn't slip back into the past.

"Need you to look at me, baby."

"Can't I do that and ride at the same time?" she complained.

No, she could not. I needed to concentrate, and her sliding her tight, wet, warm pussy over my cock was not conducive to having an important conversation.

"I was so close," she continued.

And she was. I'd felt her pussy start to spasm—that was why I'd stopped her.

Nat's nails dug into my chest as she lifted herself up and slammed back down.

"So, close," she reiterated and swiveled her hips.

"Nat," I growled. "Baby, I need you to stop a second."

"Can't."

She could, she just didn't want to and I understood why. The sex had only gotten better between us and it was pretty fucking phenomenal when it started. But as her confidence grew Nat took it to a whole new level. She was wild as fuck, but that wasn't what made it good. It wasn't even her begging for me to talk dirty to her, something I was more than happy to oblige.

It was because every touch, every word, every kiss, nibble, bite, glide, and moan was shrouded in love.

Straight-to-your-soul adoration.

The kind that had no end. It would go on forever, linger after we were both dead.

"Natasha," I grunted.

My hips bucked up to meet her downward slide and it was too late. I was too close. I'd have to have our conversation when we were done.

"You got two seconds to bring it home, baby," I warned.

"I'm almost there," she groaned.

I didn't ask her what she needed because I knew.

"Lean forward."

Her whole body shuddered and her hooded eyes hit mine.

"Not yet."

"Now, baby, I need to freshen your mark."

"But—"

I smacked Nat's ass. She jolted forward and on a long, loud purr she did as I asked.

No sooner had I sank my teeth in my woman's flesh, her pussy convulsed and tightened. Her climax detonated mine, and together we drifted into oblivion.

Sweet relief ripped through me fast and furious. Pure bliss.

Out of this world.

Every damn time.

"I love you something fierce, Owen Cullen. It's so big and so epic I can't tell you how much I love you."

My tongue soothed the new mark I'd left, then my lips brushed over it. Something I did often, whenever the mark started to fade. Something Nat had insisted never went away. She said she liked looking at it, liked touching it, liked knowing I gave it to her. So like everything else, I gave my woman what she wanted.

"You're making things easy on me," I said and turned my head to press a kiss to her throat.

Without having to look, my right arm reached out and I tagged the box off my nightstand, flipped it open, and plucked the ring free.

"Marry me?" I whispered.

"What?"

Natasha shot up so fast her tits bounced and momentarily I forgot what I was doing. Maybe this was not a good plan. Maybe I should've waited until she was fully dressed, not straddling my lap with my still-hard cock inside her.

"Marry me, baby. Become Natasha Cullen for real. Be my wife."

"Thank you."

"Nat—"

"Thank you for saving me. Thank you for forgiving me. Thank you for giving me a home and sneakers and jeans and pretty dresses and shoes—"

"Nat—"

"Thank you for loving me, but mostly thank you for letting me love you."

"Is that a yes?"

Natasha stared down at me with her pretty green eyes sparkling and at that moment I hoped she gave me five beautiful little girls all with her eyes and shiny hair. Little girls that I could spoil and she could love.

"Yes. That's a huge yes."

"Then you're welcome."

It took me a moment to pry her fingers off my chest and slide her ring on and when I did, swear to Christ the look on her face erased every minute of those fourteen hours.

Rapture.

The sweetest of smiles.

"Thank you for my beautiful ring."

"Stop thanking me," I groused.

"Thank you for making me so happy."

"One more, woman, and you'll find yourself—"

"Thank you for being—"

Natasha didn't finish. She did squeal when I flipped her over. And she definitely moaned when I made love to her. And she absolutely screamed her orgasm.

What she did not do was thank me again.

CHAPTER 28

"Thanks for meeting with me," Cruz said and offered his hand.

Whoa.

This was FBI agent Cruz Livingston?

"Thanks for coming all the way out to Maryland to meet with me."

Owen cleared his throat and I dropped Mr. Hot Stuff's hand. I glanced up at Owen and his lips were twitching.

"What?" I sassed even though I knew what.

I was totally gawking.

"Nothing."

"You know," I started conversationally. "It is not my fault all your friends are hot."

"Right." Owen smiled.

"You, of course being at the top of the hotness chart, but none of them are too far down."

I swept my arm indicating the peanut gallery who were all smirking. No, Myles and Kevin were smirking. Gabe was outright smiling like an idiot but that was Gabe's way. His over-inflated ego wouldn't let him do anything but.

Zane Lewis was sitting at the head of the long table,

which seemed to be his normal place. That made sense since we were in the conference room at Z Corps' office. To Zane's right was Lincoln Parker, Zane's brother and...well, right-hand man. Next to Linc, as he told me to call him, was Kyle. And next to Kyle was Owen's new teammate, Cooper Cain. Owen explained to me that Cooper's brother Jaxon was a member of the Red Team. He might've explained some more stuff but it flitted in one ear and out the other. Partly because I was nervous about my sit-down with Cruz. The other part was because I was surrounded by suffocating male hotness. And Cooper Cain might've been the newcomer but he fit right in.

"Right," Owen repeated.

"Maybe we should get down to business," Zane suggested.

My gaze sliced to him and I blinked. Then I blinked again. He was smiling.

Zane Lewis, Mr. Large-And-In-Charge, was smiling.

"You have dimples," I noted.

"Here we go," Linc mumbled.

"Don't be salty, little brother. Not everyone possesses—"

"I thought we were getting down to business," Owen interrupted.

And suddenly I wanted to know what Zane thought he possessed. Likely he thought he owned the world, and from what I'd learned about him that wasn't far off the mark.

Zane had plenty of politicians in his Rolodex, though unlike Wilco, Zane's contacts were made the legal way, and he was friends with them out of mutual respect, not blackmail.

Unfortunately, I couldn't sit here all day and gawk at the plentiful eye-candy. I was now gainfully employed and I had to be at work in a few hours.

"I'll make this quick," Cruz started. "I know...we all know how hard it was for you to talk to the analyst."

Cruz stopped and my heart started to flip-flop. It had

been three months since the night I killed Wilco. A month since Owen asked me to marry him, and after a rocky first week home I'd laid Sarah to rest.

She was gone. I didn't mourn her because there was nothing to mourn. Sarah Pollaski was well and truly at peace. So when Cruz had asked me to work with an FBI analyst it was not hard. It was cleansing. The last piece of the puzzle I needed to move on with my life.

"I told you then and I'll tell you now—it was my pleasure."

Incidentally, Franco had been wrong—Wilco was not as smart as he thought he was. Cruz had seen Wilco's brown-stone was wired with explosives. Later I'd learned about a man called Dude, who was friends with the three men who'd helped Owen save me—Wolf, Abe, and Mozart—who by-the-by, were total silver foxes, but that's neither here nor there. The point was, no one went *kaboom*. And Franco and the other soldiers who'd been at the retreat were in federal lockup. Franco was not talking; the other four men were. Singing like canaries now that they weren't afraid of swimming with the fishes.

Franco was screwed.

I wasn't the least bit unhappy about that.

"Right." Cruz nodded. "I also wanted to tell you the information you gave us saved lives. A lot of them, Natasha. The FBI is still trying to sort out the women who are too traumatized to talk. But the other—and the last count I got was ninety-three—women have been reunited with their families and you did that."

Ninety-three?

God, Wilco was the Devil.

"Thank you for telling me."

"It was *my* pleasure." I lost Cruz's intense stare as he looked through the room and dipped his chin. "Z, appreciate the use of your office."

"Anytime. Tell Mickie hello and have a good flight back to Texas."

"Will do."

And with that, Cruz left the room.

Welp.

That was that.

I turned to Owen but before I could ask him to walk me out, there was a buzz in the room and Zane weirdly said, "Yes, my beautiful goddess of a wife?"

"Sweet Jesus, I'm gonna puke." Kyle made a gagging sound.

"Sweet-talk will not get you out of this, Zane Lewis," Ivy snarked.

Oh, I forgot to mention. I. Love. Ivy Lewis. She is drop-dead gorgeous, has the patience of a saint—*hello* married to Zane—and she puts up with zero bullshit. She also runs the back office of Z Corps. She was in reception when I'd come in for my meeting.

"Ivy, we are not under any circumstances getting a cat," Zane responded.

I bit my lip. They were so getting a cat.

"How 'bout we talk about this at home?"

"Nothing to talk about, lovely wife. I love you to the pit of my black soul but we're not getting a cat. I hate cats. I have not kept this a secret. And it can't be lost on you, every time I pass a cat I hiss at it."

"Zane, you hiss at everything."

"I hiss at things I don't like."

"As I said, you hiss at everything. I want a cat. Eric wants a cat. Can we please—"

"Fine. Get the cat."

Lincoln busted out laughing.

Owen's body started shaking and I closed my eyes.

This was my life.

"Baby, I need to get to work," I whispered to Owen.

"I'll walk you down."

I didn't need to ask, he'd walk me down. He'd also walk me to my car. He'd kiss me silly then he'd watch me drive away. I knew this because he did it all the time. Every time I left, same thing.

I *loved* my life.

"Thank you, honey," I whispered as we stood.

Owen's eyes darkened and my body softened.

"You're lucky we're not at home," he remarked.

That comment made my body tingle because I knew what that meant. Ever since the night of our engagement, any time I thanked him he found ways to occupy my mouth. Seriously awesome, pleasurable ways. I vaguely wondered if I should call in sick. I worked in a department store; people were always looking for overtime. But I wouldn't. I loved my job and my co-workers. Besides, tonight when I got home, Owen would be there.

"I don't know, I kinda enjoy your punishment when I show gratitude."

"Not show, I love it when you show it."

"Such a man."

"Are you complaining I like the—"

I quickly lifted my hand to cover his mouth. "Hello?" I nodded toward the table.

"Baby, they're busting Zane's balls. Not a single one of them is paying attention to us."

"I am," Gabe announced.

Owen groaned and skewered Gabe with a stare. "One day, brother, you'll be trying to have a private moment with your woman and when you least expect it I'm gonna pop up and ruin it."

"Never gonna happen." Gabe smiled.

"We'll see. Payback's a bitch."

Owen took my hand and we were nearly at the door when I heard Ivy say, "There's an Evette London in reception. She says she needs to speak to you and Kyle immediately."

"Evette's down there?" Kyle asked but he was already on his feet.

Ivy was confirming there was indeed a woman named Evette downstairs but Kyle was out the door and Gabe was in hot pursuit.

"Do you know what that's about?" I asked.

"Nope. Never heard of the woman."

* * *

I WAS PINNED AGAINST MY CAR, OWEN WAS PRESSED AGAINST my front, and I was panting into his mouth. This was because he just broke an epic kiss.

Everything kept getting better and better.

"Have a good day at work," he mumbled.

"You, too. See you at home."

"Yeah, baby, see you at home."

With one last sweet kiss, he let me go.

Then I watched Owen in my rearview mirror standing next to an empty parking spot watching me go.

I was loved.

So loved.

I had so many choices laid out in front of me, more freedom than I'd ever had.

Clean and free.

And every day, I chose Owen Cullen.

CHAPTER 29

Evette London

This was a mistake.

I never should've come here. I should've called but there was no time and besides, I'd ditched my phone.

Someone was following me. Actually, now that I was out of California I could admit someone wasn't just following me —someone was trying to kill me.

I still should've called. There were still payphones, I could've called collect. Kyle wouldn't have minded the charge on the bill. He would've been grateful I wasn't bringing this issue into his wife's life.

But I needed to warn Anaya.

Besides, it was too late now—I was here.

In the lobby of Z Corps, Kyle's place of business. He was a PI or a commando or a badass, whatever he was he'd know what to do. Anaya loved me and he loved Anaya. He'd help.

God, I hoped he'd help.

I hadn't been clear-headed when I jumped on a plane. Okay, I didn't jump on a plane, I slowly walked on a plane deep breathing so I didn't have a panic attack. Apparently,

RILEY EDWARDS

the only thing I was more afraid of than flying was dying at the hands of the person who was trying to kill me.

I hadn't rented a car. I'd hailed a taxi, the old-school kind, the yellow kind you find lined up at the airport exit. Then I'd paid the fare in cash.

I'd never given much thought about things like using cash. Like everyone else, I used my card. And when you don't think about things like say, having enough cash on hand to narrowly escape across the country you run out of said cash quickly. I had three dollars in my wallet. That was it.

I really hoped Kyle would help me or I was totally up shit's creek.

"Evette?" Kyle's voice boomed.

I turned and I felt my neck muscles constrict.

My good friend Anaya had hit the hot guy motherload when she'd married Kyle. Once upon a time, I'd thought he was the hottest guy I'd ever met in person. Only being topped by Tom Cruise, who I had not met in person, but Tom was Tom so he was at the top of every list.

But I had been wrong.

Even being in the throes of a panic attack to rival all panic attacks the man standing next to Kyle demanded my attention.

Suddenly my life being in peril took a back seat and my hormones picked the *wrong* time to go into hyperdrive.

"Are you okay?" Kyle asked.

"No. Someone's trying to kill me."

I watched the man standing next to Kyle turn hard before his gaze went to the windows and started scanning.

"Ivy," Kyle barked, and the pretty brown haired receptionist looked our way. "Upstairs. Lockdown." The woman stood and Kyle continued issuing orders. "Gabe, take the front. I'll call Owen he should still be in the parking garage."

Kyle moved forward and grabbed my hand. And as wrong as it was I sighed, not because my friend Anaya's husband holding my hand made me feel inappropriate things, but because I was an independent woman who didn't need a man to take care of her. However, I had to admit Kyle's strong, warm hand wrapped around mine made me feel safe, something I hadn't felt in weeks and the relief of that swept through me reminding me how stupid I'd been.

"Not here. In California," I told him.

The man—Gabe. His name was Gabe—slowly turned his head and when his soulful gaze came to me, suddenly the death threats, car chases, and break-ins vanished. All the reasons I'd left my home in Riverton and flown across the country went up in a poof of smoke. Yes, his warm, deep, rich chocolate brown eyes were that captivating they made me forget.

"Let's get you upstairs and safe, yeah?" Gabe asked.

I nodded because I couldn't speak.

I really did need to get safe.

I also needed to tell Anaya about Kalee.

But first I needed to remember why I was in Maryland and ignore my strange reaction to the man who had spoken less than ten words to me. Though as I stood in the lobby with my eyes locked onto Gabe's I'd swear I knew him. Oh, I'd never actually met him before, but if I were one of those fanciful women who believed in love at first sight and soulmates, I'd say it felt like I'd spent a hundred lifetimes with him, that this man Gabe was born with the other half of my heart in his chest.

Yep, this was a mistake. I should've called.

* * *

FIND OUT WHAT EVETTE DISCOVERED, WHY SHE THINKS SHE'S in danger, and how far Gabe will go to protect her in the second book in the Blue Team Series. One click *GABE* now!

Nixon's Promise

Jameson's Salvation

Weston's Treasure

Alec's Dream

Chasin's Surrender

Holden's Resurrection

Jonny's Redemption

The 707 Freedom Series

Free

Freeing Jasper

Finally Free

Freedom

The Next Generation

Saving Meadow

Chasing Honor

Finding Mercy

Claiming Tuesday

Adoring Delaney

Keeping Quinn

Taking Liberty

The Masters Collection

The Awakening

The Collective

Unbroken 1 & 2 – Season One

Trust – Season Two

Standalone

Romancing Rayne

ABOUT THE AUTHOR

Riley Edwards is a bestselling multi-genre author, wife, and military mom. Riley was born and raised in Los Angeles but now resides on the east coast with her fantastic husband and children.

Riley writes heart-stopping romance with sexy alpha heroes and even stronger heroines. Riley's favorite genres to write are romantic suspense and military romance.

Don't forget to sign up for Riley's newsletter and never miss another release, sale, or exclusive bonus material. https://www.subscribepage.com/RRsignup

Facebook Fan Group

www.rileyedwardsromance.com

facebook.com/Novelist.Riley.Edwards
twitter.com/rileyedwardsrom
instagram.com/rileyedwardsromance
bookbub.com/authors/riley-edwards
amazon.com/author/rileyedwards

There are many more books in this fan fiction world than listed here, for an up-to-date list go to www.AcesPress.com

You can also visit our Amazon page at:
http://www.amazon.com/author/operationalpha

Special Forces: Operation Alpha World
Christie Adams: Charity's Heart
Denise Agnew: Dangerous to Hold
Shauna Allen: Awakening Aubrey
Brynne Asher: Blackburn
Linzi Baxter: Unlocking Dreams
Jennifer Becker: Hiding Catherine
Alice Bello: Shadowing Milly
Heather Blair: Rescue Me
Anna Blakely: Rescuing Gracelynn
Julia Bright: Saving Lorelei
Cara Carnes: Protecting Mari
Kendra Mei Chailyn: Beast
Melissa Kay Clarke: Rescuing Annabeth
Samantha A. Cole: Handling Haven
Sue Coletta: Hacked
Melissa Combs: Gallant
Anne Conley: Redemption for Misty
KaLyn Cooper: Rescuing Melina
Janie Crouch: Storm
Liz Crowe: Marking Mariah
Sarah Curtis: Securing the Odds
Jordan Dane: Redemption for Avery
Tarina Deaton: Found in the Lost
Aspen Drake, Intense
KL Donn: Unraveling Love
Riley Edwards: Protecting Olivia
PJ Fiala: Defending Sophie

Nicole Flockton: Protecting Maria
Michele Gwynn: Rescuing Emma
Casey Hagen: Shielding Nebraska
Desiree Holt: Protecting Maddie
Kathy Ivan: Saving Sarah
Kris Jacen, Be With Me
Jesse Jacobson: Protecting Honor
Silver James: Rescue Moon
Becca Jameson: Saving Sofia
Kate Kinsley: Protecting Ava
Heather Long: Securing Arizona
Gennita Low: No Protection
Kirsten Lynn: Joining Forces for Jesse
Margaret Madigan: Bang for the Buck
Trish McCallan: Hero Under Fire
Kimberly McGath: The Predecessor
Rachel McNeely: The SEAL's Surprise Baby
KD Michaels: Saving Laura
Lynn Michaels, Rescuing Kyle
Wren Michaels: The Fox & The Hound
Annie Miller: Securing Willow
Kat Mizera: Protecting Bobbi
Keira Montclair, Wolf and the Wild Scots
Mary B Moore: Force Protection
LeTeisha Newton: Protecting Butterfly
Angela Nicole: Protecting the Donna
MJ Nightingale: Protecting Beauty
Sarah O'Rourke: Saving Liberty
Victoria Paige: Reclaiming Izabel
Anne L. Parks: Mason
Debra Parmley: Protecting Pippa
Lainey Reese: Protecting New York
KeKe Renée: Protecting Bria
TL Reeve and Michele Ryan: Extracting Mateo
Elena M. Reyes: Keeping Ava

Angela Rush: Charlotte
Rose Smith: Saving Satin
Jenika Snow: Protecting Lily
Lynne St. James: SEAL's Spitfire
Dee Stewart: Conner
Harley Stone: Rescuing Mercy
Jen Talty: Burning Desire
Reina Torres, Rescuing Hi'ilani
Savvi V: Loving Lex
Megan Vernon: Protecting Us
Rachel Young: Because of Marissa

Delta Team Three Series
Lori Ryan: Nori's Delta
Becca Jameson: Destiny's Delta
Lynne St James, Gwen's Delta
Elle James: Ivy's Delta
Riley Edwards, Hope's Delta

Police and Fire: Operation Alpha World
Freya Barker: Burning for Autumn
BP Beth: Scott
Jane Blythe: Salvaging Marigold
Julia Bright, Justice for Amber
Anna Brooks, Guarding Georgia
KaLyn Cooper: Justice for Gwen
Aspen Drake: Sheltering Emma
Alexa Gregory: Backdraft
Deanndra Hall: Shelter for Sharla
Barb Han: Kace
EM Hayes: Gambling for Ashleigh
CM Steele: Guarding Hope
Reina Torres: Justice for Sloane
Aubree Valentine, Justice for Danielle
Maddie Wade: Finding English

Stacey Wilk: Stage Fright
Laine Vess: Justice for Lauren

Tarpley VFD Series
Silver James, Fighting for Elena
Deanndra Hall, Fighting for Carly
Haven Rose, Fighting for Calliope
MJ Nightingale, Fighting for Jemma
TL Reeve, Fighting for Brittney
Nicole Flockton, Fighting for Nadia

As you know, this book included at least one character from Susan Stoker's books. To check out more, see below.

SEAL of Protection: Legacy Series
Securing Caite
Securing Brenae (novella)
Securing Sidney
Securing Piper
Securing Zoey
Securing Avery
Securing Kalee
Securing Jane (Feb 2021)

Delta Team Two Series
Shielding Gillian
Shielding Kinley
Shielding Aspen
Shielding Jayme
Shielding Riley
Shielding Devyn (May 2021)
Shielding Ember (Sep 2021)
Shielding Sierra (Jan 2022)

Delta Force Heroes Series
Rescuing Rayne (FREE!)
Rescuing Aimee (novella)
Rescuing Emily
Rescuing Harley
Marrying Emily (novella)
Rescuing Kassie
Rescuing Bryn
Rescuing Casey
Rescuing Sadie (novella)
Rescuing Wendy

Rescuing Mary
Rescuing Macie (Novella)

Badge of Honor: Texas Heroes Series
Justice for Mackenzie (FREE!)
Justice for Mickie
Justice for Corrie
Justice for Laine (novella)
Shelter for Elizabeth
Justice for Boone
Shelter for Adeline
Shelter for Sophie
Justice for Erin
Justice for Milena
Shelter for Blythe
Justice for Hope
Shelter for Quinn
Shelter for Koren
Shelter for Penelope

SEAL Team Hawaii Series
Finding Elodie (Apr 2021)
Finding Lexie (Aug 2021)
Finding Kenna (Oct 2021)
Finding Monica (TBA)
Finding Carly (TBA)
Finding Ashlyn (TBA)
Finding Jodelle (TBA)

SEAL of Protection Series
Protecting Caroline (FREE!)
Protecting Alabama
Protecting Fiona
Marrying Caroline (novella)
Protecting Summer

Protecting Cheyenne
Protecting Jessyka
Protecting Julie (novella)
Protecting Melody
Protecting the Future
Protecting Kiera (novella)
Protecting Alabama's Kids (novella)
Protecting Dakota

New York Times, *USA Today* and *Wall Street Journal* Bestselling Author Susan Stoker has a heart as big as the state of Tennessee where she lives, but this all American girl has also spent the last fourteen years living in Missouri, California, Colorado, Indiana, and Texas. She's married to a retired Army man who now gets to follow *her* around the country.

www.stokeraces.com
www.AcesPress.com
susan@stokeraces.com

Made in the USA
Columbia, SC
23 September 2022